Pat

Shear Murder

A BAD HAIR DAY MYSTERY

SHEAR MURDER

NANCY J. COHEN

FIVE STAR
A part of Gale, Cengage Learning

Detroit • New York • San Francisco • New Haven, Conn • Waterville, Maine • London

Five Star Publishing, a part of Gale, Cengage Learning.

Set in 11 pt. Plantin.

LIBRARY OF CONGRESS CATALOGING-IN-PUBLICATION DATA

Cohen, Nancy J., 1948–
Shear murder : a bad hair day mystery / Nancy J. Cohen. — 1st ed.
p. cm.
ISBN-13: 978-1-4328-2554-6(hardcover)
ISBN-10: 1-4328-2554-2(hardcover)
1. Shore, Marla (Fictitious character)—Fiction. 2. Women detectives—Florida—Fiction. 3. Beauty operators—Fiction. 4. Florida—Fiction. I. Title.
PS3553.O4258S54 2012
813'.54—dc23 2011034912

First Edition. First Printing: January 2012.
Published in 2012 in conjunction with Tekno Books and Ed Gorman.

Printed in the United States of America
1 2 3 4 5 6 7 16 15 14 13 12

This story is dedicated to my fans for your continued support, encouragement, and enthusiasm. I wouldn't have finished this book without your repeated requests for more Marla Shore stories. Thanks to all of you for being my inspiration.

ACKNOWLEDGMENTS

Many thanks to Diane Davis, former chair for the Florida-Caribbean Judging Center of the American Orchid Society, and to author Sharon Hartley, avid orchid hobbyist, for sharing your knowledge of orchids. Your input added to the authenticity of this story and is greatly appreciated.

With gratitude to Detective R.C. White, Fort Lauderdale Police (retired). Thank you for answering my crime-related questions and for generously sharing your expertise.

CAST OF CHARACTERS (IN ALPHABETICAL ORDER)

Marla Shore— Owner of Cut 'N Dye Salon in Palm Haven, Florida.

Angela Moran— Senior editor for *Home & Style Magazine.*

Anita Shorstein— Marla's mother.

Arnie Hartman— Jill's groom and owner of Bagel Busters, he is also a friend of Marla's. His children are Josh and Lisa. Their nanny is Graciella.

Babs Winrow— Marla's regular client and senior VP of Tylex Industries.

Bev Hartman— Arnie's mother.

Brianna Vail— Dalton's teenaged daughter. Nickname is "Brie."

Cornelia Oakwood— Falcon's mother.

Cynthia & Bruce Rosen— Cynthia is Marla's cousin. Bruce is her husband. Cynthia's brother is Corbin.

Dalton Vail— Marla's fiancé and Brianna's father. Homicide detective in Palm Haven.

Dellene Hallberg— Senior editor for *Boca Style Magazine.*

Detective Brody— Homicide detective.

Diane Potts— Orchid class instructor.

Eddy & Alexis Rhodes— Jill's uncle, a real estate attorney, and his wife.

Georgia Rogers— Marla's former college roommate who lives in California.

Goat— A dog groomer. His real name is Kyle. He has a black poodle named Rita.

Grant Bosworth— Photographer for *Home & Style Magazine* in Palm Beach.

Griff Beasley— Photographer for *Boca Style Magazine.*

Falcon & Leanne Oakwood— Falcon is founder of Orchid Isle. Leanne is his wife and Torrie's friend.

Hally Leeds— Society columnist for *Boca Style Magazine.*

Jennifer Cater— Stylist at Cut 'N Dye Salon.

Jill Barlow— Marla's friend and Arnie's fiancée. Jill works in public relations at Stockhart Industries.

Jim Rawls— Jill's wedding photographer.

John & Kate Vail— Dalton's parents, both retired.

Kathy Wilkinson— A private investigator from North Florida.

Kevin & Dana Rhodes— Jill's cousin Kevin is a Realtor. Dana is his wife.

Lance Pearson— Marla's friend and a computer systems analyst.

Luis— Receptionist at Cut 'N Dye Salon.

Michael & Charlene Shorstein— Marla's brother and sister-in-law.

Moss & Emma Cantor— Marla's elderly neighbors.

Nicole Johnson— Hairstylist at Cut 'N Dye Salon.

Pete Schneider— A real estate agent.

Philip Canfield— Jill's wedding florist.

Rachel— Torrie's office assistant.

Roger Gold— Anita's boyfriend. His son, Barry, is an optometrist.

Samuel— Executive chef at Orchid Isle.

Sandy— Sales director at Orchid Isle.

Scott Miller— Torrie's husband who owns a clock repair shop.

Spooks— Marla's cream-colored male poodle.

Stan Kaufman— Marla's ex-spouse and an attorney.

Susan Beamer— Waitress at Jill's wedding.

Tally & Ken Riggs— Tally is Marla's best friend. Ken is her husband.

Torrie Miller— Jill's sister and matron of honor. She's a fashion reporter for *Boca Style Magazine.*

Yolanda— Owner of a fashion boutique in Fort Lauderdale.

Chapter One

If these two women don't stop arguing, one of them is bound to kill the other before the day is done. Marla Shore tucked her shears into a drawer before the leggy bride sitting in her salon chair grabbed them to stab her sister.

"Your nail polish looks like blood," Jillian Barlow said to her sibling and matron of honor. "Why did you wear such a horrid red? It'll clash with your dress."

"Who cares? It's not as if you gave us a choice with your color scheme," Torrie Miller replied, staring into the mirror from the station on their right.

"I thought lavender gowns would go perfectly with the flowers at Orchid Isle."

"So they will, for your bridesmaids. You made *me* wear plum. I don't look good in dark colors."

"It's not your wedding, is it? Oh gosh, I'm going to be sick." Bending forward, Jill clutched her stomach. Damp strands of blond hair clung to her face.

Marla picked up her blow dryer and twirled the chair around to face her client. "You'll be fine, Jill," she said in a patient tone. "You're having prewedding jitters."

Owner of Cut 'N Dye Salon, Marla had done any number of bridal parties. She'd seen attacks of nerves ranging from throwing up to throwing a fit. This was no different, except the bride and groom were friends of hers. Marla's bridesmaid gown waited in her Camry. She'd be heading to Orchid Isle along with the other wedding attendants right after their hair appointments.

"Am I making a mistake?" Jill's blue eyes misted. "I mean, there's a seven-year age difference between Arnie and me. While I adore his kids, I hope he doesn't plan to expand the family. I have no wish to get pregnant at thirty-four and ruin my figure."

Not after what you paid for cosmetic enhancements. Marla didn't want kids either, but for different reasons. She, too, had jumped into the maternal arena by sharing the responsibility for her fiancé's teenage daughter. Marla wouldn't trade her relationship with Brianna for anything, and she suspected Jill felt the same toward Arnie's family. Naturally Jill would feel nervous getting married for the first—and hopefully the last—time.

"You love Arnie," she reassured her friend. "You've even converted to Judaism for his sake. You'll be a great wife and mother. Now let me finish your hair, or we'll never get out of here." Without waiting for a reply, she switched on the blow dryer, using a round brush to lift and roll one section of hair at a time.

In the background, she heard the whirr of other dryers, the chatter of excited voices, and jazz music on the speaker system. Reflecting on her own choices, Marla hoped she'd made the right decision regarding her salon expansion. Rather than relocating to the new town center, she'd decided to remain in the same shopping strip to avoid inconveniencing her customers. Instead, she'd moved to a larger space that had become available while also renting the adjacent empty store for her new day spa.

Getting a new property manager—Marla didn't get along with the old one—had clinched the deal. She'd signed a long-term lease with favorable terms and began renovations. Despite the chaos, she'd kept good her word to do Jill's wedding party.

Finished with the dryer, Marla exchanged it for a curling

iron. All of her other operators were busy doing Jill's friends.

"That's too severe," Torrie said to her stylist, before the girl spritzed her with shine. "The upsweep works, but can't you give me some curly things around my face to soften the look?"

"You, look softer?" Jill scoffed. "That's not your norm."

Torrie, a slim brunette, shot her a searing glance. "Don't talk to me about my behavior. Look in the mirror. All that you see isn't what you get."

Jill stiffened. "You promised never to say a word—"

"I know. If you play nice, I will, too. Anyway, we need to talk about our property before we see Uncle Eddy later."

Marla began working on Jill's elaborate hairdo, trying to concentrate on her task and ignore the bantering between siblings. She hoped their fancy coiffeurs didn't frizz in the humidity. Outdoor weddings in South Florida were always risky. At least November was a better bet than summer in terms of rain.

Clipping back a section of Jill's hair, she used her curling iron to twist the remaining strands before assembling the massive waves with jeweled pins. Exhilaration swept through her. She loved using her artistic talents for bridal parties.

Her turn came next. In just four weeks, she'd become a bride for the second time. Her nuptials were set for December eighth. She swallowed hard. *How will I ever be ready?*

"Listen," Jill said to Torrie. "Kevin said we might want to consider doing a land swap."

"What's that?" Torrie squeezed her eyes shut while the stylist sprayed her hair.

"A trade-off of sorts. I'm not clear on the details, but it involves selling our property and exchanging it for another."

"No way, darling. Our lot has a great location on a busy corner. We shouldn't have any problem finding another tenant."

"Marla, give us your advice." Jill lifted her gaze to meet Marla's in the mirror. "You once owned that joint property with Stanley Kaufman. This concerns a parcel of land that Torrie and I inherited from our father."

Marla paused, comb in hand. She didn't care to be reminded of past dealings with her ex-spouse. "What are you talking about?" *If it were me, I'd be more worried about the catering arrangements at my ceremony and my groom arriving on time.*

"Torrie and I need to reach a mutual understanding before our cousin Kevin tries to smooth-talk us at the wedding. He's a real estate agent."

"Oh. Haven't you two discussed this subject before now?"

"Torrie lives in Miami. We haven't had the chance to get together. You know, what with the wedding plans and all." Jill's aloof expression told Marla that she hadn't sought the opportunity, either.

"We've been talking on the telephone," Torrie added, as though that would explain their lack of agreement.

Plucking a can of holding spray from the counter, Marla shook her head. "You don't want to involve me. Every time I get sucked into a situation, someone ends up dead."

Before either sister could reply, Nicole signaled to Marla from the chair on her left. "Babs says her scalp is burning. I used the twenty-volume peroxide like you said."

Marla glanced at the blond woman occupying an empty manicure station while her hair processed. Babs had never reacted that way before.

"Will you excuse me?" she said to Jill, putting down her spray can. Rummaging in one of her roundabout drawers, she fetched a pink packet of artificial sweetener.

Striding toward the business executive, Marla smiled. "Hi, Babs, thanks again for letting me put you in Nicole's book for today. What's this about your scalp hurting?"

Babs winced. "I can feel the dye sizzling. It's really uncomfortable, and I'm afraid it'll damage my hair. Did Nicole use the proper solution?"

"Yes, I told her what to mix. Sometimes this will happen if you develop a sensitivity. You haven't changed any of your medications lately, have you? Chemicals can affect your body as well as your hair."

Babs's face brightened. "Actually, I did. My doctor put me on something new for my blood pressure."

"Well, let me sprinkle on some sweetener. This reaction happens a lot when clients change medicines and forget to tell us. We aren't sure what the secret ingredient in the sweetener is, but it works." Marla ripped open the package in her hand, applied the granules to the woman's scalp, then kneaded it in after donning a glove.

"That feels better, thanks." Babs's posture relaxed.

"You have another twenty minutes on your timer. Can I get you a magazine or a cup of coffee?"

"No, I'm fine. Go back to your bride. She looks upset."

Jill was still arguing with her sister when Marla returned. She was so agitated that she'd begun picking at her just manicured nails.

"I told you to get a durable power of attorney drawn up," Jill told Torrie. "What happens if you're incapacitated and we have to make important decisions?"

"Scott can make them for me." Torrie watched in the mirror while her stylist patted a stray hair into place.

"Are you kidding? This is between us, not our husbands."

"Don't worry so much. We need to resolve one thing at a time. Then I'll think about the next step."

"At your pace, we'll never solve anything." Jill twisted in her seat. "Marla, is it better for us to form a limited liability company? I'm not sure a partnership agreement is the right way to go."

Oh, like I'm a legal expert? If I were, I'd have avoided marrying Stan the big-shot lawyer during a bad time in my life.

Unsnapping Jill's cape after a final spritz of holding spray, Marla shrugged. "From what I understand, the most important reason for putting your business assets into an LLC is to protect you from being personally liable."

Torrie hunched forward. "Setting up an LLC would cost us more money in attorney fees. I can't afford to keep paying these high bills."

Jill arched an eyebrow. "Oh, like the salary you make isn't enough, plus the money Scott brings in from his job?"

"Hah, that sheep is stuck in his pen. I can't rely on him for much longer."

"What's that supposed to mean?" Jill stared at her sister.

Torrie collected her purse. "A gal has to look out for herself, that's all."

Jill turned to Marla. "Did Torrie mention she's a fashion reporter for *Boca Style Magazine*? Maybe you can submit makeover photos of before and after hairstyles to her. I know you've been wanting to get some free publicity for your new spa."

"Good idea." Marla nodded. "I've been hoping to do more photo shoots but haven't had the time."

"Marla worked with Luxor Products at the Supreme Show in January," Jill explained to Torrie. "They brought models to her salon and took photos to advertise their new sunscreen line."

"We did another session in the Keys. I've been meaning to follow up with the photographer," Marla said. "I've been too busy between expanding the salon, getting ready to move into our new house, and planning my own wedding. I can't believe the date is nearly here. We haven't even—"

"I'd be happy to look at any photos you send," Torrie cut in. "Think about tying them in with a holiday issue." She glanced at her watch. "Are the other girls ready yet?"

Marla surveyed the bridesmaids. "They're not quite done. I could take them in my car if you and Jill want to go ahead."

"Karen is driving the others down." Jill brushed some stray hairs off her jeans. She'd dressed casually for her appointment, her bridal ensemble delivered ahead to the gardens where the wedding would take place.

It had been a brilliant stroke to book Orchid Isle for her wedding the same weekend as its grand opening. Since the press would be in attendance at this new attraction, the fledgling nature park would get plenty of free publicity, a boon for its developer, Falcon Oakwood.

"Is Dalton picking you up after we finish here?" Jill asked Marla.

"He's meeting me inside the park." Marla's fiancé, a homicide detective, often kept irregular hours.

"Why don't you come with us?" Jill suggested. "It's silly for you to drive by yourself."

"Who's taking Josh and Lisa? Their nanny?" Arnie had hired the woman after his wife died seven years ago. Marla assumed the children were under her supervision today.

"Graciella is coming, but Arnie is driving them all."

"I'll go with you then, if Nicole doesn't mind closing up shop."

Nicole waved her hairbrush. "You go, girlfriend. I'm cool here."

Nonetheless, it took Marla another half hour to get ready. She made sure Babs's color came out okay, went over details for the following week with her handsome Latino receptionist, and picked up her bag filled with tools of the trade.

Always be prepared for a hair emergency, especially in South Florida.

Outside, the humidity brought sweat to her brow as she walked to the parking lot. A cold front was supposed to arrive early next week, offering the break in the weather they needed. Today, scattered clouds hung overhead but it didn't look like rain. For Jill's sake, she hoped the blue skies held.

She transferred her gown and accessories to Torrie's BMW trunk before climbing into the back seat. Then she spared a moment to call Dalton and inform him she was driving with friends to the wedding venue.

"Good idea," Dalton said. "I'll see you there later."

She warmed to the sound of his deep, sexy voice. "What time do you think you'll get off work?"

"Not before five. Don't worry, I'll make it."

"Did you talk to Brie?"

"Your mother took her to the mall at Sawgrass. They're having a great time. She'll be fine without us for one night."

What would I do without Ma to occupy the teen? I want to enjoy my time alone with Dalton. Is that selfish of me?

"Don't forget to load our overnight bags," she told him. "It'll be late when we get to the hotel."

"Not too late, I hope," Dalton said in a husky tone.

Marla glanced out the window while Torrie fought the traffic heading east. "Have you checked on the dogs?"

"Your mom can handle them. I told her what time they usually go out." He cleared his throat. "By the way, my mother wants to review the seating charts for our wedding. She thinks our cousins from Arizona might be coming. We'll have to add three more seats but that leaves an odd person at one table."

Great, another headache. They'd been bombarded with suggestions from her mother and Dalton's parents, who were wintering in Florida while they searched for a condo to buy. "I gotta go. We're turning onto I-95. Bye."

Jill, sitting in the passenger seat, twisted around to address Marla. "Is everything okay with Dalton? He's going to arrive on time, isn't he?"

"Yes, he'll be there." Dalton may not have been selected to be one of Arnie's ushers, but the bridal couple counted on his presence. Plus this was Dalton's first Jewish wedding, and Marla wanted him to observe the traditions. Their own ceremony would be an interfaith marriage, but she hoped to retain some of the customs from her religion. They still had an overwhelming number of details to work out. She pressed a hand to her throbbing temple.

The sisters resumed their bickering.

"I don't want to pay a lawyer to draw up a new lease when our current tenant hasn't officially terminated," Torrie said, gripping the steering wheel.

Jill gave her a reproving look. "Kevin says we need backup, otherwise we might end up without any tenant."

"Yeah, but he won't be paying the attorney fees."

"He's promised to find us a new lessee without charging a commission. Or is that lessor? I don't understand the lingo."

"Listen, Marla," Jill said. "Torrie and I own property that's been leased to an auto lube center. Our father passed it on to us, and we never had to do anything except collect the checks every month. Then one day, I got an e-mail from a stranger who informed me the building had been vacated."

"Where is this property located?" Marla suppressed a yawn.

"In Miami, out west in the Kendall area. It used to be cow pastures and farms out there before the population exploded."

"Weren't you aware something was wrong when the rent checks stopped coming?"

"But they didn't," Jill replied. "Our lease is with the main company. We're still getting paid, but for how long, who knows? We hope to get a new tenant lined up before the company terminates their lease."

"They can do that?"

"There's an early termination clause," Torrie piped in. "And we want more money if we get a new tenant. We're not getting enough according to what the property is worth now."

"The land has escalated in value even with the volatility in real estate," Jill said. "What bothers me is, how did this guy get my e-mail address? His name is Pete Schneider, and he's a real estate agent. Or so he says."

"I looked up his firm, and it's legit," Torrie countered.

Marla leaned her arm across the seat back. "So this guy tried to get your listing?"

"We hadn't even been notified by the oil lube company that they were pulling out." Torrie's pitch rose a notch. "If it weren't for Schneider, we'd never have known the lube center closed down. I drove by there the other day. The building is boarded up and signs are posted to warn away trespassers."

"I'm confused. Didn't you just say you had a lease through the main office?"

"Yes, and I've queried them, but they haven't responded. Meanwhile, Jill called our cousin Kevin for advice. He's a big wheel in commercial real estate. Kevin said he'd find us a new tenant without charging a commission, but Schneider claimed he could get us a higher rental income. I think we should see what he can offer."

"We'd have to pay him a hefty commission." Jill glared at Torrie. "Kevin is willing to help us for free."

"What is this land-swap thing he mentioned?" Torrie shot back. "Sounds like a way for him to get our piece of land."

Turning in her seat, Jill tilted her head. "Kevin's already done some checking on the site," she told Marla, "and apparently it's not zoned for drive-ins. He'd only mentioned swapping as a means to get an equally valued location with better variances."

"I don't like it." Torrie rolled her shoulder. "Now that the property is worth so much more, everyone is out to get it."

"You're too paranoid. We have to trust someone, and my vote

is for Kevin." Jill wagged her fingers at Marla. "I asked Uncle Eddy to advise us on termination procedures with our current tenant. He's drawing up a partnership agreement for us and suggested this might be a good time to sell."

"I won't sell. I need the income," Torrie persisted.

"Then we need Kevin to find us another tenant so we won't be left high and dry," her sister said. "Give him a chance—"

"I still intend to communicate with Pete Schneider. He may come up with a better deal. It can't hurt to sound him out."

"We can't talk to him if we're giving Kevin the listing." Jill spread her hands in exasperation.

"Look, you worry about the wedding. I'll work on this."

Sensing her friend was getting upset, Marla changed the subject. "Tell me about Orchid Isle. Our rehearsal last night went too quickly for me to scout around. It looks like a beautiful park." She'd gotten a brief impression of lush tropical grounds, winding paths, and brightly colored flowers.

Torrie glanced at her in the rearview mirror. "I'm friends with Leanne Oakwood, Falcon's wife. Falcon devised the idea of a local attraction for nature enthusiasts as well as orchid fans. He hopes to finance research into advanced horticultural techniques. It's like a combo between the American Orchid Society place in Delray Beach, and Fairchild Tropical Botanic Garden."

"I can't believe the grand opening is today," Marla told Jill. "Your wedding should be one of the highlights, especially when—"

"That's how I got my magazine to provide coverage," Torrie interrupted, which appeared to be a habit of hers.

Marla didn't care for people who had to be the center of attention, but she cut Torrie some slack because of the wedding.

"I don't get it. Do you mean *Boca Style* is covering Jill and Arnie's event, or the park's opening ceremonies?" she asked the matron of honor.

"The angle is 'Where to Get Wed and Go to Bed: Romantic Locales in South Florida for Marriages and Wedding Nights.' Our magazine photographer, Griff Beasley, and society reporter, Hally Leeds, will be present."

"So you're responsible for Jill being able to book the place?"

"That's right." Torrie lifted her chin. "She doesn't give me any credit, even when I try to do the right thing. You don't know how much effort I've put into her wedding gift. It's—"

Her cell phone rang, and she grimaced. "That's probably Scott wanting to know where we are."

"So answer it," Jill snapped.

"Hello? Yes, dear, I'm with Jill now. We're at least a half hour away." A pause. "Why is Kevin telling *you* that? It's not your problem. Tell him to take a hike." She pushed the end button and stuffed the phone back into her purse.

"What did he say?" Jill pulled a compact from her handbag and checked her complexion.

"Kevin advises us to remain tenants-in-common on the deed."

"Why?"

"Who knows? It irks me that Kevin would talk to Scott about a matter concerning you and me. My husband should stick to fixing clocks in that dusty old shop of his. He doesn't have a good head for business. I'm the one who manages our finances." Glancing in the side mirror, she changed lanes.

"You brag about that all the time," Jill said, "but you haven't done any estate planning. When are you going to fulfill your promise? You told me you'd—"

"Who are you to talk about promises, darling? You didn't exactly hold true to yours in the past."

"Maybe not, but knowing why I acted as I did, you shouldn't blame me. And yet, that's all you've done through the years."

Torrie gave a heavy sigh. “I know, and that’ll change soon. Until then, let’s hope your vows mean more this time around.”

CHAPTER TWO

Marla sped down a winding brick path at Orchid Isle. Or rather, she walked as fast as she could in her dyed heels and bridesmaid gown.

Why did Torrie say Jill's vows should mean more this time around? Those words didn't make any sense.

This was Jill's first marriage. Surely Torrie must have been referring to something else? Maybe Jill had made a promise to Torrie that she hadn't kept. That could account for their strained relationship, especially since Torrie hadn't struck Marla as the forgiving sort. Then again, Jill had been known to lie in the past. She'd pretended to be an old classmate of Arnie's when they first met.

Reaching an intersection, Marla examined the signposts. Even though she had been here last night, she couldn't remember which way to go. She aimed to find the Bride's Cottage, where Jill was getting dressed.

Lugging her bag full of supplies, she swiped at her forehead, beaded with sweat. Her lavender gown swished about her ankles as she swatted an insect, cursing the humidity. She'd left behind the other bridal attendants, still primping in a private room across from the banquet hall. They had the benefit of air-conditioning, while she sweltered in the afternoon heat.

An evergreen scent pervaded the moist air, likely from the pine needles used as mulch. Colorful orchids mingled among the tropical foliage along with red crotons, pink pentas, and

Chinese fringe flowers. Dense growth peppered the area, broken by a trickling stream. Alongside the path, green liriope acted as ground cover while moss-draped live oaks and laurel fig trees provided shade. Ferns, palms, and bromeliads competed for space. The wedding would take place in the gazebo by the Rose Garden. Should she go left or right? She couldn't remember if the wedding site was by the Floral Clock or the House Museum. Listening to birds twittering in the branches, she discerned voices coming closer.

"Chill out, babe. The ceremony hasn't started yet. And anyway, I'm not the danged wedding photographer. My job is to cover the event in conjunction with the park's debut, remember?"

"So why are you in such a hurry?" a sharp female voice replied. "It can't be because you want to see the matron of honor, is it? Her husband is here somewhere. You wouldn't want him to see you having an intimate tête-à-tête."

"Get off my case, Hally. Focus on what you do best: observing other people and criticizing them."

The couple rounded a corner and fell silent when they spotted Marla. Her quick glance detected the man's scowl and the woman's taut expression. Hally, a tall redhead, wore a black dress with a deep V-neckline, an empire waist, and a skirt that fell to just below her knees. Floral appliqués at the bust and hem gave the dress a modest flare. Paired with dark heels, a shimmering metallic belt, and crystal jewelry, the ensemble fit in with the fashions displayed by Jill's well-dressed guests.

Hally's companion, on the other hand, seemed ill at ease in a tuxedo, although he'd differentiated it from the standard with a gold vest and tie. His tousled dirty-blond hair and naughty blue eyes, along with a trim beard and mustache, gave him a roguish look more befitting Robin Hood. The bulky camera in his hands revealed his trade.

"Excuse me," Marla addressed them, "are you familiar with this place? I'm lost, and I have to find the bridal cottage."

"Yo, I think it's thataway," the guy said, pointing to the left. "Near the herb garden, if I remember correctly."

"Thanks." Marla fell into step beside them. "Are you here for the wedding?"

"Sorry, I'm Griff Beasley and this is Hally Leeds." The guy tilted his head. "We're from *Boca Style Magazine*."

"Oh, isn't that where Torrie works? I met her this morning," Marla explained at their questioning looks. "I'm a friend of her sister Jill's, the bride. My name is Marla Shore, and I own a hair salon in Palm Haven called the Cut 'N Dye." She dug into her beaded handbag for a business card.

Hally took it and examined her card with interest. "Thanks. I like my current hairdresser, but you never know." She patted her sleek, straight hair, flipped up at the ends. "So tell me, what do you think of Orchid Isle so far?"

"I haven't had the chance to look around, but it's really beautiful. Are you covering the grand opening for this entire weekend?"

"Yes, we'll be here again tomorrow when the mayor shows up. We don't normally do run-of-the-mill weddings. This ceremony is newsworthy because it's the first one in the park."

"Well, I'll bet Torrie will be glad to see you."

Hally snorted. "Don't count on it."

Griff sidled up and took Marla's elbow as they approached an arch covered by winding vines with purple flowers. "Go through the arbor and hang a right at the citrus grove. Follow the brick path and you'll come to the bride's house. Be careful to watch your footing. We wouldn't want you to trip and soil your lovely gown. Maybe I should accompany you?"

She shook him off. "That's okay. Thanks for the help."

"Griff, get your paws off her and hoist your camera. Isn't

that Falcon Oakwood over by the master curator's office?" Hally pointed to a small white house with a slanted shingle roof.

"No shit? That's the big man? What's he doing talking to Torrie?" Griff squinted at the middle-aged fellow wearing eyeglasses and a formal black tuxedo.

Falcon looked as imposing as his reputation, Marla thought, observing his tall stature, wide shoulders, and graying temples. She'd figured the developer of Orchid Isle would wear an air of authority like a second skin, but it didn't seem to be working with Torrie. His hunched posture and frown indicated his displeasure with whatever she was saying.

"I hope Torrie isn't trying to edge in on my column." Hally pulled a notebook from her bag.

"I doubt it, babe. Maybe they're talking about Leanne. Torrie is friends with Oakwood's wife," Griff explained to Marla. "That's how she got her sister's wedding booked into the place."

"So where is the wife?" Hally said.

"Who knows? Let's see if Torrie will introduce us. Oakwood should be delighted to give an interview. Hey, Marla, catch ya later, okay? Save me a dance at the reception."

"She's engaged, you dolt," Marla heard Hally mutter as they hurried off. "Didn't you see the ring on her finger?"

"That hasn't stopped me before."

Marla turned away, wondering what Torrie was doing schmoozing with the park's owner instead of helping her sister get ready. *Never mind. You're here for the wedding, not to snoop into anyone else's affairs.* She hustled through the arch, veered to the right, and located the bridal cottage, another white building shaded by a Southern live oak.

"Jill, how's it going?" she called out, pushing open the door. A couple of other bridesmaids had made it inside, presumably via a different path than the one Marla had taken. They fussed over the bride, arranging her gown as she stood chewing on a fingernail in the center of the room.

"Marla, thank God. Where is everyone else? We're due to start in twenty minutes."

"They're on the way. Stop biting your nails. You'll ruin your manicure." Spotting a water cooler, Marla grabbed a fast drink and filled a cup for her friend.

"Thanks." Jill took it with a shaking hand. "Did you see Lisa and Josh outside? Their nanny phoned to say she'd arrived. They should be with Arnie."

"I didn't go by the groom's house." Marla's cell phone rang and she answered. "Hello, Dalton. Glad you made it. What? You're getting seated? Okay." She held her hand over the mouthpiece and spoke to Jill. "He says the guests have filled most of the chairs, and the rabbi is there."

"I know; he came in for me to sign the *ketubah*. The Jewish marriage contract," Jill explained to another friend.

The door opened and the rest of Jill's attendants bustled inside, followed by Arnie's mom. Since the bride's parents were deceased, Bev Hartman had been helping Jill make arrangements.

"Get your flowers, girls," Bev said. The older woman looked attractive in a lilac suit and matching wide-brimmed hat. "Jill, you look beautiful. Where's your bouquet? They'll be starting up the music soon."

A string quartet was set to play during the ceremony. The instrumentalists would move inside afterward as part of a larger band for the reception.

A man barged his way into their dominion to a muted chorus of gasps from the ladies. A couple of inches short of six feet tall, he had a narrow face, pale blue eyes, and a wide smile. He wore his longish ebony hair tied in a ponytail.

"Jill, sweetheart, you're absolutely gorgeous. Absolutely," he said, waving his hands. "Did you unpack my boxes? Is everything wonderful?"

"Marla, this is Philip Canfield, our florist." Jill raised an eyebrow. "Marla is getting married next month at the Queen Palm Country Club."

"Really? Do you have someone to do your flowers?"

"Ah, yes, thanks, but I'll keep you in mind," Marla replied.

"Bev, did you find my bouquet?" Jill called. Bev handed her the arrangement. "Oh my, it's lovely." She sniffed the white carnations and roses. "I hate to have to toss them."

"Tradition, sweetheart, tradition." Philip patted her shoulder. "Now if you'll excuse me, duty requires my attention elsewhere. Wait until you see the reception hall. It's absolutely fabulous."

Torrie breezed in, just as he departed. "Are we ready to go, people?"

Her hair was starting to wilt, Marla noted with alarm. Why had she stood outside so long in the humidity?

"Let me fix those curls in front." Marla withdrew a portable curling iron from her bag.

After fixing Torrie's hairdo, she helped Jill don her veil.

"Really, Jill, you're going all out," Torrie said with a sniff. "This getup suits a virgin more than you."

"Maybe you're not aware," Marla said, insulted for her friend, "but in a Jewish ceremony, the bride is veiled. The tradition honors Rebecca, who veiled her face when she was first brought to Isaac to be his wife."

"Oh, yeah? Veils can also be used as a disguise." Torrie leaned over and whispered a few words in Jill's ear.

Jill jerked back as though she'd been burned. "How dare you mention her name to me? If you say one word to anyone, you'll be sorry. It'll be the last thing you ever say."

"I'd better run along," Bev said, after glancing at her watch. "It's almost your turn. Good luck, girls."

While Arnie's mother charged out the door, Marla wondered

what Torrie had said to Jill that visibly upset her. Or maybe Jill's trembling was simply due to nerves. Marla could easily sympathize. Soon she'd be in the same position. Along with a matron of honor, she'd have four attendants, including Dalton's daughter, Brianna. Since it was her second wedding, she didn't want a fancy affair. Their relatives had different ideas, though. Their guest list kept climbing.

Summoned outside, Marla took her place in the procession. She grasped the flowers, their scent heavy in the heat. Her palms sweated but she dared not wipe them on her gown.

Swallowing, she scanned the rows of seated guests, the rabbi up front in his white robe, and the gazebo decorated with flowers to become a chuppah. She looked forward to standing under one herself again, and hopefully the canopy held up by four poles this time would symbolize a better home for her and Dalton than her previous marriage.

Josh and Lisa, Arnie's children from his first wife, paraded down the aisle scattering rose petals. Music played in the background, drowning out the drone of an airplane overhead.

She braced herself, and then it was her turn to walk down the aisle. She held her head high, hoping she wouldn't trip, her gaze finding Dalton among the seated guests. He looked magnificent in a dark tuxedo, tall and broad-shouldered with his usual air of authority. She swallowed. In just four weeks, they'd be man and wife. Taking her place in the lineup with the other attendants, she turned to face the audience.

Jill acquitted herself admirably to the awww's and ahhh's of the assembly. Once under the chuppah, she circled the groom seven times. Not being particularly religious, Marla would readily forego this ritual during her interfaith ceremony, but she respected its meaning nonetheless.

As a convert to Judaism, her friend Jill didn't expect her relatives to understand. She'd explained the traditions in the program, which she had showed Marla last night at the rehearsal dinner. Marla had learned something new, having tuned out at Sunday school to imagine different hairstyles on her friends.

Just as the world was created in seven days, the bride, representing Mother Earth in her seven turns around the groom, reminded people that marriage was part of the creation process. At the same time, she symbolically built the walls of the couple's new dwelling, embodied by the chuppah.

Facing away from the assembly, Jill settled at Arnie's right side. Once they were in place, the rabbi recited several psalms before beginning a series of blessings that conveyed the holiness of marriage.

"Blessed are You, our God, King of the Universe, Who created the fruit of the vine." The robed clergyman paused while the bride and groom drank from a cup of wine.

Smiling, Marla felt a surge of joy. She always liked to recite the Kiddush, the special sanctification prayer over wine included on Shabbat and festivals. Marriage demonstrated the ultimate sanctification of a man and woman to each other. Too bad her ex hadn't extended that belief to her.

Marla blocked out the rabbi's words when her attention caught on Falcon Oakwood in the front row. Perched at the edge of his seat, he was flanked by a younger woman with short reddish-brown hair in a pixie cut, and a stern-faced matron with snowy white hair and a pearl satin suit. Which one was his wife, Leanne? Surely not the older lady. From the similarity in their prominent noses and double chins, Marla would guess she and Falcon were related. The younger woman, wearing a low-cut cream shift under a lacy black dress, looked markedly unhappy.

Marla swung her gaze back just in time to see Arnie place a gold ring on Jill's finger.

"Be sanctified unto me with this ring according to the Law of

Moses and Israel," he said in a clear, firm tone.

Seeing the joy radiating from his eyes, Marla blinked back a swell of tears. Her dear friend had found happiness at last, and she mentally wished him and his bride years of conjugal bliss.

While the rabbi read the marriage contract out loud, she wondered if it was true that a *ketubah* existed for interfaith ceremonies. She'd have to look into it for her own nuptials.

Time sped while the rabbi recited more blessings. After the bride and groom took a sip from their second cup of wine, Arnie bent his knee and stomped on the traditional wrapped glass.

Marla's heart exulted. Even though this practice was supposed to remind people of the holy Temple's destruction in Jerusalem, she assigned it a happy connotation. Her mother said this was the last time the groom got to put his foot down.

Accompanied by shouts of *mazel tov!* and applause, Arnie and Jill faced the audience, smiled broadly, and strode down the aisle.

The cocktail hour got into full swing on the porch attached to the main building. Marla and the others in the wedding party lingered behind, having been corralled by the photography team for more outdoor shots. Griff and Hally hovered nearby, the former snapping pictures for their magazine while the reporter scribbled notes. As the group broke up, Hally scurried after Falcon Oakwood to get an interview.

Griff attached himself to Marla, offering to get her a drink. "Like, you can tell me about your salon."

"Thanks," she said, aware of his seductive undertone, "but I have to find my fiancé inside." They trudged along the path together, while Marla took care not to soil her shoes.

"Griff, where are you going?" Torrie snapped, catching up to them. "I need you to take photos of what everyone's wearing for my fashion column."

"That isn't my job," he replied with a hint of annoyance. "We're covering the wedding in its nature setting."

"What do you mean, *we?*"

"Me and Hally." He scraped stiff fingers through his unruly blond hair. "You know we got this assignment for today."

"Yeah, at whose suggestion to our senior editor?" Torrie's voice rose, while Marla pretended to hurry on ahead. She put a stretch of distance between them and then slowed her pace so she could remain within hearing range. "Dellene is aware I'm writing up the event."

"Bug off, babe. This isn't your gig. I saw you talking to Falcon Oakwood earlier. He say anything about his enterprise that Hally can use as a quote?"

"Why should I help her?"

"Because some cooperative spirit might advance your cause better than your usual bitchy attitude?"

"Oh, right, like I'm gonna boost Hally's career."

"I thought you were friends with Leanne Oakwood. Surely you got enough of a scoop from her."

"My discussion with Falcon was private, you moron, so stop pressing me. Hally can interview him if she wants to pepper her article with his words of wisdom." Her voice turned sugary. "Now behave, darling. When are we going to meet again?"

"I'm tied up for the next few weeks," he replied in a sullen tone. "Can't pin down any dates right now."

"You're not avoiding me, are you? I'd hate to think you were lying, Griff, especially when I've put myself at risk for you. Scott hasn't said anything, but he's given me odd looks lately."

"So let's chill for a while."

"Are you kidding? I'm ready to make my move."

"I'm just saying it may be too soon."

"You're not backing out, are you? Because if you've made empty promises to me, you'll be sorry."

"Don't threaten me, babe."

"You know what I can do."

"Oh, yeah? Well, let me give you a word of warning. If you rat on me, you're dead."

Marla heard scuffling noises, then smooching. "Now that's better," Torrie crooned. "You always did like it rough."

Griff laughed, but it sounded more like a sinister snicker.

Wondering about their discussion, Marla zoomed ahead to join the gaily dressed guests sampling hors d'oeuvres on a shaded porch. Drinks in hand, Dalton waited for her by the steps.

"Here, I thought you'd need this." He handed her a wine glass filled with a light golden fluid.

"Thanks." She stood on her tiptoes to give him a brief kiss before greedily gulping the dry white wine. After quenching her thirst, she moved under a ceiling fan to cool off. "Have you seen Jill? I wonder if she needs help."

"She's fine, sweetcakes. Did I tell you how ravishing you look?" His smoky gaze dropped to her figure.

"Thanks, but pastels aren't really my color."

"No? What are you wearing to *our* wedding? You still haven't found a dress, have you?"

"I'm looking for the perfect outfit." Someone bumped her rear, and she turned to face a stout man in a tuxedo. He had thinning gray hair, florid skin, and deep-set oak brown eyes under prominent brows.

"Oh, I'm terribly sorry," the man said in a slurred tone. He held a wine glass that was empty except for a few dregs.

Jill chose that moment to sidle up to them. "Uncle Eddy, I see you've run into my friend, Marla and her fiancé, Dalton Vail. Marla, this is Eddy Rhodes and his wife, Alexis."

"Nice to meet you," Marla said to the large-boned woman by his side. Eddy's wife had rather masculine features, like a cross-dresser wearing heavy makeup. Marla couldn't help staring, while inwardly berating herself.

Alexis addressed her husband. "Come on, Eddy, you need to sit down." She grasped his elbow.

He shook her off. "Nonsense, I'm always delighted to meet friends of my niece. How are ya, folks? Isn't this a grand wedding? Except for the liquor. Cheap stuff, but whaddya expect?" He signaled a passing waiter. "Hey, my good man. Can you kindly get me a refill?"

"You've had enough." Alexis gritted her teeth.

"Hell, no, I'm just getting started." He elbowed Dalton. "If you want a real vintage, you should see my wine cellar."

"Thanks, but I'm not a connoisseur." Dalton stepped back a pace.

"Kevin appreciates a good bottle, don't you?" Eddy drew over a long-faced man with short tobacco hair and sallow skin. "Kevin is my brother Luke's kid. Tall fellow, isn't he?"

Kevin's ears turned red. "Hi, Uncle Eddy, Aunt Alexis. Jill, allow me to congratulate the bride." He kissed her on the cheek. "I hope you'll be happy. Arnie seems like a nice guy, even if he is Jewish."

"So am I, cousin," Jill reminded him. "I hope you respect my choice. Where is Dana?" Her blond head twisted to regard the company. Arnie waved to her, and she gathered her skirt prior to hastening over.

"My wife is chatting with Torrie and Scott," Kevin said. "Yo, Jill, before you go, we have to talk. I drove by your property on the way here and—"

"Not now, please. I think it's almost time to go in to dinner." She moved off, and Marla trailed along to offer her congratulations to the groom.

Events followed in a whirl. Guests paraded into the magnificent reception hall decorated in dark lilac, lavender, and cream, with tiny white lights strung throughout lavish floral centerpieces. Tea candles on the tables and chiffon ceiling drapes added to the romantic ambience.

Marla and Dalton didn't make the head table, reserved for the bride and groom, Arnie's parents, and Jill's sister and brother-in-law. Instead, they found their places among the other attendants, mostly recent acquaintances.

"I'd rather seat people at our affair with their friends and family," Marla whispered to Dalton.

"Later," he rasped back as Arnie and Jill marched in to a round of applause before starting the dancing with their special song. Marla recalled the elaborate reception she'd had with Stan. Too bad she hadn't saved her dream wedding for Dalton.

"Come on," she yelled to him when the band started playing a lively tune. She grabbed his hand and pulled him into the circle being formed, kicking her legs and sidestepping with the rest of the laughing crowd dancing the hora.

Meal courses intermingled with the music. When it was Arnie's turn to be lifted in a chair in joyful celebration, she pushed Dalton onto the dance floor to assist. At first reserved, he'd mellowed after several drinks, and he gamely joined Arnie's friends in hoisting the wedding couple to shouts of cheer and rousing music.

Hours later, after the entrée had been cleared, Jill approached their table. "Have you seen my sister?" she asked Marla. "I want to do the bouquet toss before people leave."

Marla glanced at Torrie's husband, whom she'd met earlier. The man stood alone, staring morosely at his drink. His face reminded her of Edward G. Robinson when the actor played Dathan in *The Ten Commandments,* one of her favorite films. He wore round eyeglasses, a mustache and goatee, and a permanent hunch.

"Maybe she's gone to the ladies' room. You haven't cut the

cake yet. Don't you want to do that first?" Marla glanced at the alcove where the tiered wedding cake was displayed on a decorated table. "I can get a waitress to wheel it over."

She looked for the young woman she'd seen earlier, who had appeared fascinated by the bride. The girl's creamy complexion didn't match her severe black hair, making her stand out to Marla's expert eye. Something wasn't quite right about her appearance, but she didn't see the girl anywhere now.

"Where's the photographer?" The bride craned her neck to survey the room. "I'll have to drag Arnie over."

Marla spotted Dalton talking to one of Arnie's relatives and signaled that she'd be occupied. "Go look for them. I can take care of the cake."

"Torrie shouldn't just disappear like that." Jill shook her head. "I hope she isn't talking to Kevin about our property without me. He's not here, either."

Marla left her friend muttering to herself as she headed for the recess at the side of the stage. A slow, romantic tune played on the speaker system. She noticed a service door right behind the clothed round table on which the cake sat. The confection was beautifully done, with three layers culminating in a ceramic bride and groom at the top. The buttercream frosting was embellished with edible ribbons and rosettes that made her smack her lips in anticipation of a sugary treat.

"There's no knife," she said in dismay, figuring she'd have to get a waiter after all.

Until she stepped behind the table with her back to the wall. Until she saw the woman's arm poking out from under the tablecloth. And until she pushed back the drape and saw the cake knife embedded in Torrie Miller's chest.

Chapter Three

Oh, God. She must be seeing things. But when Marla lifted the drape again, Torrie's body lay there, unmoving, in the same spot.

Was the woman dead? Making that determination would decide her next action.

Thinking fast, she clutched her ear and said aloud to any passersby, "Oh, my, I've lost an earring back." That should justify her dropping out of sight for a few seconds.

She crouched quickly, drew in a deep breath, and felt Torrie's clammy wrist for a pulse.

Nothing.

She couldn't bear to touch the woman's neck, not with her glazed eyes half-open. Torrie's chest—dear Lord, Marla had to force her horrified glance away from the knife—wasn't rising, but the bile in her own throat choked her.

Coughing, she covered her mouth and stood upright. *Come on, don't throw up. Think what you should do next.*

Regret swelled within her. Jill expected Torrie to watch the cake-cutting ceremony. How awful. She may not have gotten along with her sister, but this presented a horrible end to their troubled relationship.

Uncertain how to proceed, Marla nudged Torrie's arm under the table and released the cloth so nothing showed.

Catching Dalton's eye, she signaled frantically. He'd know what to do. When he reached her side, she sagged against him.

"Don't look now, but there's a dead body under the table," she murmured under her breath.

"What?"

"You heard me." She smiled tremulously at a couple who strolled past. Could they tell she was sweating? That her face had lost its color? That she was about to lose her dinner?

Dalton half bent, his dark hair falling forward, but then he straightened with a grin. "Good one, Marla. You almost got me."

She shuffled her feet. "I'm not kidding." Any minute they'd call for the cake, or Jill would broaden the hunt for her sister. Chewing on her bottom lip, she lifted a portion of the drape so Vail could see for himself. Her stomach heaved as she almost stepped on a trickle of congealing blood. Forcing down the acid reflux, she grimaced.

"Holy Mother, you aren't joking." He gave her an incredulous glance that she read as, *Not again.*

"I didn't feel a pulse. Can you believe this? I mean, it's bad enough that Torrie met her end this way, but couldn't it have happened after Jill and Arnie left? Their wedding has gone so smoothly until now." She didn't intend to sound callous, but she felt so bad for her friend, considering the unpleasant events that would follow.

Dalton's lips compressed. "Let me take a look. Anyone watching?"

"Not right this minute."

"Good." He bent, muttered an expletive, then straightened. "I have to call this in."

She let the cloth fall back into place. "Can we do it quietly? I hate to put a pall over everything, at least until Jill concludes the ceremonies. Give her a few more happy memories for the wedding album, if you will."

"Are you proposing we should keep the lid on an obvious

crime scene?" Dalton asked, flabbergasted.

"I'm proposing that we don't let anyone move this table to disrupt the evidence. Think about it."

Dalton's glance met hers, and she saw by the stormy gray in his eyes that he understood Marla's overwhelming concern for her friend.

"Stay here. I'll go out in the hall to make the call." He started toward the door behind the alcove, appeared to have second thoughts, and veered in the opposite direction.

Marla gave a sick smile to anyone who passed, saying she was guarding the cake table until Jill and Arnie had rounded up the photographer.

"We'll leave the table here," Dalton said upon his return, "and just move the cake. That should buy us about fifteen minutes or so before the shit hits the fan."

"Thanks, Dalton. We can do this."

Steeling herself, she lifted half of the cardboard base holding the tiered confection while Dalton gripped the other side. Together they started a slow shuffling dance toward the head table. Her breath came short and rapid from the labor, or maybe she was hyperventilating out of fright that someone would discover the body.

"Hey, guys, what are you doing?" Philip Canfield intercepted them. His ponytail had come loose, and he looked hassled.

Marla hadn't realized the florist was still around. "It's time for the cake ceremony."

"What happened to my beautiful table?" He gestured toward the nook. "Didn't you see the flowers I put around the rim? My magnificent orchids? They match those candied violets to perfection." He air-kissed his fingers for emphasis.

Marla paused before she tripped and sprayed the crowd with buttercream frosting. "Uh, one of the legs is broken. We were afraid the table would topple over if we wheeled it out. Can you imagine the disaster?" She gave a nervous laugh.

"Good heavens, then allow me to assist you. I'll get a tray. Don't go anywhere."

"Never mind, we'll be all right," Dalton reassured him.

"I'm sorry, I didn't introduce you," Marla said hastily, hoping to distract the man. "Philip, this is my fiancé, Dalton Vail. We're getting married in four weeks."

"Yes, I remember. I should give you my card in case you run into a snag with your decorator." He fumbled in his pocket and handed her a business card. "December is such a busy month, what with holiday parties and all. I'd find a way to fit you into my schedule."

Seeing that she had her hands full, he tucked the card into Dalton's tuxedo jacket. *Leave already,* Marla commanded silently, her arms trembling. If she didn't put the darn cake down soon, she'd splatter it all over the floor.

"Your centerpieces are fabulous," she said, hoping to spur him on his way. "And I loved how you decorated the gazebo into a chuppah. You did a wonderful job."

Dalton inclined his head, meaning they should resume their pace. She picked up speed, her grip slick with sweat. Biting her lip, she concentrated on their destination.

"Don't forget," Canfield said, dogging their steps. "Call me if you need me. I'm tops in the business."

She grunted with relief when he strolled away and they'd put their burden to rest at the bride's place of honor. Her body shook from head to toe. She dreaded the scene that would follow.

"Where's the cake knife?" Dalton's brow creased in a perplexed frown.

She stared at him, aghast. "Didn't you see? That's what . . . it's in Torrie's chest."

"Hell. Wait here."

He ran off and returned a few moments later brandishing a meat knife. "This will have to do. Let's move things along. Yo, Arnie," he hollered to the groom, dancing to an oldie but goodie at arm's length with an elderly matron.

Arnie's expression, a sort of weary resignation, brightened. "Come and join us on the dance floor."

Dalton shook his head. "Can't. Time to cut the cake. Where's the bride?"

Marla spotted Jill across the room, chatting with Leanne Oakwood while the wedding photographer jostled with the man from *Boca Style Magazine* for the best angle to snap pictures. She could just imagine Falcon's reaction to a murder on Orchid Isle's opening weekend. Then again, sensational news coverage often brought curiosity seekers to a site. Attendance might increase as a result.

"Excuse us, please," she told Falcon's wife, steering Jill away by the elbow. "Arnie is waiting for you to cut the cake," she informed the bride. "We moved it over to the center where everyone can see better."

"Thanks, hon. I saw you chatting with Philip. Aren't his flower arrangements magnificent? Leanne was telling me how he keeps her vases filled at home. I gather he was instrumental in helping Falcon obtain some of the rarer orchids for his collection."

"Is that so? He must have good suppliers. Tell me, how are you holding up?" *You'd better be strong, considering the bad news that's about to ruin your day.*

"I'm fine." Jill bustled forward, her gown sweeping the floor. "The cake looks so beautiful, it's almost too perfect to destroy. Don't forget to save the top layer for me to take home and freeze."

"Here." Dalton shoved the knife handle at her and Arnie. "Smile for the camera."

Arnie stared at the knife but didn't make a move to take it. "What's this? It isn't the one we picked out at the store."

"What do you mean?" Marla's heart skipped a beat.

"We bought a special cake knife. Jill liked the ribbons and engraving. You must have left it on the table."

"I don't know why you moved the cake, Marla," Jill added. "The lighting over there was better for photos."

"It's good here, too. Why don't you go ahead with the ceremony, since your guests are waiting? I'll find your knife later. You can use it on your anniversary when you defrost the remains."

Her unfortunate choice of a last word brought a different type of remains to mind. Gulping, she pushed that thought aside with another unpleasant memory.

She'd frozen the top layer from her wedding to Stan and easily recalled its bitter taste one year later when their marriage dissolved.

"Arnie, will you look on the other table?" Jill said in a peevish tone.

"I'll go." Dalton loped off before anyone could object. He returned a moment later, shaking his head. "Sorry, can't find your knife anywhere. We'll ask the caterer later. Meanwhile, I'd suggest you proceed. It's getting late, and people will start leaving soon."

No bride wanted to see her guests depart before she'd completed all the rituals.

As Jill and Arnie fed cake to each other and the assistant photographer caught them on video, Marla reflected how Jill seemed more concerned about her missing cake knife than her sister. Nor did the bride comment on the matron of honor's absence during the garter and bouquet tosses. How odd, unless she figured Torrie was occupied elsewhere.

Dalton had gone out to make a second call for backup. He'd

just reentered the ballroom when a shriek rent the air. A young blond waitress, attempting to move the round table in the corner, stood rooted to the spot with an expression of horror on her face. A pair of legs stuck out from beneath the floor-length cloth, plum high heels stained with a sickly crimson.

"Hold on." Dalton rushed over. He whispered a few words to the woman, who then stumbled from the room. "Listen up, people," he said to the shocked assembly, while the musicians on stage froze, instruments in midair. "There's been a, er, an accident. Why don't you gather your belongings and wait on the porch where we had cocktails?" His commanding tone brooked no arguments. "The police are on their way, and they'll want to ask questions before you leave."

"Who is it?" Jill asked, the words barely escaping her lips. Arnie's mouth compressed as he put an arm around her waist.

Marla scanned the room. Fortunately, his kids were nowhere in sight. They must be outdoors with the other youngsters. "I'm afraid it's Torrie," she said, feeling she should be the one to break the news. "I'm so sorry, Jill."

"My sister? Oh, my God. Did they call an ambulance? I'll go with her to the hospital."

Her next stop is likely the morgue. Marla's heart went out to the newlyweds. How she'd wanted this day to be joyous.

When Jill started to move toward her sister, Marla blocked her path. People filed past them toward the patio in a somber and silent fashion. In the periphery of her vision, she saw Dalton barring anyone from going near the crime scene.

Marla exchanged a glance with Arnie. There was no avoiding the truth. "Jill, your sister's been stabbed. Torrie is beyond help. I'm sorry," she repeated.

"She's . . . she isn't . . ." Jill sputtered to a stop.

"Yes."

"Oooh." The bride sagged against Arnie, whose eyes reflected painful awareness.

"Look, why don't you guys wait in the bride's room? We'll tell the detective in charge to question you first. There isn't anything you can do by hanging around here," Marla said.

"I should find our nanny and let her know what's going on," Arnie told Jill. "She can take Josh and Lisa home."

"Call her on your cell phone," Marla suggested. "Dalton and I will handle the traffic at this end. Go on, you two. At least you can have some privacy while we're waiting."

"Shouldn't I at least look at her? For identification, I mean." Jill's eyes filled with tears.

"Scott can do that. See, Dalton is talking to him." Torrie's husband stood with his shoulders slumped and a hand on his mouth while Dalton spoke to him alone by the raised platform.

After more coaxing, Jill finally acquiesced. Watching Arnie lead her away, Marla slouched. She wanted nothing more than to crash at the hotel with Dalton. That wasn't about to happen any time soon, especially when the cops arrived.

Dalton held a private conference with the paramedics on the scene. They had to wait another half hour before a detective showed up, along with his team of crime lab technicians.

"Marla, this is Detective Brody." Dalton signaled her over from where she drooped by their dinner table. The staff, told not to clear the room yet, hovered by the perimeter.

Brody, in his forties, wore creases beside his eyes like a badge of honor. "I'd like to get your statement, ma'am, before I interview the bride and groom."

"How can I help you?" Her throat went dry. They sank onto seats draped in lavender.

"Tell me how you discovered the victim." Brody's deep baritone was worthy of a radio announcer.

Glancing at Dalton for comfort, Marla folded her hands in her lap. "It was time for the cake-cutting ceremony. I meant to help by rolling out the side table, but then I saw an arm sticking out from underneath."

Brody scribbled in his notepad. "You were able to ID this person?"

"Yes. I took a peek beneath the cloth. Torrie, the bride's sister, had been stabbed with the cake knife."

"Torrie Miller, right?" He squinted at her, his gaze keen. "Tell me what you know about the deceased."

"She's married, works for *Boca Style Magazine* as a fashion reporter, and drives a snazzy BMW."

"I'm guessing this is a crime of passion, because whoever did it grabbed a handy weapon and didn't put much thought into hiding the body." Brody tilted his head. "We won't know the cause of death for certain until the medical examiner's report. In the meantime, can you think of anyone who had cause to harm her?"

"Can I!" *Just about everyone I met today.*

Her comment drew a snort from Dalton. "You're asking my unofficial deputy here. She'll tell you more than you want to know, buddy. And if you don't stay on top of things, she'll find the bad guy before you get anywhere close."

She swiped at a couple of stray hairs cutting her vision. "No way. I'm keeping my ears clean on this one. We have too much to do planning our own wedding." Smiling sweetly at her betrothed, she waited for the detective to prompt her again.

"I'd like to take brief statements from everyone and then let them go home," Brody said, "so if you have anyone in mind that I should interview further, please share that information."

A flash of light drew her attention to the forensic guy snapping pictures. The cake table had been moved out of the way, and Torrie's body lay in full view. Someone had drawn a chalk outline around it.

A wave of dizziness assailed her. "The photographer," she

murmured. Dalton's warm hand squeezed hers, giving her strength. "Not the man doing wedding photos, but the other one. Griff Beasley. He works with Torrie at the magazine."

"He's here?" Brody said with a puzzled frown.

"Yes, apparently Griff and Hally Leeds were assigned to cover the wedding because it takes place the same weekend as the grand opening for Orchid Isle. Hally is a society reporter," she explained. "They came as a team."

"When did you meet these people?" Dalton inserted, as though wondering why he'd been left out.

"Outside, just before the wedding ceremony, when I was headed toward the bride's house. I overheard a brief conversation between them."

"And?" both men said in unison.

Marla folded her arms across her chest. "Hally implied that Griff had more than a professional interest in Torrie. Hally didn't seem happy about it either."

"You're saying she acted jealous?" Brody held his pen poised over his notebook.

"I can't be sure. After all, I don't know these people very well. Hally also said something about Torrie edging in on her column. When Torrie spoke to Griff later, she sounded less than eager to boost Hally's career."

"Friendly rivalry between colleagues is nothing new," Dalton commented.

"Right, but if you're looking for motives, Hally came across as resentful either way."

"Had you noticed any hint about more than a professional relationship between this Beasley character and the deceased?" Brody asked.

Marla's face pinched in thought. "Actually, yes. Torrie said something to Griff about putting herself at risk for him and that she hoped her husband hadn't noticed. She said Griff would be sorry if he backed out on his word."

"What did he say in return?"

"That if she ratted on him, she's dead," Marla ended in a hushed tone.

Brody scribbled madly. "Those two sound like persons of interest. Who else?"

"Um, Torrie had a conversation with Falcon Oakwood. I know she's friends with his wife, Leanne. That's how Jill was able to book the wedding at Orchid Isle."

"So?" Dalton yawned.

The poor man looked exhausted. Marla felt bad, embroiling him in another murder investigation. It wasn't his district, but he wouldn't let go so easily.

"Whatever Torrie and Falcon were discussing wasn't making the real estate developer happy," Marla said. "Then again, they could have been talking about the weather, for all I know."

"Anything else?" Brody gripped his pen.

"Well, there are the family issues."

"Oh?" Brody straightened, his keen eyes alert.

"Jill and Torrie own a piece of commercial property together. It's been rented on a steady basis until recently, when their tenant left. Their cousin Kevin, who's in the real estate business, offered to get them a new lease without charging a commission."

"This property, is it worth much?"

"It's increased in value. Torrie and Jill were in the process of drawing up a partnership agreement. I believe their uncle, an attorney, was helping them."

"I see," Brody murmured, adding Jill's relatives to his expanding list of guests to interview more thoroughly. "Thanks for your cooperation, Miss Shore. You've been very helpful. Lieutenant," he said to Dalton, "you and the lady can go now. We'll talk more later. I may have more questions, plus I'd appreciate your insights."

Dalton didn't have talking on his mind when he unlocked their hotel room door, unfastened his bow tie and cummerbund, and loosened his shirt. With a gleam in his eyes, he pulled her close after she'd kicked off her shoes.

"I'm sorry for what happened today." He stroked her hair. "This should have been a happy occasion."

"It's horrible. I can't imagine how Jill feels right now."

She closed her eyes, relishing the feel of his strong arms around her. She needed to feel alive, to know that her own world felt stable. Raising her stockinged feet, she met his lips with a passionate kiss.

He deepened the embrace. "These clothes are in the way," he murmured, raining kisses down her cheek. "Do you think Torrie got in Jill's way?"

Dalton's sexy tone distracted her from his words. "What?"

He drew a corner of her gown off her shoulder and kissed her bared flesh. "I mean, could your friend Jill be glad her sister is out of the picture?"

Marla jerked back. "How could you think that?"

He didn't drop his hands from where he held her. "I saw you fidget when you mentioned the partnership issue."

Her temples throbbed. "I was wondering who stood to inherit Torrie's share, that's all."

"You think Jill has something to gain by her sister's death?"

"More likely Torrie's husband Scott is her heir."

"Depends on what Torrie's will states. She could have left her portion to either one."

"I'm not privy to that information, nor do I care." She smiled up at his concerned face. "All I care about right now is this." Moving her hand, she showed him what she meant.

His breath hitched, and their conversation ended abruptly as he sidestepped her to the bed.

Tomorrow, she'd think about what Jill had whispered to Torrie just before the ceremony.

If you say one word to anyone, you'll be sorry. It'll be the last thing you ever say.

Chapter Four

Marla and Dalton lazed in bed the next morning, sharing pillow talk. They faced each other, Marla in her silk nightgown, and Dalton in his boxers. He traced his fingers idly along Marla's arm while she stroked his chest nested with soft hairs.

"The wedding yesterday got me thinking," Dalton said, his gaze half-lidded.

"Mmm, what about?" Still groggy, she was loath to get out of bed to make coffee.

"You and me. How you've brought me back to life and given me focus again. After Pam died—"

She touched his lips. "Hush. You don't have to say it."

He brushed her hand aside. "Yes, I do." His eyes shone with a warm sheen. "We had the dream church wedding. Ten years later I watched her die a slow, agonizing death from cancer. My work is ugly. I see things that make you wonder about the worthiness of the human race. When Pam was alive, I came home to a place where I could find peace. With her gone, our daughter was the only thing that kept me going . . . until I met you."

"I know," she said softly, glad she'd made a difference. Her eyes misted as she remembered their early days together, when he refused to discard any item in his house that had belonged to Pam. She'd come to love the man, recognizing his loneliness and helping him to move on.

He wasn't the only one who'd had to adjust. After a tragedy

in her past, when Marla was babysitting a toddler and the child drowned in the backyard pool, Marla had vowed never to have children. She couldn't bear to risk the pain of loss. Never mind that the child's parents had told her to take the expected phone call. She'd looked away for mere minutes, and that's all it took for the kid to climb out of her playpen and into the water.

Even though the accident had happened years ago, it seeded Marla with doubts about her own abilities. She had Dalton and his daughter to thank for helping her grow beyond her past mistakes.

"If you stick with me," she told him, "I don't know how much peace you'll have. I've become a jinx. People around me end up dead."

Dalton tapped her nose. "That's not what gets you into trouble. You're likely to play amateur sleuth again. Leave the police business to the professionals."

Sitting upright, she clutched the sheet to her body. "You're the one who asks for my help now."

"Yeah, but this isn't one of those occasions. I understand you feel bad for Jill and Arnie, but you already have a full plate."

"Tell me about it. That reminds me, I have to talk to the painter regarding my day spa tomorrow. I'm not happy with his color selection."

"Speaking of colors, what about our wedding? Have you made a final decision yet?"

"I want to talk to the florist again first. What should we do today? Lie out by the pool?" She'd feel terribly guilty taking the entire day off. But then again, they *were* at a beach resort and should get their money's worth. "Actually, that's not a bad idea. Let's forget about everything and just relax."

Dalton's cell phone rang, putting a crimp in their plans. "Hello, Detective Brody." He stood, his shoulders hunching as he listened. "That is interesting. Thanks for the update." Clicking off, he regarded Marla from beneath his thick brows. "The knife handle was clean of prints."

"Meaning?"

"Someone was smart enough to wipe it, or they wore gloves."

She got up, pulled on her underwear, and set about making coffee on their in-room coffee maker. While waiting for it to brew, she opened the blackout drapes. They'd slept late. Morning sunbeams penetrated the room.

"That smacks of premeditation," Marla said, "but Brody assumed it was a crime of opportunity. The killer couldn't have foreseen the cake knife would be sharp enough to do the job until he'd actually held it."

"If the cause of death was from chest trauma."

"You're saying she might have been killed by other means first?" Marla shook her head. "I saw blood. She wouldn't have bled if she'd already been dead."

"True. Let's say it was a crime of passion," Dalton said, pacing the floor, "and the bad guy was smart enough to clean the weapon of choice. Did he use a cloth napkin, a handy dish towel, or perchance wear a pair of disposable plastic gloves obtained from the kitchen?"

She held up her hand in a stop signal. "Whoa, you're hurting my brain. I haven't had my caffeine yet." At the coffee stand, she broke open a condiment package and added sugar and powdered cream to one of the mugs. The smell of freshly brewed java made her mouth water.

"Well, think about it." He scratched his bristly jaw. "What would you do if you'd just stabbed someone on the spur of the moment, and the knife was still stuck in her? You couldn't risk pulling it out and having blood splatter all over your evening wear. So you leave the knife in but need to wipe the part you'd touched."

"I'd grab a dinner napkin from a nearby table. I don't think

I'd get a glove from the kitchen first. That might be traceable if the police talked to the cooks."

"So where did that napkin end up?"

Halfway to putting the filled coffee mug to her lips, Marla paused. "Good question. In the killer's pocket? To trace that, you'd have to contact all the tuxedo rental places or dry cleaners in the tri-county area. Or did the napkin land on another table, where it got picked up and sent to the facility's laundry service?"

"I'd like to take a look at the seating arrangements," Dalton said. "I suppose Jill has a copy?"

"So does Arnie's mother. But shouldn't you pass these theories on to Brody? It's his investigation, not yours."

"Right," he replied a bit too hastily.

She gave him a suspicious glance but didn't pursue the matter, hoping to cast aside the shadows from the previous evening and enjoy their day. She'd like to call Jill, but didn't want to intrude. Despite the tragedy, last evening was her friend's wedding night.

After breakfast in the hotel restaurant, she and Dalton spread their towels by the pool. Some of the other wedding guests had stayed overnight, too, judging from a few familiar faces.

She recognized Alexis, Jill's aunt by marriage, wearing a one-piece swimsuit over her big-boned form. Scrunching her eyes behind a pair of dark sunglasses, Marla watched the older woman. Alexis poised at the deep end of the pool and then dove in with the grace of a practiced diver. Impressed, Marla wished she could swim laps with such little effort.

Dalton sat oblivious at her side, shades propped on his slightly humped nose. "Where should we go for lunch?"

"Lunch? We just finished breakfast." *Typical man to think about his next meal.*

"We could go to South Beach or Lincoln Road."

"Or we could go home. Did you talk to Brie?"

He nodded. "She's fine. Anita is taking her out to eat after she finishes her homework. And before you ask, Spooks is behaving himself. He likes the new dog treats I bought."

"Good. Oh look, here comes Alexis." Marla waved.

Dalton gave a grunt of recognition. "I remember them. Her husband is the wine snob, and she's the workhorse."

"Dalton, that's not nice." Marla plastered a friendly smile on her face as Alexis strode over, a towel wrapped around her torso. Her sculpted arms made Marla wonder if she lifted weights for exercise.

"Marla, isn't it?" Alexis said in a throaty voice.

"That's right, and this is Dalton."

"I haven't seen many people from the wedding party today," Alexis replied. "Either they're sleeping in, or they left early. That wouldn't surprise me, considering what happened last night."

Marla tilted her head. "We all had quite a shock. What a terrible tragedy. I feel so bad for Jill."

Alexis scraped a chair over while Marla shot a glance at Dalton. The corners of his mouth turned down. No doubt he'd rather relax without the encumbrance of company.

"Heavens, child, I know," Alexis said. "It was such a beautiful wedding. Just like Torrie to ruin things. Used to be the other way around, from what I understood."

Marla's ears perked up. "Meaning?" She scrutinized Alexis's hair with a critical eye. Her auburn tint could use some shine. Copper highlights would do the trick.

"Jillian was the one who caused trouble in her younger days. I'm glad she's turned into a straight arrow. Changed her looks, too." Alexis waggled her eyebrows. "Got a boob job, bleached her hair. I could use the opposite," she said, chuckling and lifting her bosom.

"Tell me, how is your husband Eddy related to Jill? I know

he's her uncle, but through which parent?" Marla hoped to delve into Jill's background without seeming too nosy.

A thoughtful gleam entered Alexis's expression. "Well, now, let me see." She tapped her chin. "Sarah and David Barlow were Torrie and Jill's parents. Eddy was Sarah's brother. Jill brought her folks a lot of grief back then, and Eddy kinda feels bad that he didn't step in to help."

"Is that why Eddy is helping the girls with this property thing?" Marla guessed.

"Uh, huh. That child has a lot of gumption, I have to say. I never thought Jill deserved . . . well, that's water under the bridge. Obviously, she's gone through a lot of changes."

"Arnie's a good man and a friend of mine. I wouldn't want him to get hurt."

"Jill will do well by him, and she loves his kids. They'll be fine. It's too bad she and Torrie got dropped that bucket of worms, though. Eddy was just working on an agreement for them. Now Kevin has gotten himself involved."

"Kevin is their cousin, right?"

"Kevin is Luke's son. He's the other sibling. Luke, Sarah, and Eddy, that's the three of 'em. Can't say much for the other two, but my Eddy has done me proud. You have to come by our place sometime, child, and see our house. We have an extensive cellar, if you're into wine."

"Where do you live?"

"In Coral Gables. We have our own pool, of course, but I have to get my early morning swim, or I'm ruined for the day." She gave a trill laugh that sounded oddly like a neighing horse.

Dalton uttered a strangled cough. At Marla's glare, his face puckered and his lips clamped to suppress a grin. Okay, maybe he'd put that unkind image in her head.

"I suppose Torrie's funeral will be in Miami," Marla said. "Is her home anywhere near yours?"

"Heavens, no. They live in Kendall. Poor Scott. He tries so hard but always seems to be struggling. Or at least, that's my recent impression. They used to be quite well-off."

"Really? What happened?"

Alexis shrugged. "Beats me. It's probably a good thing they never had kids. Scott's a good-looking guy. He won't be alone for long, although he'll mourn his wife. The man truly loved her."

"I'd like to attend Torrie's memorial service. Will you give me a call when you get the information?" Marla rummaged in her bag for a business card. "Although, I suppose I could ask Jill. Arnie couldn't take off from work this week, so they're delaying their honeymoon."

"You don't want to bother the child. She'll be distraught, not that she isn't already. Jillian was positively shaking when I saw her in the ladies' room yesterday. You'd think she'd have been more relaxed with the wedding winding down."

"What time was this?"

"Oh, I dunno. Sometime after dinner but before she cut the cake. She's a bundle of nerves, that girl. If you ask me, this business with their property is driving her over the edge. She stood there, scrubbing her hands at the sink, muttering to herself. She's got too much on her mind."

"Such as?" Dalton cut in. Marla recognized his deceptively smooth tone. He could be a sly fox when interrogating suspects. Odds were in their favor that Alexis didn't know his occupation.

"That's for Jillian to say." Alexis rose. "Are you folks sticking around much longer?"

"Nope, checkout time is eleven o'clock." Dalton stood, and Marla followed suit. She really wasn't in the mood for sunbathing anyway.

"Aren't you two getting married next?" Alexis wagged her forefinger. "You should consider Philip Canfield if you don't have a wedding decorator. He did a terrific job last night. I just loved the orchids in the centerpieces."

"The flowers were beautiful, weren't they? Someone told me he works for Falcon Oakwood."

"Phil helps Falcon obtain his orchid specimens. Are you into plants, Marla? I can't abide the things. Too much trouble."

Marla gave an empathic smile. "I have a black thumb myself. Plants wilt if they come near me."

Alexis sighed. "I'd better trot off and nudge Eddy awake. Nice chatting with you people."

"You hear?" Dalton poked Marla after Alexis left. "She has to *trot* off and *nudge* Eddy. What did I tell you?"

"Give it up, Dalton. I'm more interested in hearing what she has to say about Jill."

"Interesting remark she made about Jill washing her hands. Almost reminds me of Lady Macbeth."

She glared at him. "I trust Jill, but there are things about her we don't know. If it's something she hasn't told Arnie, that's not a good way to start a marriage."

On their way indoors, Dalton hummed a classic Disney tune. "Not your business, oh no," he sang, "but if I know you, you'll know what to do, and it won't be making stew."

"So now you're a poet like my neighbor, Moss? Come on, aren't you the least bit curious?"

"Curious, yes. But not enough to take time out from my job, wedding planning, and packing to move into our new house in less than a month. And that reminds me. I need to talk to you about which toilets to order."

Her mouth dropped open. "I'm concerned about Torrie's murder, and your mind is in the toilet? Really, Dalton. What's happened to you?"

Marla had little time to think about the case on Monday, when she met her mother, Anita, and almost mother-in-law, Kate, to show them the facility at Queen Palm Country Club and review the menu. For the cocktail hour, she and Dalton had chosen a mixture of live stations manned by chefs, various hors d'oeuvres laid out buffet-style, and waitresses circulating with hot specialties. Maybe she'd gone overboard. She wanted their opinions.

"It's impressive as far as banquet halls go," Kate said, as they walked through the parking lot after their appointment. "The view of the golf course is lovely, but I'm afraid the space for the cocktails will be cramped. It's too bad that other section is already booked."

"I'm glad you cut out the turkey station," Anita countered, raking her short, layered white hair. Her fingernails flashed with bright red polish, a color that would look garish on Kate. "That was totally unnecessary. I still think you could have negotiated a better price on the liquor."

Although younger, Kate colored her hair an attractive auburn that complemented her fair complexion. Dalton's mother had liked how Marla feathered her hair about her face while on their cruise aboard the *Tropical Sun.* Kate had gotten her hairdresser in Maine to maintain the style.

"I told you cost wouldn't be an issue," Kate said. "John and I are very willing to pitch in."

"Actually," Anita retorted, "the kids could use any money saved for more important things, like better window treatments in their new house. All they get are those standard white blinds. Drapes are so much more insulating."

Yeah, as well as being dust magnets.

"Thanks for your generous offer, Kate, but you've got your own investment in a condo to consider." Marla dug out her car keys from her purse.

"You're right, but we're still willing to contribute." Kate rustled in her handbag for a tissue and wiped her face. "Whew.

Is it always this hot in November? Maybe we should stay in Maine until December next year."

Marla unlocked the car doors and slid into her seat. "We're supposed to get a cold front tonight. That counts as our change of seasons. It should be refreshingly drier in the morning."

"How is your house hunting going?" Anita asked Kate. She sat on the passenger side, while Kate folded into the rear.

"I like the condo we're renting," Kate said, "but it's too expensive to buy, especially with all the other bargains out there. We're taking our time. Insurance is the other issue. Homeowners policies in South Florida are wickedly expensive."

"Tell me about it." Marla started the engine. Soon she'd be paying insurance on two places—her townhouse, which she hoped to rent out, plus their new residence. Not to mention property taxes. Ma was right. She should pare back the wedding costs to save money for future expenses.

"What's next on the list?" Kate fastened her seat belt as Marla drove toward the exit.

"The florist. I want to show you his sample arrangements." This was the first day she'd been able to get both of the elder women together. Previously, she'd made the rounds with Dalton to sign the contracts and make their basic choices. "Then we'll go to the bridal shop to look at dresses."

"I hope you're not looking for anything too extravagant," Anita commented. "Gowns can be awfully expensive."

"I know. There's one I like, but I want your opinion on it before I decide."

"You'll look lovely in white," Kate said dreamily.

Anita clucked her tongue. "Ivory goes better with your complexion."

Uh, oh. Marla sensed another argument brewing. "Kate, I wonder if your real estate agent knows Kevin Rhodes, Jill's cousin? Or are you still using that woman from Tampa?"

On their recent cruise, Kate and her husband, John, had met a Realtor with connections in the art world. Dalton's retired father hoped to exhibit his stained-glass designs at shows around the country, a plan that didn't earn Kate's enthusiasm.

"We're working with someone local now. I can ask her. Why? Does it have anything to do with that bride's sister who died at the wedding?"

Keeping her eyes on the road, Marla nodded. "Remember how I told you that Jill and Torrie co-owned a piece of commercial property? Kevin is trying to find them a new tenant."

"Did Jill inherit her sister's share?" Anita cast an innocent glance in Marla's direction.

Marla smiled inwardly. Anita rarely encouraged her crime solving, usually warning her against getting involved. However, Ma wasn't about to let Kate monopolize her daughter's attention.

"I don't know if Torrie had a will or what it says. I haven't spoken to Jill since her wedding. Now that it's Monday, I presume she and Arnie are back to work, unless she's taking time off. Scott's the one who will be making funeral arrangements after his wife's body is released, although Jill might have offered to help him."

It sounded so horrible to speak of a person she'd known that way. Poor Torrie. She hadn't warranted such a brutal death, no matter how badly she'd provoked someone.

"Why do you want information on Jill's cousin?" Anita persisted. "Do you think Kevin has a motive?"

"I just thought I'd ask, since Kate is consulting real estate agents in town. Kevin might have a reputation, that's all. If I heard anything useful, I'd pass it on to Jill or Detective Brody."

"Could Torrie's death be related to this property issue?"

"Ver vaist?" Marla replied in Yiddish. "Who knows? Torrie earned her share of enemies." She glanced at her watch. "Bless

my bones, it's after twelve. We'd better grab a bite to eat. I'm supposed to meet the painter at four-thirty in our day spa."

"Speaking of painters," Kate said in a bright tone, "Dalton needs you to pick a color."

"I told him we're going to the florist today to make a final decision."

"No, he means for the toilets in your new house. Dalton says the plumber is waiting for your selection."

"Toilets? I should have known." *Don't tell me I'm marrying Hardware Harry.* "I'll call him later, along with everyone else on my list." Her cell phone rang, and she answered.

"Marla? It's Jill. We have to talk."

Chapter Five

Jill came rushing up to Marla on Tuesday in the middle of a furniture delivery at her spa. They hadn't been able to touch base again the day before, no matter how hard Marla tried to free herself. Dalton's mom had insisted on taking the family out to dinner, and Ma's boyfriend, Roger, had joined them. Marla winced when she recalled John's taciturn silence during the meal and Roger's boisterous bellows.

"What's the matter?" she asked Jill, distracted by the furniture mover who brought in a desk shaped like a lima bean. She had chosen wood furniture so the reception area would feel like someone's living room, inducing a comfortable, homey ambiance. A credenza would hold a coffeemaker and a plate of pastries from Arnie's Bagel Busters restaurant next door. The whole idea was to give guests a pleasant experience so they'd want to return.

"It's Scott." Jill grimaced. She wore her long blond hair in a ponytail, jeans and a sweater for the cooler weather, and ankle-high boots. "My sister isn't even in her grave yet, and he's bugging me to sell our property."

Marla motioned to a sofa, letting her aesthetician direct the delivery guy. Facing Jill, she took a seat in an armchair. The smell of fresh paint entered her nose. Their massage rooms were on the painter's agenda today.

"Who owns Torrie's share now?" she said.

"He does, the jerk. Torrie and I were on the deed as tenants-in-common, meaning we can leave our share to our heirs. Apparently, Torrie has a will naming Scott."

"Have you seen it?"

"No. Scott says Uncle Eddy has the original."

"Isn't Eddy a real estate attorney?"

"He handles family stuff sometimes. What am I going to do?"

Clasping her hands, Marla leaned forward without voicing her opinion. Why had Jill come to her instead of Arnie? "I thought your cousin Kevin was hunting for a new tenant."

"He is." Jill blinked, her lashes heavily darkened. "He sent letters to his company contacts, including banks, since that other fellow had mentioned getting a bank building on the site."

"You mean the real estate guy who first alerted you?"

"Yep. We could get a decent income by renting to a new tenant, better than the old lease. Whereas if we sell, we'll have to pay commissions and capital gains taxes and attorney fees. There wouldn't be much left to invest, and we'd never generate the same monthly amount."

"Do both co-owners have to consent in order to sell?"

"Scott says we do." Jill wrung her hands. "Torrie and I never got around to signing the partnership agreement. This is exactly the reason why I wanted one, so the rules would be clear. I can't deal with Scott, Marla. I can't."

"He might be reasonable if you pointed out the pros and cons for selling versus renting the property. It's worth the wait to try and find a tenant."

"Absolutely. The lube center has to give us one year's rent up front as a condition of early termination. That will help us pay our expenses. Kevin isn't charging us a commission, and Eddy's law firm will give us a discount, but it'll still cost us. What did you and Stan do when you both owned your property?"

Marla winced at the mention of her ex-spouse. "We were in

agreement on most issues. It sounds as though you know what you want."

"Maybe so, but I'd be grateful if you could talk to Scott."

"Me? What for?"

Jill's blue eyes took on an imploring look. "You're good with people. Pay him a condolence call and then steer the conversation to the topic. Tell him the advantages of renting. You're getting good income on your property, aren't you?"

"Well, sure." That's why she had bought Stan out. "I'll fit it in somehow. I'm booked with hair appointments today. Tonight, I wanted to discuss gifts with Dalton for his ushers. And we still can't agree on a place for the rehearsal dinner."

"Where have you looked?"

Marla mentioned some local restaurants. "Dalton's mom insists on paying."

"That's generous of her. You're talking about December. You'd better hurry or nothing will be available."

"Tell me about it. Dalton doesn't care, and my mother is more concerned with the price tag for the reception."

"Heck, sugar, sounds like both your mamas are being bullish."

"It's like a competition between them. We should have gone to Vegas and eloped."

Jill rose, swinging her ponytail. "No fair. You came to my wedding. I wouldn't miss yours."

Marla grinned. "You're right." Standing, she stretched. "At least we've got the basics covered. In the meantime . . . I hate to bring this up, but when is Torrie's funeral?"

"Probably on Friday. The police said they're going to, uh, you know, release her on Wednesday. Scott is still making arrangements. I offered to help, but he likes to do things on his own. He's letting me order food platters for the people afterwards."

"Is he working this week?" She couldn't imagine he'd go into his shop right after his wife died.

Jill shrugged. "He's been home when I've called." Her gaze shifted. "Nice paintings. Very colorful." She pointed to the wall where a couple of framed pictures hung on display.

"I bought them at an art auction on board the *Tropical Sun* during the final blowout sale," Marla replied with a hint of pride. She'd deserved it, after solving the murder of an artist whose work had been the cause of scandal.

"Those romantic scenes match your furniture." Jill glanced around with approval. "This looks charming. I hope you'll invite me to the grand opening. I'll bring my friends."

"Arnie has agreed to cater the event, but I'll have to supply the wine." Marla bustled to the armoire and grabbed a brochure listing spa services. "Twenty percent off your first facial, massage, or paraffin wax treatment." She smiled. "Try the foot reflexology. It's relaxing after work."

"Maybe for you. I sit at a desk all day." Jill gave a weary sigh, as though her shoulders had taken on a burden of heavy weights. "Thank goodness I took this week off. I couldn't have worked under the circumstances."

"I'll talk to Scott." Marla walked her friend to the door. "In the meantime, let me know if you learn anything new."

Twenty minutes later, while she was lifting a strand of damp hair on her next client, Marla remembered what she'd meant to say to Jill. With so many other things on her mind, she'd forgotten.

"Holy highlights," she called to Nicole, cutting a customer's hair at the adjacent chair. "I forgot to ask Jill the most important question."

"What's that?" Nicole flicked a glance her way.

Marla began telling her about recent events but was interrupted by a phone call from her best friend, Tally, and then by

Dalton, who discussed the virtues of different door handles for their house. It would have been easier to go with the standard package instead of customizing every accessory. As the cost escalated, so did Marla's sense of regret over their decision. She wondered at Dalton's sudden obsession with toilets and door knobs. Was this his way of escaping wedding anxiety?

"I meant to ask Jill who may have hated her sister enough to stab her," she told Nicole later, after finishing her story when they both had a few minutes in private. "And where did the napkin go, assuming that's what the killer used to wipe off the knife handle?"

"On another table?"

"I thought of that. Presumably, the detective has spoken to the waiters. There's a door behind the alcove, which means someone could have entered from the corridor behind and shoved Torrie under the table in the reception hall."

"They could have escaped down that same corridor." Nicole busied herself stacking foils for her next client. "Was anyone missing from the wedding party earlier, before you discovered the body?"

"I'm not sure. I should talk to the catering staff. It's always best to go firsthand to the source." Besides, they might provide more information about Falcon Oakwood. Marla remembered Torrie speaking to him earlier that day, and he hadn't appeared pleased by their conversation.

Maybe she could persuade Dalton and Brie to accompany her. They enjoyed walking in parks and identifying the trees. That notion appealed to her a lot more than another trip to a hardware store.

Then again, Philip Canfield, the wedding decorator, had a connection to both Torrie and Oakwood. Would Torrie's husband know anything about the guy?

She sought a way to bring up the subject that evening when

she stopped by Scott's house at six-thirty. Schlepping a sack with an aromatic roast chicken in one hand and her handbag in the other, she rapped on his door. She'd had to leave work early in order to beat rush-hour traffic and was glad she'd had the foresight to grab a burger before getting on the turnpike.

Scott greeted her at the door of his ranch-style home in the Kendall area of South Miami. The days were getting shorter and the sun had begun its descent, leaving a chilly breeze in its wake. Marla admired the blue plumbagos and hot pink lantana plants decorating his walkway.

"Nice house," she commented, her gaze sweeping to the white tile roof, sandpaper exterior, and impact-resistant windows. His gutter had a dent, possibly made by a flying coconut in the last storm. A palm leaned nearby, dead fronds hanging down.

"Thanks." He ushered her inside. She swore he looked like an older-era movie actor with his goatee and mustache.

Suppressing the urge to blurt her impression, she followed him into a living room furnished with a leather sofa, loveseat, and two armchairs. "Here, I brought you some dinner." She handed him the bag. He accepted it with a small nod. "I'm so sorry," she started when he'd returned from the kitchen.

"Thank you for—" He stopped, waiting to let her speak. When she remained silent, he continued, "Thanks for stopping by." Rubbing his forehead, he scrunched his small, dark brown eyes. "It's been a tough week."

"Jill said the funeral might be on Friday?"

"Not anymore. There's a delay in releasing her, uh, you know. It'll be on Sunday at eleven o'clock."

"If you give me directions, I'd like to attend. Jill is a good friend of mine, and I'm sure she'd appreciate the support."

Scott tugged on his tie, making her wonder if he'd gone to work that day. Why else would he wear a dress shirt and good pants, unless it was to impress visitors like herself?

Remembering that he wasn't Jewish and had different customs, she wanted to ask about a wake but didn't care to sound ignorant. *Jill will tell me,* she decided, avoiding the awkward topic.

"Sorry, please take a seat." Scott gestured at the furnishings.

As she crossed in front of him, she noted a stain on his shirt. Maybe he wasn't as collected as he tried to appear.

"That's a great photo of you and Torrie." She pointed to a framed picture on the cocktail table.

"It was taken at a benefit dinner last March." Dropping into an armchair, he hunched forward. "Torrie attended a lot of social events for her job. Sometimes she would take me along with her."

Marla sniffed at a hint of tobacco, like from a pipe or cigar. "What kind of work do you do?"

His challenging gaze met hers. "I own a clock repair shop. I know it doesn't sound like much, but I've always had a fascination with time pieces. We fix everything from watches to chime and cuckoo clocks to antique long-case models. Those are especially beautiful in mahogany."

From the passion lacing his voice, she could tell he truly enjoyed his occupation. "How you do train for that type of job?"

"I studied horology in Pennsylvania."

"What?"

"Horology. It's the study of time, timekeepers—meaning clocks and watches—and timekeeping. I'm certified as a master clockmaker and master watchmaker."

Her ears picked up the sound of clocks ticking. She followed their direction to a wall unit displaying several models. "That's a nice collection. Are they antiques?" She knew nothing about the subject. Her clocks at home were either battery run or digital, certainly unlike these decorative objects.

"Those are my vintage Atmos clocks." He got up and strode to a rectangular-shaped case. Inside the housing was a round dial. "This is the tall-case version. It's nickel-plated, as you can see." His fingers traced the silver in a caress worthy of a lover. "The movement works perfectly. Over here, we have a regulator model." He pointed to a square case where another round clock filled the interior.

She noted the Tiffany & Company name on its face. "I like the one next to it."

"That's by Kirby, Beard & Company of Paris. See the porcelain dial with the gold case? I've never come across another one like it." He indicated a dome-shaped model at the end of the row. "This bell-jar is my favorite. Isn't she a beauty?"

"It's amazing they're still working." If he'd showered as much attention on his wife, they might have had a happier marriage.

Scott beamed proudly. "All of these have a mercury motor. It's inside the round box behind the movement. The motor transforms thermal energy into mechanical energy, which the clock movement uses to drive the balance and display the time. The Atmos clock consumes sixty times less energy than a wristwatch."

"No kidding? You mean the old wind-up type, don't you?"

He frowned in response. "I have modern timepieces, too. You'll have to stop by my shop to see the Jubilee model. It was created in 1983 to celebrate the one hundred and fiftieth anniversary of the manufacturer. They produced a limited run of fifteen hundred units. This is number two hundred and twelve."

"They're all very attractive." Marla admired the round- and square-shaped dials inside the glass and metal housing.

"I have so many more. Grandfather clocks, mantle clocks, carriage and cuckoo clocks, master and electric models. I could start a museum." His voice sped up, like a train gathering speed.

If she didn't stop him now, Marla would never be able to change the topic.

"How did Torrie feel about your business?"

"She never understood my passion." He cleared his throat. "Sorry, I forgot to offer you something to drink. Or I have lots of cake. The neighbors have been generous."

"No thanks, I've just had dinner. But go ahead if you're thirsty." She watched while he poured himself a Scotch and soda from a bar in his wall unit. His hand shook as he held the bottle. Was their conversation disturbing him?

"Torrie yelled at me for wasting money on inanimate objects," he said, his back to her. "So I asked, what about those rocks she wore around her neck? 'Oh no, they count as wardrobe, and as a fashion reporter, I have an image to project,' " he mimicked in a high falsetto.

"Did she ever help you in the shop?"

"Are you joking?" He whirled around to face her. "Torrie never wanted me to give up the insurance biz. I sold life insurance when we met," he said, responding to her questioning glance. "Got quite a good income, too. Then I got burned out on telling people they were gonna die someday."

"So you turned your hobby into a business?"

"Exactly. I'd hoped our investments would make up the difference, but things don't always work out the way you plan."

"Tell me about it." Wondering which thread to pull, his financial status or the property issue, she decided to come at either of them from an oblique angle. "You couldn't have foreseen what happened at the wedding. I'm so sorry."

Grasping his whiskey glass, he sank into an armchair. "Torrie thought it was so cool she got Jill's wedding booked at Orchid Isle. She's friends with the developer's wife, you know."

"Yes, I met them briefly at the reception. Leanne seems like a nice woman."

"Nice but flighty. She needs a man who's fully devoted to her, but Falcon's balls are cut off by his mother."

"Excuse me?"

"Didn't you see Cornelia at the wedding? The older lady who sat next to him in the pew?"

"Oh, yes." Marla remembered the white-haired lady with the stiff coiffeur.

"Cornelia rules the nest in their household, and she makes her disappointment clear that Leanne hasn't conceived. According to what Torrie told me, Leanne planned to end Cornelia's interference in her life."

Oh yeah? How so? Not wishing to stray from their current focus, Marla targeted her next question to Scott's relationship with his wife. "You and Torrie never had children, right?"

"We're childless by choice. I always wanted to do more traveling, but Torrie has been consumed by her job. She wanted that editorial position real bad. Now it looks like Hally will get it by default."

"What do you mean?"

"There's an opening at their magazine for a higher level job, and they both were contenders." He drew his mouth down in derision. "Torrie won't have to worry about that anymore." Hanging his head, he appeared lost in his own memories.

"Am I tiring you?" Marla didn't wish to overstay her welcome. Why had she come? Oh, right, Jill had asked her to put in a good word regarding the property issue.

"No, no." He waved a hand. "I'm not used to being alone, so I'm glad for the company. My brother is supposed to come over later and help with the arrangements."

"Jill said you could call her if you need anything."

"Ha. More likely the other way around. She put you up to this, didn't she?" He took a drink at Marla's protesting shake of her head. "She's hung up over their land. Doesn't care that her sister is dead, just what's gonna happen to her income."

"I think Jill cares a great deal about her sister's death," Marla said quietly, "but this was an unresolved issue between them. She'd feel better if the two of you reached an agreement."

"You mean she'd feel better if I didn't step into her sister's shoes and usurp the family business. She thinks Kevin can find another tenant. Well, good luck. That land is contaminated, and it's gonna take a lot of money to clean it up."

"Isn't that the oil company's responsibility? Jill says you can make more money through a land lease than by selling and investing the proceeds."

Scott shoved to his feet. "Thank you for coming, Marla, but this is where we say good night."

Okay by me. At least I fulfilled my promise to Jill.

She stood upright, her joints stiff from a day's work and then sitting in the car. "I hope the police figure out what happened. Do you have any theories?" Rolling her shoulders, she sighed. The motion loosened her muscles and restored her circulation.

His expression soured. "None that I'm willing to share. Say, aren't you getting married soon?" He led her toward the door.

"In less than a month. My fiancé and I are still making plans. I made an appointment with Jill's florist. His flower arrangements were magnificent."

"Yes, Canfield did a good job."

"We need a photographer, too," Marla lied. "I remember Jill's guy had an assistant who did the videos, but then there was that other man from Torrie's magazine."

"Griff Beasley?" Scott's mouth turned down. "I'd steer clear of him, if I were you."

Marla halted. "Why is that?"

His dark eyes snagged hers. "He's a shark who'll bite when the opportunity strikes. It should have been him, not my wife, who died that night."

Chapter Six

"Scott didn't think too highly of Griff Beasley," Marla told Nicole the next morning at work while they waited for their ten o'clock appointments.

"Oh no?" The dark-skinned stylist glanced at her with a gleam of curiosity. Nicole relished a good mystery and kept urging Marla to read one of the whodunits she knocked off in a week.

"He advised me to avoid Griff. Obviously, Scott doesn't like the fellow."

Nicole plugged in her tools while Marla set out the foils she'd need for her first customer. "Why is that?"

Marla's gaze swept the salon. Luis, their receptionist, had set up the coffeemaker and obtained their usual order of bagels from Arnie's deli. Countertops glistened and music played softly in the background.

"I don't know, but I'd like to find out. I'll give him a call later when we have a break."

"Didn't you say Torrie had something on Griff and that he'd threatened her?"

"He wasn't the only one." Lowering her voice, she told Nicole about the incident in the bridal room.

"Shut up, girlfriend. You did not hear Jill say that to her sister."

"Jill couldn't be guilty. She stayed in the ballroom throughout the reception, dancing and greeting guests."

Nicole's brown eyes pinned her. "Didn't you tell me she went to the little girls' room to scrub her hands?"

Remembering what Alexis had told her, Marla put down the rest of her foils. "So? She took a break for a few minutes."

"Jill didn't want people to discover something Torrie knew about her. Now Torrie is dead."

Marla refused to think ill of her friend. "Scott has a better motive. He's inherited Torrie's share of the property she owned with Jill."

"Yet he seems to be mad at Griff for some reason."

"Griff is a suspect by virtue of his association with the magazine where Torrie worked, and so is Hally. According to Scott, Hally and Torrie were vying for a promotion. Now that Torrie is out of the picture, guess who leaps up the totem pole?"

"Are you relying on hearsay, or do you know this for a fact? Shouldn't you be checking your sources directly?"

Marla sniffed the brewed coffee. She could use a second cup. "I'll have to go see Hally."

"And why are you skipping around like a piece of bacon in the fry pan? Hasn't Dalton told you enough times to leave the investigating to the cops? You have plenty to do with your own wedding three weeks from Saturday."

"So true." She beamed at her friend. "You'll be proud of me. I finally made my choices at David's Bridal."

Nicole's eyebrows lifted. "And?"

"The bridesmaids will wear a satin strapless tea-length dress in persimmon with a rhinestone belt. It was on sale for eighty dollars, and it's something they can wear to other parties, so I think everyone will be pleased. The matron of honor will wear the same dress in coral."

Marla hadn't asked any staff members from the salon to be in her bridal party. It wouldn't be fair to include some of them and not the others.

"What about your gown?" Nicole asked.

Her face softened. "I found a beautiful ivory dress that's absolutely perfect. I love it."

"Take some photos next time you go for a fitting. Did you decide on a place for the rehearsal dinner?"

"I put Dalton's mother in charge of that one. The seating charts for the reception are driving me crazy. Ma keeps finding relatives I didn't know existed."

"Like your entire clan that showed up for the reunion at Sugar Crest resort? After the ghosts you encountered, you'd think they'd steer clear of family events."

"Unfortunately, that's not the case. They're all coming."

Focusing on her customers kept Marla busy until one o'clock, when she finally found a few minutes to gobble down a turkey sandwich. Sitting in the back room to garner some privacy, she considered her conversation with Nicole.

Why *was* she concerning herself with Torrie's murder?

Because she'd discovered the body. Because Jill may have a motive, but Marla didn't think she'd done the deed. Because Jill had asked her for help.

Give up the excuses. You do it because it's your calling. "Justice, justice, shall you pursue." Her bat mitzvah Torah portion had become her driving force.

Besides, Marla couldn't turn down a friend in need, and she had a feeling Jill was going to need her more than ever in the days ahead. Arming herself with knowledge could only be viewed as foresight.

Thus, she felt no twinge of guilt when she phoned *Boca Style Magazine* and asked to speak to Griff Beasley.

"I can give you his cell," the woman on the other line said. "He doesn't come into the office on a regular basis."

Marla felt a swell of excitement when he answered his phone. Feeling like a hunter on the chase, she identified herself and then threw out her gambit. "I'd like to follow up on some things we discussed at Jill's wedding. Can we meet later? I'll buy you a drink."

"Well, sure, babe. I'm stuck in Miami, though. Gotta cover a party at the Venetian Pool."

"I've heard of the place but I've never been there. When do you think you'll be finished?"

"This whole shebang starts at five. Maybe by seven? I can leave after I take my photos." His drawl deepened. "Hey, here's an idea. Let's meet at the Biltmore. Then after a few drinks, if you don't feel like driving home, we'll see if they have a room."

Gritting her teeth, Marla forced herself to make a sweet reply. "All right, but I'll need directions."

As soon as she hung up, she phoned Dalton to see if he'd care to join her. Her blood surged when she heard his rich, masculine voice.

"Sorry, I have to work late tonight. Weren't you supposed to make dinner?"

She winced, remembering her offer to keep Brianna company until her dad got home. "You're absolutely right, and I'll pick up something on my way over." The phone remained silent. "Dalton, are you still there?"

"Yeah, I'm thinking. Probably you should talk to Griff if he's willing to meet you. I don't want you to go alone, though. You can't ask Jill, or anyone from the wedding for that matter, because he might clam up. Take someone innocuous."

"I'll call Tally." She needed to update her best friend and matron of honor on the wedding details anyway.

But Tally wasn't available either, and Marla didn't want to take Brianna for such a long ride when the teen had homework to do. As she found herself on the road again after a day of work, she felt guilty that her poodle, Spooks, and Dalton's golden retriever, Lucky, were Brie's only company.

Sighing, she gripped the steering wheel and focused on her

current mission rather than all the obligations she was avoiding.

What did she hope to gain from this interview? The reason why Griff had threatened Torrie, for one thing. What caused Scott to dislike him? If he'd taken pictures of the wedding cake and when. Who might have been in the vicinity?

As she sped west on I-595, veered south on I-75 to State Road 826, Marla reflected on what she knew about the man. Not too much. Society photographer for *Boca Style Magazine.* Dashing good looks with his blondish beard and mustache and bad-boy smile. Tension between him and Hally. Tension between him and Torrie. Did this reflect upon their personal relationships or work rivalries?

Her gaze lifted to the palm trees dotting the industrial landscape along the Palmetto Expressway. Oh, look. She didn't know they had a Bijoux Turner outlet there. That might be worth a return trip.

Her exit came up past the airport, and she got off at Coral Way. Soon she entered luxurious Coral Gables. Streets lined by overhanging live oaks, two-story homes with Spanish barrel-tile roofs, lush tropical vegetation, and gated properties filled the bill for this deluxe community.

Squinting in the twilight, she tried to read the stone street signs close to the ground. She'd finished work earlier than expected, printed out directions to the Venetian Pool, and decided to stop by there first. Likely Griff wouldn't have left yet for their appointment at the Biltmore. She came to the fountain in the middle of a circle and followed her map.

Driving down a side street, she admired a hacienda-style villa sporting orange trees on its rooftop, iron-grille balconies, and potted plants.

After finding a parking space, she emerged into the cool evening air, where birds twittered but insects hadn't yet started their nightly chorus. Normally closed by this time of day, the

Venetian Pool had remained open for the private party, likely a charity fund-raiser from the looks of the expensively attired patrons, colorful lanterns, live music, and linen-swathed tables.

"May I have your ticket, ma'am?" said a uniformed attendant at the door. He wore white gloves and a tuxedo.

"I'm with Griff Beasley from *Boca Style Magazine.*" Marla flashed a business card so quickly he couldn't read it. "Where can I find him?" Hopefully he hadn't finished his assignment and left the premises.

"Check on the beach side. Just be careful walking over there; the path can get slippery when wet." The attendant waved her through.

She breezed across a small bridge with salmon-colored grillwork toward a Venetian-style building. One short flight of stone steps led downward toward clusters of crotons and a grotto-like space beyond. Another staircase rose into a tower.

She descended to the ground level, ducking her head beneath an arch to enter a reception area with an unmanned admission desk. No doubt she'd find Griff mingling among the revelers. Not a soul lingered indoors here.

The main entrance segued into an anteroom lined with blue-colored tiles and boasting a central fountain and historic photos mounted on the walls. Formed from a limestone quarry in 1924, the pool was listed in the National Register of Historic Places. It held 820,000 gallons of water from a natural spring.

Impressed, Marla thought how lucky the community was to have this facility for its residents. It reminded her of the swim clubs up north where she grew up.

Past another stone archway, she stepped into an open-air courtyard set with tables and chairs. Couples stood around laughing and sipping champagne, while waiters strolled by carrying trays of hors d'oeuvres. Marla spared a glance at the barracks-like buildings bordering the courtyard. Their concrete exterior, high windows, closed doors, and heavy wood beams gave her the creeps. They looked too much like prison walls in some third-world country, except for door frames and garbage cans painted bright tangerine. A meager sign read *café* on one door, no doubt leading to a concession stand during the day.

Directing her attention toward the grotto-like pool, she followed the tile path to a covered loggia where wood beams crisscrossed overhead. It faced the water on one side and the courtyard on the other. Elbowing her way through the partygoers, she didn't see Griff anywhere.

Across the water's emerald expanse, an enormous waterfall gushed into the lagoon. The roar of cascading water resounded along with the chatter of guests and the clink of glasses. She spotted an empty lifeguard chair shaded by an umbrella in the middle of a cobblestone bridge. Behind it looked to be a coral cave. Could Griff be in there?

She made her way over and peered inside. A bunch of nattily dressed folks sat on wood benches while balancing plates of food. No sign of Griff. *You'd think he'd be circulating and snapping pictures, unless he already finished his job here.*

"Excuse me, have you seen a photographer around?" she asked a patron. "He works for *Boca Style Magazine.*"

The woman, surveying Marla's simple skirt and knit top, lifted her nose. "I saw him last by the beach, dear. Tell him I'd be happy to pose for a picture, will you?"

Marla didn't deign to answer. Instead, she strode toward a stretch of sandy beach facing the cool emerald lagoon fringed with palm trees and dotted with lampposts that looked like they came straight from Venice, painted a whimsical apricot and melon.

Some guests sat on lounge chairs, but Griff wasn't among them. Her gaze followed the pathway as it rimmed the pool, but she didn't spot his tall figure. She must have missed him.

Disappointed, Marla turned back while rustling her car keys from her purse. She'd have to drive to the Biltmore after all. When the keys slipped through her fingers, she crouched to retrieve them from the grass. Her gaze fell upon a partially hidden grotto through a stone archway covered by a leafy vine.

Stacked lounge chairs, pool cleaning tools, and a huge ceramic planter lay inside the gloomy interior . . . from which a man was stumbling toward her. She straightened quickly.

"Marla, is that you?"

Good God, it was Griff! He had a dazed look on his face as she rushed over.

"What happened?" She noted a nasty bruise on his temple.

"I dunno. Must have hit my head." He touched the spot. "Ouch, that hurts."

"Are you dizzy?"

"I'll be okay."

"This arch is awfully low. Did you forget to duck?"

"Nope, I heard somebody call my name from inside. That's the last thing I remember, babe." His face flooded with awareness. "My camera . . . do you see it?"

"Just a minute. It's too dark in there." Withdrawing a penlight from her purse, Marla shone it around the grotto. "Here it is." She pounced on a case lying in the corner.

Griff grabbed it from her and rummaged through the contents. "Yo, everything seems to be intact." He patted his pocket. "My wallet is still here. Couldn't have been a thief."

"Maybe the intent wasn't to steal anything."

Brushing off his clothes, he regarded her intently. "No? What then? And why are you here?"

"I came early. Maybe this was a warning of sorts. Or your attacker was spooked by some nearby guests and didn't have time to finish the job."

Griff stared at her. "I'm not even sure it was a *he.*"

"What about the voice?"

"No one I recognized, nor could I be clear on the gender." His eyes, reflecting the lamplight, darkened. "Now that I think on it, the raspy tone sounded like a person who phoned me earlier."

"Say again?"

"I got a call about covering another gig this afternoon. That was kinda weird, actually."

"What do you mean?" Marla offered him a tissue and a squirt of hand sanitizer to clean his wound.

"Someone called to ask if my magazine would allow me to take photos at an event in Palm Beach tonight. When I said I was tied up, the person suggested I stop by if I was in the area. I replied that I couldn't; I'd be at the Venetian Pool in Coral Gables."

Schlemiel, you told a perfect stranger where you were going. Recognition dawned on his face while she studied him with a smirk.

"Shit, I screwed myself, didn't I?"

"If it were me, I'd be concerned about someone bonking me on the head, especially coming on the heels of Torrie's death."

Ducking under the arch, they emerged from the grotto. The moon had come up, spraying the water with sparkles of light.

Griff didn't choose to comment on her remark. "I need a drink or two," he growled. "Are you still up for the Biltmore?"

"If you can make it. Maybe you should see a doctor."

"No, thanks."

"How about if I drive us to the hotel then? I'll give you a ride back here when we're done."

"That'll work for me."

She followed his instructions to Anastasia Avenue, where she spied the hotel's center tower rising above the trees. After parking in an adjacent lot, they entered the main building on the ground floor. Expensive furnishings graced the cool, refined interior. She heard the clacking noise of high heels on the marble floor along with the clash of silverware from a café overlooking the pool.

They veered left, past a clothing boutique and a gift shop, toward a bar with cozy armchairs and subdued lighting. The chatter of patrons competed with the *ding, ding, ding* for a bellboy from the front desk.

"Let's go upstairs," Griff suggested. "There's a quieter lounge."

Evidently, they'd been on the lower lobby level. She followed him up a flight of carpeted stairs into a cavernous hall with marble floors and columns, mahogany paneling, potted palms, a baby grand piano, and ornately decorated high ceilings.

Groupings of couches and armchairs ranged across the expanse. Glass cases held historical memorabilia such as postcards, porcelain china, old room keys, and silverware.

Here stands another monument to the 1920s, like Sugar Crest Plantation Resort on Florida's west coast, Marla thought.

Once they were settled in an intimate lounge, she waited until they'd received their drinks before introducing the reason for her interview.

"Speaking of Torrie's tragic end," she said to provide a link to their prior conversation, "I paid a condolence call on Scott yesterday."

"So?" Griff gulped down his beer. Some of the foam dribbled onto his mustache. He wiped it off with his sleeve.

"I presume you guys had met before through Torrie's work? Scott said he'd been to a couple of business affairs with her."

"Torrie didn't like to bring her husband. The man would sit stiff as a log and rarely joined in conversations." Griff plowed a hand through his tousled hair, wincing when his fingers touched the congealed wound. "Bumped my head," he explained to a passing waiter who gave him a sharp look.

"How did the two of you get along?" Marla sipped her chardonnay.

"We didn't. That cold fish didn't even get along with his own wife."

"Oh? What do you mean?"

"Scott probably found out Torrie planned to leave him." Griff cast her a pained glance. "Don't you know? That's why he murdered her."

Chapter Seven

Marla rushed through her Thursday morning appointments so she could keep the date she'd made with Hally. Perhaps Griff's colleague could shed light on his passionate declaration the day before. Did he really believe that Scott killed his own wife? The photographer had refused to elaborate, claiming it wouldn't be in his best interest to stoke the fire, whatever that meant.

Bursting with impatience, she yearned to tell Dalton about her interview. She hadn't had time last night, between driving to his house, where she stayed most of the time now, taking out the dogs, and catching up on Brie's news while he worked late.

She'd e-mailed Hally Leeds just before going to bed and had been surprised to find a response this morning. Certainly, Hally would be happy to mention the grand opening of Marla's day spa in her column, especially in conjunction with their fund-raiser for Locks of Love, the group that provides wigs for financially disadvantaged children who have lost their hair because of a medical condition. She meant to fill Dalton in later. In between snipping and coloring her clients' hair, running over to the day spa to consult with the new massage therapist, and fielding a call from her mother about the wedding, Marla barely had time to breathe.

"I hope you can fix this," her next customer said, plopping into the salon chair after a shampoo.

"What were you thinking?" Marla riffled through the woman's damp strands. Her ash-blond hair looked as though a weed whacker had attacked her head.

Lynn, a regular client, gave a sheepish grin. "The ends were getting long, so I thought I'd save time and trim them myself."

Looks like it, too. Marla fastened a drape around her. "I can do some layers, bring it up here, and that should complement your bone structure. It'll be flattering but shorter than your usual cut."

"Go for it, hon. Whatever you do will be better than this."

"At least you didn't dye your hair eggplant purple like my last client." Marla grimaced. "People find that home remedies cost more in the long run because then they need to come in for corrective treatments."

"I've learned my lesson." Lynn gave her a smile fraught with curiosity. "How are your wedding plans coming?"

Marla picked up her comb and shears. "We still have so much to do." Just thinking about her mental list made her shoulders sag. "We've got the basics covered, but the details are overwhelming. My mother and Dalton's mom keep adding people to the guest list."

"It's late for that, isn't it? Didn't your invitations already go out?"

She separated a section of hair and fastened it aside with a clip. "Yes, but they figured most of the out-of-town relatives wouldn't come. They were wrong. Jill and Arnie didn't have so much grief." Lynn frequented Arnie's deli next door.

"Didn't you find someone stabbed with a cake knife at his affair?"

Marla paused, hand in midair. "Where did you hear that?"

"I read it in the newspaper."

"Oh, joy." She'd made headlines again. Maybe that's why the phone kept ringing up front. Thank goodness Luis fielded all their calls, when he wasn't flirting with their clients.

"Hey, girlfriend, isn't that gal's funeral on Friday?" Nicole called, eavesdropping from the next station. Wearing a glove, she applied a relaxing solution to her customer's hair.

"It's been moved to Sunday at eleven."

"You learn anything new from that photographer yesterday?"

Marla lifted a shank of hair, snipped at an angle, then let the strands fall back into place. "Griff made some interesting remarks about Torrie's husband."

"Oh, yeah? Maybe he wanted to throw you off track," Nicole suggested. "You know, to take the heat off himself?"

"I doubt it. We met at the Venetian Pool in Coral Gables where he'd been assigned to cover an event. When I found him, Griff was injured. He'd been mugged, and his head wound was quite real."

"Shut up." Nicole stared at her. "Was he robbed?"

"No, and the peculiar thing is, he didn't seem that concerned. I offered to buy him a drink, so we went to the Biltmore afterward. He said Torrie planned to leave Scott, and that's why Scott killed her."

"Holy guacamole, Marla." Lynn caught her gaze in the mirror. "You're always in the thick of things. How do you do it?"

Marla grinned. "I wish I knew. So essentially, we have Griff saying Scott is to blame, and Scott saying Griff can't be trusted. Which one do I believe?"

"Unless Griff bashed himself on the head, you have to wonder why someone assaulted him." Lynn looked thoughtful while Marla shaped her hair. "Didn't he make any guesses?"

"I don't think Griff wants to know, although I'm wondering what made him a target. If robbery wasn't the motive, could this have been an attempt to scare him off?"

"Good point," Nicole contributed. "That means he knows something that's a threat to the killer. Maybe he snapped a picture of the guy with Torrie at the wedding."

"So then why wasn't his camera bag stolen?"

"Because he'd already turned in the film for developing or uploaded his digital photos."

"He wasn't the wedding photographer," Marla reminded Nicole.

"Doesn't matter. He must have caught something significant on film. Ask his magazine editor if she has the pictures."

"Hally might have seen them. She's the society reporter who works with him. I'm hoping she can shed more light on Griff's character, because he's an enigma to me. He'd seemed morose, talking about Torrie in the hotel lounge last night as though he cared. But when I overheard their conversation at the park, he threatened her."

"About what?" Lynn asked.

"I don't know, but I'll find out." Setting down her implements, Marla grabbed a blow dryer and switched it on.

Four hours later, she switched off the ignition on her Camry and emerged from her car at the magazine's address in Boca Raton. Entering the brick building, she faced a warren of cubicles beyond a wide reception desk. So much for privacy. Maybe Hally could step away for a cup of coffee.

The sleek redhead glanced up from a computer when Marla approached. "Hello, darling. Come to see me at my digs?" She waved a hand. "Hey, girls, this is Marla Shore. She operates a beauty salon in Palm Haven."

Marla nodded her greeting. "Actually, I'm here to talk about my new day spa. You e-mailed me that you might be interested in covering our opening celebration. We're raising money for Locks of Love, donating ten percent from all our spa treatments that day."

"Write me up a press release, and I'll see if I can get approval to cover the story."

"Thanks, I'd be grateful."

"Is that really why you came to see me?" Bending forward, Hally straightened a framed photo on her desk. It showed a pair of kittens playing. Marla glanced at a couple of other framed shots at her station. No people, she noted. Were these pets more important to Hally than her actual family members?

Marla's arm brushed against a potted plant at an adjacent cubicle. There wasn't an empty chair in sight. Noise from clacking computer keys and workers' subdued chatter competed for volume in the background. This was no place to hold a private conversation.

"Can we go somewhere else?" she asked Hally, who studied her with a speculative gleam. "I want to discuss a mutual acquaintance who was at the wedding."

Hally's blue eyes narrowed. "Griff, I presume? As you can see, I'm rather busy."

"Did you happen to see his pictures from the wedding?"

"I don't do the layouts, darling. That's our editor's job. Dellene puts the whole piece together."

"When is the issue coming out? Can I get a sneak peek? Those photos may show something the police should know."

"I'm afraid that's not possible." Gathering her Kate Spade handbag, Hally rose. She tugged at a cobalt-blue top that she wore over a silky flowing skirt. Marla wasn't that familiar with designer labels, but this looked like Dana Buchman. It could be worth hundreds of dollars, unless she'd bought it on sale at the outlet mall.

"What's this?" Marla pointed to an open magazine on Hally's desk. Photos from a recent society ball jumped out at her. Squinting, she tried to read the byline, but the print was too small.

Hally's face took on an ugly sneer. "That's *Home & Style Magazine* from Palm Beach. Their photographer takes really good pictures. I've never met Grant Bosworth, and some say neither have his editors, but somehow he always seems to get the scoop ahead of our publication."

A young woman with a blond ponytail stumbled in their direction, nearly dropping a pile of papers. Her face reddened. "Here are your page proofs, Miss Leeds."

Marla stared at her. For some reason, the girl looked familiar. Had they met before?

"Put them down before they end up all over the floor," Hally snapped. "We're going into the break room. I don't want to be interrupted, Rachel. You got that?"

Marla saw the flash of anger in Rachel's sharp brown eyes. "Sure, Miss Leeds. And Dellene says, I mean, she said to tell you the article on the diabetic society event was great."

"You should show more respect, kid. Our editor is Mrs. Hallberg to you."

"Yes, ma'am." Dumping her burden on Hally's desk as instructed, the girl swung away.

Marla, appalled at Hally's rudeness, stood watching with her mouth hanging open.

"Come on, no one should be in the break room right now." Hally wove through the office maze with Marla at her heels. Empty coffee mugs, stacks of paper, and glossy magazine pages were piled everywhere. Staff members scooted here and there or sat frozen at their computer stations, typing madly.

How could anyone get their work done with this continuous clamor? Marla considered the noises in her salon and how they would sound to a stranger. The whirr of blow dryers, the chatter of customers, and the splash of sink water were comforting to her. She supposed the same could be said of background work noise anywhere. Depending on if you liked your job or not, the sounds would either bring pleasure or raise your stress level.

"Do you work with Griff often?" she asked Hally over a cup of coffee in the break room, where they sat on opposite sides of a marred wood table.

Hally pursed her lips. "We try to team up when we can."

Her lofty tone made Marla instantly suspicious. "Oh? And are these all local assignments, or do you sometimes travel together?"

The reporter's eyes glimmered. "Any overnighters we pull are strictly on our own, if you know what I mean."

"I'm not sure that I do." Marla could play coy, too.

"Then let me put it bluntly, darling. Griff and I are together. Or at least we were, until *she* butted in. That won't be a problem any longer."

"She? Do you mean Torrie?"

Hally bared her teeth. "The bitch knew he had the hots for me, and she still tried to chisel in on my territory. In more ways than one. I'm sorry she had to die the way she did, but I won't miss her."

"Are you saying she tried to lure Griff away from you?"

"Torrie and Scott were having problems, in case you didn't notice. A little thing like being married wouldn't stop her."

"I visited Scott, and he warned me away from Griff. Was Scott aware Griff had been fooling around with his wife?"

"I don't know Scott well enough to answer your question."

"How about Griff, then? Which one of you two did he favor? Or do you think he snuggled up to Torrie because she knew something damaging about him?"

"Where did you get that idea?"

"I overheard them talking at Orchid Isle. She was upset about Griff going back on his word. They threatened each other, actually."

"I'm not surprised." Hally's gaze turned thoughtful. "Torrie knew things about people, things they wouldn't want others to learn. Hanging around high society like we do, we hear stuff. Torrie collected a lot of dirt. She wasn't as careful as she should've been."

Meaning what? Torrie blackmailed people? Then what secret did Griff have to hide?

Marla didn't voice her thoughts aloud. She still needed to clarify the issues between Scott and Griff. Which one had the most to gain by Torrie's death?

"I ran into Griff the other day," she mentioned casually. "He nearly accused Scott of murdering his wife. You don't know Scott that well, but did Torrie ever seem scared of him?"

"Hell, no. All she did was put down the poor guy. He wasn't assertive enough. He spent more time with his clocks than with her. He didn't care if his clothing was out of style. She didn't have one good thing to say about her husband."

Sometimes the meek types were capable of the most violence.

"Did Griff tell you he got mugged? Nothing was stolen, so robbery couldn't have been the motive. That's why I was interested in the pictures he took at the wedding. Maybe one of them shows Torrie's murderer."

Hally took a gulp of coffee. "What else would you expect, darling? The killer had to be someone familiar to her, and we're all in the photos. I know it's not me, so that leaves everyone else." She wrinkled her brow. "What happened to Griff?"

"Someone conked him on the head."

"Is he okay? I haven't seen him in . . . since we worked together at Orchid Isle."

"Oh, he'll be fine." Marla wrapped her hand around the insulated cup. "Weren't you also covering the park's grand opening? How did that go?"

Hally lifted her nose. "I got a great interview with Falcon Oakwood. Watch for my story in the next issue of our magazine."

"He wasn't the first owner of the property, was he?" She'd been unable to find much information on the Internet about that tract of land.

"Nope. After he acquired the site, it took him five years to develop the exhibits, plant the gardens, carve out the nature trails, and design the buildings. He wanted a place to showcase his orchid collection, to support research for new hybrids or whatever they're called, and to provide a native plant habitat."

"You sound like an admirer."

"I respect his goals, that's all."

"Was Torrie scoping him out for an interview, too?"

Hally's expression shuttered. "She may have had other things on her mind."

"Wasn't she friends with his wife?"

"Just so."

"I wonder how much they confided in each other."

"You'll have to ask Leanne that question. You might want to talk to her anyway."

"It was nice of Leanne to put in a word to her husband about Jill's wedding. The garden setting worked out perfectly."

"Purely a publicity move, darling. Falcon knew it would bring people to the park." Finishing her beverage, Hally tossed the empty container into a nearby trash can. "Leanne can tell you other things, but I'm not sure you want to hear them. Too much knowledge can be a liability." With an air of dismissal, she stood.

With more questions tripping on her tongue, Marla followed Hally from the break room. Jumping aside as a staffer scurried past, she regarded the bustling scene with a sense of guilt. Time to go back to her salon.

"I appreciate your taking the time to see me," she told Hally. "Please give me a call if you think of anything else that would be helpful. I can always pass information along to my fiancé, who's with the police. I suppose the crime scene guys already examined Torrie's computer files and such?"

Her skirt swishing, Hally strolled along at her side. "They were here the next day."

"And?"

"I don't know if they found anything relevant."

They might not have, but did you? Hally would have had time to come by the office on Saturday night. Had she discovered which file contained the supposed "dirt" on people that Torrie collected? And if this file truly existed, did it contain material that someone would kill to keep secret?

Marla parted amiably and walked, deep in thought, toward the front door. If only she could get a look at this place when no one was here. She'd search for Griff's photos as well as hidden files on Hally's computer, and Torrie's as well, if the police had returned the dead woman's CPU.

Lost in her musings, she bumped into someone as she breezed past the reception desk.

"Oh, I'm sorry," said Rachel.

Now Marla saw that she wore a name tag indicating her status as an intern. The poor thing must be so used to apologizing that she automatically assumed her own guilt.

"No, it's my fault. I wasn't watching where I was going." Anxious to move on, Marla shifted her handbag to her other shoulder. "Are you okay?"

Rachel regarded her with large, round eyes. "I'm fine, but can I have a word with you?"

What's this about? Maybe the girl hadn't collided with her by accident.

"Sure, honey. Would you like to step outside?" Whatever the girl had to say wouldn't be for Hally's ears. Marla gave the receptionist—a lady with a beehive hairdo and a wad of gum in her mouth—a brief wave at the exit.

Retrieving her sunglasses, Marla propped them on her nose. The temperature had risen toward eighty and the air was dry, making for a glorious afternoon. Too bad she didn't have the rest of the day free.

Leaning her back against the wall, Marla confronted the intern. "What can I do for you, Rachel?"

The girl shaded her face with a hand. "I thought you'd like to know that Hally has been talking about you. She told us how you were eavesdropping on her conversations at the wedding and that you're a close friend of Torrie's sister."

"So?"

"Hally said that Jill had a reason to want her sister dead. But the truth is, so did Hally."

"I gather Hally and Torrie didn't have much love for each other." Marla eyed the girl curiously. Whose side was she on?

"They were both under consideration for a promotion. Like, I'd hate to see Hally get the post. Torrie deserved it more." Rachel's eyes welled with moisture.

"Is there any truth in Hally's statement? Her implication that Jill had a motive to kill Torrie is pretty drastic."

"Jill wouldn't hurt anyone. Maybe she didn't want Torrie to tell anyone about . . . at least, not yet, until we . . . you know."

No, I don't. Fill me in, will you? Gritting her teeth, Marla sucked in a deep breath to calm her nerves.

"You shouldn't let Hally get you down," she advised, breaking an awkward silence. "I'm sure she's under pressure, especially with a promotion at stake."

Rachel leaned inward. "That's what I mean. I'm not sure how far she would go to move up the ladder."

"Hally is ambitious, but she isn't stupid. You know, it would really help if I could get a look at her computer."

"What for?" Rachel gave a furtive look over her shoulder.

"I'd like to check out her article on Orchid Isle, for one thing. Have you seen any of the photos lying around the office? Are they printed out, or is everything done with digital images?"

"Gosh, I don't know."

"I understand Hally has worked with Griff Beasley a number

of times. Have you met the guy?"

"She talks about him a lot, but he doesn't come around too often. Anyway, I didn't have much contact with Hally before now. Torrie's the one who hired me as her intern."

Interesting. Torrie hadn't struck Marla as the kindhearted type. Maybe she'd simply wanted a minion to do her bidding.

"I appreciate your confidences," she told the girl. "All I want is justice for Jill's sister."

"Me, too." Rachel hung her head. "I owe her a lot, so it's the least I can do."

"Will you be going to the funeral?"

"Sure. Like, the whole office gang will probably be there."

"Good, then I'll see you again. If anything turns up in the meantime, please give me a call."

After she handed the intern a business card and turned away, Marla remembered where she might have seen her before. A mental image flashed in her mind: the black-haired waitress at the wedding who had taken such an interest in Jill. Rachel shared an uncanny resemblance to the woman.

Nah, it had to be a coincidence. Didn't it?

CHAPTER EIGHT

"What do you mean, you want to snoop inside Hally's office?" Dalton asked with a frown of disapproval.

"You heard me." Sitting across from him in a local café where they'd gone for early dinner, Marla leaned forward. "She knows something. Can you find out if the detective in charge of Torrie's investigation got any information off her computer? I think Hally copied her files."

"So? Hally is the society maven, right? What would she want, Torrie's fashion descriptions?" He cut the snicker that escaped his lips when the waitress delivered their coffee and desserts. Glancing at his watch, he dug in without hesitation, doubtless not wanting to waste time before picking up his daughter at dance class.

"Hally implied that her rival collected gossip on people, things they wouldn't want others to hear." The aroma of baking brownies made her mouth water. She dipped a spoon into her chocolate soufflé, feeling an instant of regret. The dish looked so artistic, she hated to ruin it. Oh, well. Like the cheese at the end of a mousetrap, this treat was meant to be consumed, not merely admired.

The chocolate crust puffed over its container, a white ceramic bowl. Raspberry sauce was zigzagged across the powdered sugar–sprinkled plate. Like a volcano, the soufflé's outer crust yielded to molten chocolate lava inside. Its rich semisweet flavor exploded in her mouth with an eruption of pleasure.

"Umm, this is heavenly," she mumbled between bites. "How is your Chocolate Indulgence?"

"Try some," Dalton offered.

She bent toward him, opening her mouth so he could give her a taste. Rolling the velvety smoothness on her tongue, she swallowed, savoring the sweet aftertaste.

Her gaze locked with his. Oh, my. The blatant desire in his eyes caused liquid heat to surge through her veins.

"Maybe eating chocolate at night isn't such a good idea. I forgot what we were talking about."

Dalton gave a wicked grin. "Come over my house later. I'll relieve your hunger."

I wish. "Sorry, but I have work to do at my place. I still have some cartons to finish packing."

"So you were joking, right? About finding a way to get into the magazine's building after hours?"

Her mood sobered. "Surely you don't think I'd do anything that dumb? You know me better than that."

How true, and that's what worries me, read the look he returned. "So what do you want from my end?"

"Besides asking if the cops found anything in Torrie's computer files? I'd like you to investigate Falcon Oakwood's background."

"Why?" His smoky gray eyes bored into hers.

"There's a connection between Torrie and Leanne Oakwood. That's enough of a reason. Someone killed Jill's sister, and everyone associated with her qualifies as a suspect." *You taught me that much, pal.*

"Even your friend?"

"Hardly." Marla stiffened. "Jill is terribly upset about her sister's death."

"Is she more upset about Scott landing Torrie's share of their jointly owned property?"

Marla's gaze slid away. "That particular issue concerned her before the tragedy."

"Exactly. Maybe she thought her problems would be solved with Torrie out of the way."

"That's absurd. Both of them were upset over losing the tenant. If anything, Torrie was adamant about finding a new renter. Jill seemed more uncertain. Now she's under pressure from her relatives to follow their advice."

"I suppose we'll see them again at the funeral."

"Tell me about it. I wonder if Griff Beasley will come. Torrie's colleagues, including Hally, will likely be there."

"Hally actually admitted there was a love triangle between those three?" He drank a sip of water.

She nodded. "Professional jealousy, as well. Hally's assistant made it clear she isn't happy about the society reporter getting a promotion. Since Torrie is gone, that's all but assured."

"Interesting."

Lifting her coffee cup, Marla tilted her head. "I feel bad for Jill, having to attend her sister's funeral so soon after her wedding. If I can help her survive this, I'll do what it takes."

"Speaking of things to do, sweetcakes, Mom is bugging me."

"Now what?" She suppressed a grimace. She loved Kate, but their tastes often clashed.

"She thinks we should register for gifts at Bloomingdales as well as Macy's and Bed, Bath, & Beyond."

"It's too late. We're already receiving packages."

"People are asking her what to get us."

"So? I don't have time to go to the mall again or to fill out online forms. I have an appointment with Jill's florist tomorrow. Maybe he noticed something important at the wedding."

Dalton reached across the table to pat her hand. "Just don't get so caught up in Jill's affairs that you forget about your own. You have a tendency to get tangled in investigations when personal pressure takes its toll."

"Do I? I didn't know you were a psychologist."

He winked, his mouth curving in a sexy smile. "That's part of my job, so watch out. I can anticipate your moves before you make them."

His words were as much innuendo as warning. How could he know she was sorely tempted to use those lock picks her cousin Cynthia had given her? If only another method for getting into Torrie's office undetected would present itself.

She didn't have a chance to follow through that evening, being overwhelmed with e-mails and phone calls to her mother, Dalton's mom, and her friend Tally.

Tally picked up the receiver after two rings. "Hi, Marla. Thanks for returning my call. I went down to the bridal shop for my final fitting. I love the dress, and I especially like that I'll be able to wear it afterwards at cocktail parties."

Marla sank onto her bed and leaned against the pillows. "I'm glad you're happy. I still have to pick up my gown one of these days. Ma is lending me her pearls for the occasion."

"What's happening otherwise?"

Marla cradled the phone by her ear. "I told you what happened at Arnie and Jill's affair. I'm trying to help Jill so she can put this tragedy behind her. It seems as though everyone who knew Torrie disliked her for some reason."

"Holy smokes, Marla, you've got enough to do. Ken and I would like to get together with you guys, too."

She felt a flush of guilt. "I'm pretty swamped right now."

"It's important, Marla."

"Why? What's the matter?"

"I need to tell you in person."

Uh, oh. People usually came to her with their problems. What now?

"Tomorrow night is out. I'm going to services with my mother and Roger." The thought of spending time with Anita's boyfriend made her gag, but he pleased her mother and that's what counted. "I'm spending Saturday night with Dalton's parents, and Sunday is the funeral."

"Maybe I should make an appointment at your salon," Tally said in a disgruntled tone.

"I'm sorry. It's just a busy week, unless . . ."

"What?"

"Are you interested in joining me for a B and E?"

"Say again?" A pause. "Oh, no, Marla. You can't be thinking of involving me in your escapade." Then a note of curiosity. "Who's your target?"

"*Boca Style Magazine.* I want to look in Hally Leeds's drawers."

"By breaking into her office building? Dalton would have a cow if he finds out."

"I won't get caught." Marla filled the tall blonde in on her latest investigative findings.

"You're insane. Do you really think the society columnist found something significant in Torrie's files?"

"It's possible."

"You want to see if Griff's photos are there, too, don't you? Otherwise, why would someone bonk him on the head?"

"Maybe Hally did it out of jealousy." Marla crossed her legs. "She may have heard about his assignment, although he said someone phoned him, and he gave away his location. He couldn't identify the speaker."

"Hey, I have an idea." Excitement laced her friend's voice. "Do you have Hally's e-mail address? You could ask your computer pal if he can access her files from a remote location."

"You mean, hack in? I suppose I could ask Lance." The techno nerd had helped her before.

"In the meantime, is Jill aware you're running around town

for her sake?"

"She asked for my advice."

"Yeah, over the property matter. How about her uncle Eddy and cousin Kevin? Do they benefit from Torrie's death?"

"I'll try to get more out of them at the funeral." Marla switched tactics. "So what is it you're dying to tell me?"

Tally gave a low chuckle. "Oh, no, you have to see me in person for that information. Call me when you're ready to set a date. In the meantime, keep your focus. Your wedding is almost here."

Hanging up, Marla moaned. If only people wouldn't keep reminding her of that fact, but everyone seemed to be a yenta these days. Maybe Dalton was right. When the noose around her personal life tightened, she ran after crooks. It was a lot easier to deal with the black-and-white aspects of life rather than the gray areas with all their distractions.

Eddy Rhodes's name came up again the following day when Marla visited the florist at his shop in downtown Hollywood. She'd forgotten how attractive Philip Canfield was, with his ebony hair tied in a ponytail, warm blue eyes, and dazzling smile.

"How are you, luv? It's so nice to see you again." He strode around the counter to air-kiss her on both cheeks. "Don't you adore our holiday decorations? December is my favorite time of year."

"They're wonderful. You've done a beautiful job." She even spotted a menorah on a small table with a blue cloth.

A fragrant cinnamon aroma mixed with pine wafted through the shop. Christmas wreaths competed for space with buckets of cut flowers, floral baskets, and green plants. In a refrigerated case, orchids and roses burst with vibrant colors, while on a high shelf around the perimeter of the shop stood sample centerpieces for various celebrations.

"What brings you in today?" Canfield asked, while an assistant added a vase filled with carnations to the refrigerated storage.

"As you know, my wedding is coming up in a few weeks. I'm sorry I didn't meet you earlier. I've already hired someone, but a friend of mine is getting married next, and I thought I'd scout you out for her." She chuckled nervously, hoping he'd buy her story.

"When is the date?"

"It's in June, so they have plenty of time." She thought of Nicole, trying to talk her boyfriend into tying the knot.

"That's a busy month for weddings, so you'd have to tell her to put down a deposit without delay. We're already booking a year ahead. How many are in the bridal party?"

Marla clutched her purse. "Four to six? I'm not sure she's asked anyone yet."

"Have a seat at that table in the rear, and I'll give you some information you can bring back to her."

Marla ducked past a flowered archway into an alcove where he indicated she should go. More sample centerpieces were scattered around the tight space, making her feel as though she'd entered a fairyland. Tiny glittering lights decorated towering potted trees, while ivory tulle draped from the ceiling. Huge albums littered the tabletop, where a vase sat with an elegant arrangement of white roses, carnations, ferns, and baby's breath.

One album was open to a page showing a bar mitzvah where the theme was pirates and the entrance was through a replica of a sailing ship. Taking a seat, Marla riffled through the books until she came to a wedding album. How could she steer the conversation to Jill's affair? Was that making her heart thud so fast, or did thinking about her own nuptials make her breathless?

"I was impressed by the flowers at Jill's wedding," she said after the florist joined her. "The centerpieces were magnificent."

"Thanks so much. They were fabulous, weren't they? Would you like some wine, luv? We have cold chablis and freshly baked chocolate chip cookies."

"How can I resist?" Marla accepted the treats, while conceding his marketing skills could teach her a few pointers. He made her feel special. "Jill was lucky to find you."

Canfield beamed with pride. "She liked my orchids, so we worked those into her arrangements. They're so much more divine than lilies, in my opinion." He gave a high-pitched giggle. "Of course, I'm an orchid enthusiast. I was so pleased that her affair was held at Falcon's new park. What a stroke of genius on his part to book her function on their opening weekend. Talk about a publicity coup in his favor!"

"Torrie set that up, and now she's dead."

His face crumpled into a sad frown. "How true, and how tragic. I felt so sorry for the poor bride. Her own sister."

Marla gave him a shrewd glance. "You stayed pretty much until the end. Do you usually do that at weddings?"

He shrugged. "I like to make sure everything is perfect for the reception. It's my reputation at stake, understand. Each signature event must be unique and memorable." Opening a notebook, he withdrew a printed sheet of paper. "Now if I can just get your friend's name and the name of the groom, along with their addresses and phone numbers."

"Uh, Nicole will have to contact you herself. I didn't write down that information."

"All right. Is her affair similar to yours? How many attendants will you be having? Don't forget, if you run into any last-minute problems, give me a call. I'm good at managing unexpected snafus."

Like murder? She blinked. "Thanks, I appreciate that. I'm having four bridesmaids plus a matron of honor." Her brother's wife, Charlene, two friends, plus Brianna made up the bridal party, along with Tally. She'd been hesitant to ask Brie, unsure how the teen would react, but fortunately, the girl had been thrilled to be included.

He smiled. "Will you walk by yourself in the procession, or with your father?"

"My mother will precede me. My father is deceased." No way she'd ask Roger to participate. She could just imagine Anita's stocky boyfriend waddling along, ruffling the rug underfoot so she'd trip when her turn came.

"What about the lucky groom? Who's attending him?"

Marla smiled at the way Canfield inspired confidences. How much had Jill told the man? "Dalton doesn't have any siblings, so my brother Michael will be his best man. He's asked four of his friends to be ushers."

"They'll need boutonnieres. The groom's parents will be participating?"

"Yes." How did they get on the subject of her wedding? Wasn't he supposed to be giving her information to take home to her hypothetical friend?

"Of course you're doing corsages for the mothers?"

"That's right." She'd already made her selections.

"So that's seven boutonnieres, two corsages, one bridal bouquet, and five for your bridesmaids and maid of honor."

Numbers swirled in her head. "Correct. Anyway, much as I would like to discuss my own details, I came to get info for my friend, remember?"

He pursed his lips. "So sorry, but I love to discuss weddings. Here are some pictures of the most common bouquet styles." He pulled another book from the stack and flicked open the pages to a classic all-white collection. "The round nosegay is always popular. People used these back in the fourteenth century to mask odors. That's where the nosegay got its name.

Get it? Nose?" He giggled.

"I see." What she saw was that he made her lose concentration. If she didn't focus their conversation, she'd never get out of there.

"If your friend chooses to wear a formal gown, I'd suggest this cascade bouquet." He showed her another picture. "Or for a more contemporary design, we can do wonders with calla lilies, orchids, and anthuriums. These can be simple but sophisticated."

"How about candles, like at Jill's wedding?" she said in a desperate attempt to steer the conversation.

"At the ceremony, she can have flowers alone, or flowers plus candlelight. We have lots of options for the dinner tables, depending on the look she wants."

"Could you give me price sheets for the different choices?"

"We have various packages available if your friend is cost conscious, but everything can be customized. I've included the info in this material." He waved a packet. "Also, I can suggest colors for the table linens and chairs. It would help if your friend brings in swatches from the bridal dresses."

Mute, Marla merely nodded.

"May I refill your wine glass, luv? You're looking a mite stressed."

"I'm okay, thanks," she said, her stomach roiling. All these details drove her mad on top of everything else: the new house, the day spa, the parents.

"We can do gifts, too. You know, for the bridal party, as well as small remembrances for the wedding guests." He twirled his hand in the air. "It depends on how elaborate your friend cares to go. Who's doing the cake? We can scatter rose petals on the cake table, or we could use orchids, my favorite."

Ah, there's the opening she needed. "Speaking of wedding cakes, I'm wondering where Jill and Arnie bought their cake knife.

Would you know? Was it from a gift shop or did you supply it?"

He shut the bridal album with an abrupt snap. "They bought their knife elsewhere, but I can show you our selections if you wish."

"Who's responsible for setting it on the cake table?"

"That depends on your decorator." Something flickered behind his gaze. "I can lay it out and surround it with flowers, or the bride can make arrangements with the caterer."

"I see." She folded her hands together. "Who was responsible at Jill's event? Pardon me for asking, but I'm wondering who touched it last."

"Arnie gave the knife to me beforehand. I brought it in my van along with everything else."

"So you placed it on the table beside the cake, before the ceremony even started?"

"My dear, I finished doing the ballroom before the bride even arrived."

"Tell me about the orchids at Jill's affair. Her centerpieces were so magnificent. Is it hard to obtain such a large amount of orchids? Aren't they super costly?"

"I have good suppliers. Look at Orchid Isle if you want an example on a grand scale." He beamed proudly. "Who do you think supplies Falcon with his plant stock?"

"Isn't that a job for a nursery?"

He cocked his head. "I guess your friend Jill didn't tell you. I'm part-owner of a nursery out in Davie. Her uncle helped me realize that ambition of mine."

"I had no idea. So you don't just own a flower shop?"

He waved his hand. "My resources go much deeper, luv. I have collectors come to me, like Mr. Oakwood."

"You said Jill's uncle was involved?"

"Eddy Rhodes made my dream possible. That real estate attorney can move mountains. He's amazing."

"I suppose he'll be at Torrie's funeral on Sunday." *Interesting how Eddy's name keeps popping up.*

"I'm glad you reminded me. I'm planning to attend." His eyes misted. "Poor lady. I still can't believe such a tragedy could happen at one of my weddings."

Poor you, you mean. "Did you notice Torrie talking to anyone who might have upset her?"

He shook his head, shuffling the papers in front of him into a neat pile. "My focus was on the bride, and on my exquisite designs. Have you heard anything about the investigation? I can't imagine who would have wanted to harm that unfortunate woman."

"I'm not privy to the police reports."

"Didn't you say your fiancé was a detective?"

So you noticed. "In Palm Haven. Dalton doesn't have jurisdiction on this case. Tell me, had you met Torrie before the wedding?"

"I ran into her a couple of times at Leanne's house."

"Oh. I understand Torrie used her influence with Leanne to book her sister's wedding at Orchid Isle."

"The dates worked out perfectly."

"Hally said I should talk to Leanne if I wanted to learn more about her relationship to Torrie."

"Who?"

"Hally Leeds, the fashion reporter from *Boca Style Magazine.*"

"When did you speak to her?"

"Yesterday."

"You're getting around, aren't you?" He must have realized from her expression that he'd sounded snippy, because then he tapped her arm and grinned. "I mean, you have so much to do with your own wedding coming up. I'm surprised you're wasting time chasing around town for your friends."

"I'm glad to help out. I guess I'll see you on Sunday, then.

Thanks so much for this information. My friend will be grateful. I'll tell her to get in touch with you and book her date as soon as possible."

"That would be wise." He stuffed the documents into the packet folder and handed it over. "Take these, and have her call me with any questions. We'll make sure her event is fabulous."

His giggle followed her out the door, but it sounded hollow, like an insurance salesman trying too hard to be convincing.

Chapter Nine

Marla and Dalton filed into a row holding two empty spaces at the funeral home in Coral Gables. Already the pews were filled, many of them with familiar faces. Muttering her apologies as she slid her feet in front of several people, Marla gratefully sank onto the cushioned seat.

Now that she had time to look around in the hushed silence, broken only by the sounds of an organ playing in the background, she noted the generous flower displays surrounding the casket in front. Different colored orchids were among the varieties. Had Philip Canfield donated those baskets? A table off to the side held framed photos showing Torrie in happier times.

"We do photos at Jewish funerals." She leaned toward Dalton so no one else could hear her. "However, we don't send flowers. Usually, people bring food to the family afterward or give charitable donations in the deceased's memory."

Looking darkly handsome in his fitted sport coat, he gave her a glum glance. "Thanks, I'll remember that."

"Jill said she'll be sitting shivah at home until Thursday. I'd like to get over there tomorrow."

Patting her hand, he nodded. "You're a good friend."

"Speaking of friends, I got so busy yesterday that I couldn't call Tally back. I can't wait to find out what she has to tell me." She studied the lock of his peppery hair that stubbornly tumbled onto his forehead. His temples had gotten grayer since she'd met him. "Do you think she's pregnant?"

He lifted his eyebrows. “They’ve been trying long enough.”

“Tell me about it.” She’d be thrilled for Tally but feared it would separate them further. Tally had gone New Age on her, and now she’d talk about cribs and diapers and all that production that went along with babies.

Her attention diverted when the music swelled and the minister walked in. Jill and Arnie sat in the front row along with Scott Miller and some other people Marla didn’t recognize. She crossed her legs, preparing for the eulogies to follow. Loathing funerals, she checked her watch at frequent intervals, hoping they could make it to their appointment at the country club. She and Dalton needed to review several details with the caterer.

Despite her resolution not to get teary-eyed, she couldn’t help herself from getting choked up when Scott spoke about his wife. In the front row, Jill’s shoulders shook with silent sobs. Marla cast a subtle glance around. She spotted Leanne Oakwood with tears trickling down her cheeks. Her husband sat stoically at her side, his mother flanking him. Sitting directly behind the Oakwoods was Philip Canfield, wearing a somber suit.

“This isn’t that much different from a Jewish funeral,” Marla commented to Dalton on their way to the cemetery after the service concluded. Police cars escorted their procession, sirens blaring, traffic being held at intersections until they passed. “The minister conducted the service, and then Torrie’s close family and friends spoke about her life. What’s different seems to be the flowers and our customs in the days that follow.”

“We had three-hour wakes for two days before my grandfather’s funeral.” Focused on the road, Dalton gripped the steering wheel. “When Pam died, we had calling hours at the funeral home for a couple of nights before the service.”

“So Christians have friends stop by to express their sympathy in the days before the funeral,” Marla said, trying to understand, "whereas we sit shivah afterward—three days for Reform Jews, and seven days for more religious denominations."

Gentiles even sprinkled dirt on the casket, she noticed at the graveside ceremony. Bowing her head while the minister recited a prayer, she remembered sprinkling Israeli dirt on her father's coffin.

When the service concluded, people dispersed. She almost liked that better than Jewish funerals, where the guests lined up in two parallel rows and mourners walked down the aisle between them, accepting their condolences and pats on the back, along with their scrutiny. Here friends and family stood in different groupings speaking quietly before commuting to Scott's house for food and drink.

Marla saw they had time to spare, so she angled toward the Oakwoods. Jill and Arnie were surrounded by family, including Eddy and Alexis and their cousin Kevin. They appeared to be involved in an earnest discussion, so she didn't want to interrupt. Leanne looked somewhat lost, standing aside while her husband and his mother carried on a conversation.

"How are you, Leanne?" Marla said, alone since Dalton had wandered off to make a phone call. "We met at Jill's wedding, remember?"

"Sure, you were one of the bridesmaids." Leanne smiled, lines crinkling her eyes. She wore her tinted reddish-brown hair in a cute pixie cut with bangs feathering her arched eyebrows. A cool breeze blew, and she tightened the maroon scarf around her neck. It provided the only splash of color against a black suit.

Feeling chilled, Marla folded her arms across her chest. She'd worn a short-sleeve dress and should have brought a sweater. Hopefully, it would warm up soon. Her stomach growled; one o'clock meant she was due for lunch. "It was kind of you to help Jill book her wedding at Orchid Isle."

Leanne's mouth turned down. "What a disaster. Falcon was upset about the negative publicity."

Oh, yeah? Every time my name is linked in the news to a murder, I get a surge in business.

"I'm so sorry."

"Don't feel bad for us. Poor Torrie." Leanne dabbed at her eyes with a tissue. "She didn't even have the chance to spread her wings that she'd so longed for."

"What do you mean?" Was Leanne talking about the possible promotion at work? Torrie may have been hopeful, but her ascension up the career ladder had not been assured.

Leanne shot a venomous glance toward Griff Beasley, who stood among a cluster of employees from *Boca Style Magazine.* A couple of young females appeared to be enthralled with whatever he was saying. "She thought that two-timer was her ticket to adventure. She couldn't have been more wrong."

Marla opened her mouth, but before she could pose another question, Philip Canfield sauntered in their direction. He'd draped a bright red scarf around his neck. "Lo and behold, my two favorite ladies." He air-kissed each of them in turn. "Leanne, my lovely, cheer up. Our dear Torrie wouldn't want her friend to look so sad."

To Marla's surprise, Leanne grasped his arm. "You're always around for support. I don't know what I'd do without you."

A private look passed between them, making Marla wonder about their relationship. Wasn't Philip gay? He certainly gave that impression with his flamboyant clothes and effusive gestures.

Falcon's mother took them in at a glance and strode over. "Do I know you?" She wore an expensive black dress and veiled hat.

"I don't believe we've formally met." Marla extended her hand. "I'm Marla Shore, Jill and Arnie's friend."

"You can call me Cornelia." She turned to her son. "Falcon, I'm getting chilly. It's time for us to leave."

"Yes, Mama." His shoulders hunched.

"How are you, Mr. Oakwood?" Marla regarded him with a level glance.

"How can anyone feel under the circumstances?" He glared at her from behind his spectacles. "Terrible affair, this. Who'd have thought such a beautiful wedding would end in tragedy?"

The man sounded as though the only tragedy was the inconvenience to his schedule.

Philip slipped away, while Leanne stood with her eyes downcast. Cornelia's gaze narrowed, scrutinizing her daughter-in-law. Marla could sense the palpable tension in the air.

"My fiancé is waiting." She pointed to where Dalton stood, signaling to her. "I'd love to chat with you some more, but I have to go. Please excuse me."

Leanne gave her a genuinely warm smile. "You know, it made me feel better to talk to you. If you're ever in Coconut Grove, stop by and we'll have tea."

"Could I have your number so I can call first? I may take you up on your offer." *Sooner than you think, pal.*

After exchanging business cards, Marla turned and bumped elbows with someone.

"Sorry," said Kevin, Jill's cousin. He introduced Marla to his wife, Dana, a woman with strawberry-blond hair and rosy cheeks, who looked like she'd come off the boat from Scandinavia. Her low-cut black lace dress seemed too risqué for a funeral, by Marla's standards.

"How do you do?" Dana fingered the pearls on her neck. "Jill was just talking about you."

Marla smiled when Dalton caught up to her. "Really? This is my fiancé, Dalton Vail. Dalton, you've met Kevin Rhodes, and this is his wife, Dana."

Dalton lifted his eyebrows. "You're the guy who's in real estate, right?"

Kevin gave a vigorous nod. "Jill mentioned that you knew about our quagmire with the oil lube company. I understand you own a rental property yourself?"

Marla shifted her purse, her heels sinking into the soft earth. They stood on a grassy expanse at the edge of the street so as not to trespass on anyone's grave. "My ex-husband and I bought it together. He sold me his share, so now it's all mine." Only after she'd kept Stan from going to jail by solving his third wife's murder.

"If you're thinking of bailing out, come to me," Kevin said. "I can get you a good price."

"Is that what you told Jill about her piece of land?" she asked as Dalton's cell phone trilled.

"It's Mom," Dalton told her, rolling his eyes. "She's asking if we're free yet. Meet me at the car." He stalked off while Marla switched her attention back to the older couple.

"My cousin insists upon finding another tenant." Kevin's forehead crinkled. "She says that's what Torrie would have wanted. I can certainly do that for her and Scott, but it may take some time. The environmental issues have to be dealt with first."

"Isn't that the responsibility of the oil company?"

"Depends on the wording in her lease. She's working with Uncle Eddy's law firm on the termination procedures. Meanwhile, I've gotten a few nibbles on our listing. Some are crank calls but there's one fast food place and a bank who are interested."

"It's good that she has you to help her. She's been very upset over the whole thing."

"That's because she never had to lift a finger before," Dana cut in with a pout. "Her grandfather started the business."

Kevin gave his wife a quelling glance. "I've sent letters out to all the head honchos in the area," he told Marla, peering at her as though she should be impressed. "It's what I do."

So you're not trying to trick her into selling or trading the property? Or was he using a different ploy, making finding a tenant so difficult that she'd decide to sell in desperation?

"I've heard Eddy's name crop up in relation to Philip Canfield." A breeze lifted the hairs on Marla's arms. "The florist said he owns a plant nursery that Eddy helped him obtain."

"He needed more space to cultivate his orchids."

"So he grows his flowers there, or does he import them like most other florists?"

"You'd have to ask Canfield."

"I understand he also supplies many of the plants for Orchid Isle."

"I believe he and Falcon Oakwood share a passion for orchids. Falcon is one of those fanatic collectors. That's how Canfield got involved in Jill's wedding. Falcon's wife, Leanne, introduced the man to her friend, Torrie."

"It's such a shame that Falcon's grand opening was marred by Torrie's death. It appears to have been a crime of opportunity." From the corner of her eye, Marla spotted Dalton trudging over to a dark sedan. Detective Brody. She wondered if he had attended the funeral service. If he stood in the back, she might not have noticed him.

"Is that so?" Kevin's ears turned red. "I wonder if the investigation has turned up anything. Would you know?"

She shook her head. "Not me. Do you have any information that might be relevant? Like, who was the last person you saw Torrie with at the reception?"

"She was talking to some waitress," Dana blurted, shooting a glance at her husband. "They were outside. I couldn't hear what they were saying but the girl seemed distraught."

"Really?" Marla searched the crowd but didn't see Rachel anywhere. She hadn't seen the office intern at Torrie's funeral service. Had she just imagined the girl's resemblance to the waitress at Jill's wedding?

Perhaps the catering staff could shed light on the waitress's identity. She'd been wanting to revisit Orchid Isle. If she needed an excuse, she could scout out the place for her hypothetical friend.

Eddy and Alexis sauntered over. After giving them a perfunctory greeting, Marla left to rejoin Dalton, deep in conversation with the police detective.

"Any prints on the doorknob?" Dalton asked him.

Detective Brody scratched his jaw. "Nope, wiped clean. But the bugger didn't get the spot on the carpet."

"Excuse me? What am I missing?" Marla shifted her handbag to her other shoulder. It was getting late. After their stop at the country club, she and Dalton planned to meet Kate and John to discuss the rehearsal dinner. So much to do; not enough time. Wasn't that her life story?

"Torrie's body appears to have been dragged from the corridor on the other side of the service door to under the cake table in the banquet hall," Dalton told her. "Presumably she was killed in the hallway and then moved to avoid detection."

Her mouth dropped open. "What was she doing back there?"

"Meeting someone? Coming from the restroom? Who knows?" Dalton turned to Brody. "What about the staff? I assume you've interviewed everyone on duty that day."

The detective's brows folded together. "Naturally. I'm trying to locate one staff member in particular. The other people say she vanished about the time of the murder."

"Don't tell me," Marla said. "I'll bet it's a waitress with dark hair."

"How did you know?" Brody replied in his baritone voice.

"Dana Rhodes just told me how she saw the waitress talking to Torrie outside, and the girl seemed upset. So you're saying she's missing?"

"The woman's name is Susan Beamer, and she was a temp hire. Trouble is, her background doesn't check out. Now I can't get a trace on her."

"That's too bad," Dalton said. "Keep working it, though. Something might turn up."

"You bet. Nice seeing you folks."

"Thanks, Detective. I'll be in touch." Dalton shook his hand in farewell.

As she and Dalton walked back to his car, Marla clamped her lips shut. Should she share her theories with him, or wait until she had hard evidence?

It seemed absurd, but perhaps Rachel had shown up at the wedding disguised as this waitress. For what purpose? To keep tabs on her idol? Torrie had given her the job as an intern. Rachel could have become obsessed with her mentor.

Maybe they'd argued that day after the ceremony. Torrie might have been annoyed at Rachel's deception, perhaps even threatened to fire her. Had they proceeded indoors to the service corridor behind the reception hall? And then did Rachel, aka Susan, get so riled that she jabbed the cake knife into Torrie's chest?

There was one thing wrong with that idea. How did she obtain the knife from the table in the ballroom? Or had Philip lied about putting it there?

The only way to tell would be to see the wedding pictures. If she couldn't access the photos in Hally's office, she urgently needed to consult the wedding photographer. Jill had given her the name of the guy who did her event. While Marla was in his office, maybe she could sneak a peek at Jill's proofs.

She'd better hurry, because whoever bumped off Torrie might

decide to cover his or her tracks even further. Griff had already been attacked. Who would be next?

Chapter Ten

Marla hit a dead end when she attempted to contact Jill's wedding photographer the next day. Surrounded in her townhouse home office by empty boxes, she hung onto the receiver.

"I'm sorry," said the receptionist on the line, "but he's gone on vacation. You can come in and look at our albums in the meantime. Jim is booked solid through May of next year, though."

"That's okay, this affair isn't until June. Mr. Rawls just did my friends' wedding: Jill and Arnie Hartman. I was hoping to see how their proofs came out."

"You could stop by and view the digitals. The prints won't be ready for several weeks. Excuse me, I'm getting another call. Just drop by if you want to see samples of our work."

"Thanks." Marla put the receiver back on the hook and surveyed the papers piled on her desk, the screen saver twirling on her computer monitor, and the packing materials cluttering the floor.

She didn't fathom how she'd be ready to move by their closing date in January. Between the wedding and her spa's grand opening, she'd be a wreck by the end of the year. Thank goodness today was Monday. She had the day off from the salon to get things done.

She did some bookkeeping and wrote a press release about the spa opening as promised for Hally. Paying a shivah call to Jill was also on order for today.

Heading into the kitchen, she refilled Spook's water dish and made sure the poodle had an adequate supply of Science Diet Light Small Bites before letting him in from the back yard.

"Come here, precious." Scratching Spooks behind his ears, she gave him a sausage treat and watched him run into the living room for privacy. Fortunately, he got along well with Dalton's golden retriever. Two dogs would be a handful, in addition to a teenager. If Marla's life was busy now, soon it would get a lot more hectic. She embraced the change, though. It was time.

Hoping to touch base with Brianna before the girl left for school, Marla dialed Dalton's house. "Hi, honey," she said when the teen answered. "Do you still want me to get tickets to the *Nutcracker* ballet? If so, I'll order them online today."

"Sure, that's cool." Brianna sounded breathless, as though she'd rushed to answer the phone. "Are you and Spooks coming over later?"

"Yep, I've made shepherd's pie for dinner."

"Awesome." Brianna paused. "Dad says you need to work on the seating charts for the wedding again."

"I know. We keep getting more RSVPs. Why do people wait until the last minute to respond?"

"Guess you didn't expect so many cousins would want to come."

"I can't wait for them to meet you."

"Uh, huh." Brianna sounded less than thrilled. "By the way, I've been thinking about taking acting lessons. Will you talk to Dad for me?"

What am I, the buffer zone between you two? "Why don't we discuss it later? You need to get going, or you'll miss your bus. Love you."

An inner glow filled her as she shut down the computer and snatched her purse. Who'd have thought becoming a stepmother would be so gratifying? It flattered her beyond belief that Brianna sought her advice and that Dalton finally listened to her opinions about teenage girls.

The phone rang before she could escape.

"Hi, *bubula,* it's me," said Anita. "I thought I'd catch you before you ran out. Remember, Roger and I are meeting you and your *mechutonim* for dinner Wednesday night at the Vienna Café. If you get there first, tell them we have a reservation for seven people."

Oh, joy. Marla tried to muster some enthusiasm but failed. Ma's boyfriend Roger and Dalton's father were as unlike as a blonde and a brunette. Changing the subject, she blabbered about Brianna.

"She got an A on her math test. I'm so proud of her. That was my worst subject."

"Protsent fun kinder iz tei'erer vi protsent fun gelt," Anita said in Yiddish. "Dividends from children are more precious than money. Maybe now you'll consider having kids of your own."

"No, thank you. Brie will keep me busy enough. What time is your doctor appointment this afternoon? Do you want me to go with you?"

"Roger is driving me, thanks. We're going out for a bite to eat afterwards. Gotta go now, bye."

Roger, Roger, Roger. That's all she heard from her mother lately. It's a good thing Anita didn't bring him along on their excursions with Kate, or she'd *plotz.*

Well, okay, maybe she wouldn't have a fit, but she'd certainly complain.

Never mind that now. What could she bring as a gift to Jill and Arnie? People usually brought food, but Arnie owned a restaurant and had supplied platters from his deli, including dessert. Cold cuts could get tiring after a while, though. She'd like to bring something nutritious that their kids could enjoy.

How about a lasagna dish for variety?

She picked up a prepared casserole at Doris's Market and headed over to Arnie's modest ranch-style home in nearby Sunrise. Several cars blocked the driveway, so she had to park along the grassy swale. Having hoped for a private conversation with the bereaved couple, she swallowed her disappointment. She wouldn't be able to discuss Torrie's case with strangers present.

Arnie greeted Marla at the door. His mustache tickled her cheek as he gave her a bear hug inside the foyer.

"Where's Dalton?" Arnie glanced at the driveway.

"He's working, so I came alone." She handed Arnie the covered foil pan. "Here, can you give this to Jill, please?"

"She'll join us in a minute. She's in the kitchen talking to Kevin about her property. Go on and make yourself at home."

Marla glanced at the dining table laden with bagels and lox, Swiss cheese slices, tomatoes and onions, *rugelach,* and other goodies. Tempted to make herself a sandwich, she took a seat in the living room instead. She always felt odd about eating during condolence calls. How could people stuff themselves when their hosts were experiencing such pain?

"It's nice of you to stay home to support Jill instead of going in to work," Marla told Arnie when he returned.

His face weary, he dropped onto the sofa. "Yeah, well, it's the least I can do. Funny how we'd postponed our honeymoon and now we have to take time off from work anyway."

"You'll enjoy your New Year's cruise. I'm just so sorry that this had to spoil your wedding."

"Most of it was over by the time . . . you know. Jill is taking it pretty hard. She and her sister had been estranged for so long, and then they had just started getting back together, thanks to their inheritance."

Marla crossed her legs. "Do you know what came between

them initially? I visited Scott, but he mostly rambled on about his clocks. He's obsessed with his timepieces, isn't he? He gave me the impression that Torrie didn't like his occupation. She'd rather he stayed in the insurance business."

"I wouldn't know about that. We haven't had much contact."

"Now that Torrie's gone, I suppose you won't see much of him in the future."

"My wife will have to communicate with Scott because of their co-ownership. She's doing all the work, while he sits back and tinkers with his toys. I can't tell you how many hours she's spent looking through her grandfather's papers for the original lease and all its amendments, the easements granted, the survey, insurance certificates, and more."

"She would've had to deal with this anyway. It's just coming at a bad time, and Torrie isn't here to help her." Marla leaned forward. "She can always call on me. You know that I'm here for you if you need anything."

He gave her a warm smile. "You're a good friend. I'm glad you and Jill get along so well."

"We've come a long way, baby." Marla laughed, remembering how she and Jill had first met. Friendship had been the farthest thing from her mind. Her only thought was to protect Arnie from the woman who claimed to be his former classmate. Jill had pretended to be Hortense Crone in order to collect information regarding a murder victim. She'd done a good job but hadn't counted on falling for Arnie in the process.

"I should ask Jill about her acting career," she said. "Brianna wants to take lessons."

"Jill has given up going to auditions. She doesn't have time anymore, between her job at Stockhart Industries and the kids. She's so good to them."

"I'm happy for you, Arnie."

His gaze held hers with unsaid words. There had been a time

when he had courted Marla, but she hadn't wanted to be burdened with children. Besides, while she loved Arnie as a friend, he'd never lit her fire. Her body sung to Dalton's song, and she missed him even now.

"Can I get you some coffee?" Arnie glanced at the laden buffet. "Or would you like something to eat? Jill should be out momentarily."

"No, thanks, I'm okay." She folded her hands. "Have you spoken to Detective Brody lately? I wonder how his investigation is going."

She also wondered if he'd shared his findings with them about Torrie being killed in the corridor behind the banquet hall. Had the culprit slipped into the reception and mingled among the guests, or had he run outside through the exterior door? In that case, the police should have dusted *all* the doorknobs for prints.

Arnie stroked his mustache. "We hear they're looking for some waitress who disappeared. Jill has been acting funny since she heard about it. Actually, she's been upset since we got that bouquet." He pointed to a flower basket on the sideboard.

"Who's it from?"

"Someone named Rachel."

Marla sat up straighter. "What did the card say?"

" 'You're in my thoughts. From, Rachel.' I don't recall Jill knowing anyone by that name."

Should she tell him about the intern at Torrie's office? The girl hadn't been present at the funeral. Why not, when so many of Torrie's pals were there? Had she been afraid the police detective would attend, or was there another reason why she didn't want to show her face?

"Why would Jill be disturbed by the note unless she knew the sender?"

"*Ver vaist?* Who knows?"

"Does she talk much about her life when she lived in Vero Beach?"

"Actually, it was Hortense who lived in Vero Beach. Jill came from Orlando."

"But she grew up in Miami. So how did she end up in Orlando working in public relations?"

"What does it matter?" He jumped to his feet. "I'll see what's keeping her. It isn't polite to keep a guest waiting."

Oh, now I'm a guest instead of a friend? What's the matter, Arnie? Have I touched upon a sore subject, or do you not know as much about your bride as you should? She rose and stretched.

Jill greeted Marla with an effusive hug, while Kevin gave her a curt nod. He held a stuffed manila envelope in his hand.

"You'd better make sure that Scott understands how much it's going to cost you," Kevin advised Jill. "You could be paying up to fifty thousand dollars in attorney fees by the time you're done, and that doesn't include the commission I could be charging."

Jill's eyes glazed as she pushed a limp strand of hair off her face. "We're very grateful to you, Kevin. I'll talk to Scott about setting up a joint bank account. We'll have to wait until he has access to Torrie's funds. Keep in mind that neither one of us has received the final payment from the oil company. That'll help pay the lawyer bills." She led Kevin to the exit.

"Let me know as soon as you get the official termination letter from the oil lube people." He tugged his tie into place. "I've called, but the yahoo in the Florida office says it takes a while for the paperwork to go through National. They're such a big bureaucracy that they don't care about little folks like us."

"They're holding everything up. What if somebody trips and falls on the property in the meantime? What if we have to pay property taxes while we're waiting for them to accept their responsibility? The longer the delay, the longer we have to wait for a new tenant to take over."

Kevin patted her shoulder. "Don't worry, I've dealt with dozens of similar situations before. It'll happen."

"I hope you're right." Jill watched him leave and then shut the door. "This is making me sick. Marla, do you have as much aggravation from your rental property?"

"Sometimes, but it's worth the effort in the long run. You could never invest the money from a sale and make the same income."

"So what?" Arnie jabbed his forefinger at them. "Look at all the trouble it's causing. I say you should sell and be done with it."

"Torrie didn't want to sell, and neither do I." Jill sniffled. "We've talked about this. Josh and Lisa could benefit from my inheritance, especially if we enroll them in private school when they're older. That'll cost us over ten thousand dollars per year for each child. I could use your encouragement, Arnie. Instead, you sound like Uncle Eddy."

"His firm will make plenty of money whatever you and Scott decide. Maybe you should have retained independent counsel."

"Eddy is giving us a discount."

"You call five percent a discount? Big deal, when he charges three hundred sixty dollars an hour."

"I can't talk to you. You won't listen."

Marla heard voices chattering from the patio. "Is someone else here?" She'd seen more cars than Kevin's.

"A couple of my cousins and a lady from the foster care system where Torrie volunteered her time," Jill said.

"Interesting. Scott didn't mention Torrie's volunteer work to me when we spoke. His disapproval of Griff Beasley came through loud and clear, though." Marla tilted her head. "That reminds me, when you get your proofs, could you let me know? I'd love to see them. I might get some ideas I can pass on to our wedding photographer."

"The prints won't be ready for a few weeks." Jill's statement confirmed what the photographer's receptionist had told Marla.

The other visitors chose that moment to join them in the living room. After a round of introductions, the gray-haired lady addressed the group.

"I don't know who we'll get to take Torrie's place. She was very devoted to her role as a court-appointed guardian in our foster care program. We need more people like her."

"What prompted her to get involved?" Marla asked. Understanding the victim's motives could lead to the killer. You never knew which action might trigger an explosion of bottled-up rage in an acquaintance.

"I'm not sure, actually," the woman said. "She just wanted to do something for the children, maybe because she had none of her own."

"Are you kidding?" Jill planted her hands on her hips. "That may have been her initial reason, but guilt became her main motivator."

"Guilt over what? I thought you and Torrie didn't share confidences," Marla pointed out with a meaningful glare.

Jill's face blanched, and she glanced away.

"Can I get you anything to eat?" Arnie inserted quickly. Serving people food seemed to be his coping mechanism.

"Not me, thanks. Again, please accept my condolences for your loss. I have to go," the lady said.

"So do we," chimed in the cousins.

The guests made their farewells, leaving Marla alone with her hosts in the living room.

"So how are your wedding plans going?" Jill asked, after Arnie excused himself to make a phone call. Feeling awkward, Marla perched on the edge of the sofa.

"Oh, gosh, we still have a million things to do." Marla

described their progress and what remained on her to-do list.

"You'll be relieved when it's all over," Jill reassured her with a wan smile.

"Not really. Then I have the grand opening of my new spa, followed by our move in January. I won't be able to relax until well into spring."

"Aren't you taking any time off for a honeymoon?"

She shrugged. "We've talked about it. Ma offered to watch Brianna if we want to go away, but we haven't made any plans."

"I hope we're still able to go on our cruise."

"Maybe the case will be solved by then." Marla hesitated. "Torrie's funeral service was lovely. It was similar to a Jewish funeral. There aren't that many differences between the traditions." Except when the person was cremated instead of buried. She didn't say that aloud.

"Yes, I was surprised Scott had so many good things to say about my sister." Wringing her hands, Jill studied the floor.

"I think he truly loved her."

Jill's gaze flew to meet Marla's assessing glance. "Then why was she unhappy? Torrie didn't talk about Scott with any fondness. She always seemed to put him down."

"He told me she'd have preferred for him to stay in the insurance business. It's my guess he makes less money with his clock shop than he did in his prior job."

"Money may have been an issue. Or it could be that Scott regarded his timepieces with more affection than his wife."

Marla tilted her head. "Do you believe Torrie turned elsewhere for attention?"

"Why would you think that?" Jill narrowed her eyes. "Or do you know something I don't?"

I could ask you the same question, pal.

"Hally Leeds was jealous of Torrie. I spoke to the reporter after your wedding, and Hally made it clear she has the hots for

Griff Beasley, their freelance photographer. I overheard Torrie and Griff arguing at Orchid Isle. It can't help but make me wonder if they had a thing together."

"Weren't Torrie and Hally both contenders for a promotion? That's plenty of reason for rivalry."

"True, but what if Scott thought his wife was carrying on with Griff? Do you think it would make him mad enough to kill her?"

"I'm sure the police are considering that angle." Jill's fingers plucked at the upholstery.

"Someone murdered your sister." Her tone hardened. "Haven't you considered who might have done the deed? Or that you might be in danger? What if it's related to this property you both owned?"

"That's absurd."

"Scott has Torrie's share now. That gives him even more reason to do her in, especially if he's hurting for money."

"I may not be fond of Scott, but he's too meek to commit an act of violence."

"Clark Kent hid behind his mild-mannered exterior, too."

"Come on, what proof do you have?"

"Then again, maybe Hally did it to secure her promotion." Marla hoped to provoke Jill into revealing her secrets. She could help with damage control before the police took interest.

"You're forgetting about Leanne." Jill bent her head, strands of blond hair shielding her face.

"Excuse me?"

"Leanne Oakwood, Torrie's friend." Jill gave her an oblique glance. "Torrie once mentioned how she knew things about the Oakwoods that they wouldn't want to get around."

"Funny you should say so. When I spoke to Hally, she said your sister kept files on people. I imagine the cops checked her computer, but not before Hally copied the data."

Jill paled. "What kind of files? Did she have personal stuff in there?"

"Why are you so alarmed? Afraid Torrie took notes on you?" Marla chuckled as though that were a joke, but she studied Jill's reaction.

Jill shot to her feet. "She might have written down things only my family knows, things they promised never to speak of again. Not that Torrie ever let me forget." Her eye shone with venom. "At least now she can't haunt me with my past mistakes."

"What does that mean?" Marla's pulse rate spiked. Maybe now she'd get some answers.

She never got a reply. Arnie strode into the room, holding the telephone receiver. "It's for you," he told Marla, his tone grim.

Marla jumped up and snatched the instrument. Who would be calling her here? "Hello?"

"I dialed your cell phone," Dalton's deep voice said, "but you didn't answer."

Marla regarded her purse on the floor by the armchair. "It's in my handbag. I didn't hear it ring, sorry. What's wrong?"

"Bad news. Hally Leeds is dead. Strangled."

Chapter Eleven

Marla drove south on I-95, pondering the news she'd received a mere fifteen minutes ago. She'd blurted the reason for her abrupt departure to Arnie and Jill before storming out the door. She had a long drive ahead and wanted to accomplish her mission so she could proceed with her errands for the day.

Leanne Oakwood had vital information. Marla must talk to the socialite before the police got to her.

A colleague had found Hally's body that morning in the company parking lot, where it appeared she'd been accosted late last night. Marla could think of a number of people who might hold a grudge against the woman.

Gripping the steering wheel, she counted them on her mental list. First there was Rachel, who didn't like that Hally was usurping Torrie's place in terms of a promotion. Or maybe Hally had found out what Torrie and Rachel had been discussing so heatedly at the wedding, if Rachel was indeed the waitress in disguise.

Torrie had known something about Griff Beasley that he didn't want to get out. If Hally knew about it, he could have done her in. But then, who would have bopped him on the head at the Venetian Pool unless he had cracked his own noggin for show? That didn't make any sense, because he'd expected to meet Marla at the Biltmore.

Hally had hinted that the Oakwoods had something to hide. Hence Marla's visit to Leanne, who'd asked her to drop by anyway. Leanne might be able to give her the heads up on Philip Canfield, since she'd recommended the florist for Jill's wedding. Marla also wanted to learn more about Orchid Isle and Falcon's relationship to Eddy Rhodes.

The scenery in Miami passed by in a blur as she sped down the highway toward Coconut Grove. I-95 segued into Route 1 at Biscayne Bay. She followed the signs past Vizcaya and the Museum of Science, taking a winding back road and admiring the overhanging foliage. Tropical trees and hibiscus blossoms graced the villas she passed. According to her directions, she was looking for a gated community off Old Cutler Road.

Having called ahead, Marla got buzzed in by the guard. Then she wound down several streets before reaching her goal. The house turned out to be a two-story structure in a cul-de-sac facing a broad lake. She parked in the driveway of a multi-car garage, pausing a moment after turning off the ignition to admire the brick façade and sloped tile roof. More northern in flavor, the place distinguished itself from its hacienda-style neighbors.

Leanne answered the doorbell, smiling a genuine welcome.

"Marla, how nice of you to visit," she said in her throaty tone. She wore a teal silk blouse, black slacks, and a jewel-studded belt. Her reddish-brown hair looked fluffed as though she'd blow-dried it that morning. Marla's glance dropped to her fingernails, perfectly manicured with coral polish.

I should look so put together when an unexpected visitor shows up, she thought.

"Hi, Leanne, thanks for seeing me."

"Come on in. Let's go into the living room. Carla," she hollered, "my guest is here. Bring us some refreshments, please."

An acknowledging cry came from what Marla surmised was the kitchen area. Shifting her purse, she followed Leanne into a high-ceilinged room decorated like a northwestern lodge. She couldn't help gaping at the stuffed animal heads on the walls.

"My, you have quite a collection." She swallowed.

"Falcon enjoys hunting." Leanne made a moue of distaste. "Me, I'm a member of PETA and I don't eat meat."

Marla sat in a wing chair while Leanne dropped onto a faux suede couch. "You must have interesting dinner conversations," Marla remarked.

"Not really. Cornelia doesn't support my views."

"Cornelia? Isn't that Falcon's mother?"

Leanne didn't answer, tightening her lips when a maid shuffled in bearing a tray. The woman set her burden down on the coffee table, while Marla wondered if she could eat those cut sandwich triangles with a moose head staring at her from above.

"Care for some tea?" Leanne asked, lifting a fine china teapot. "It's lemon grass green tea, organic of course."

"Yes, thanks." Marla raised her teacup, yielding to hunger. She thought of the laden table at Arnie's house with regret. All that food would go to spoil if no one ate it.

She made small conversation while chewing on a couple of egg salad sandwiches. "I saw Jill earlier," she said, after wiping her mouth with a paper napkin. Might as well cut to the quick. "She and Arnie are sitting shivah for three days."

"How is she?" Leanne's eyes scrunched in sympathy.

Her makeup shone in the bright sunlight streaming in the windows. Blush highlighted her cheeks, a bit too rosy for Marla's taste. With her attractive features, Leanne could get by with a more subtle touch.

"Jill is managing," Marla answered, "but she'd like to see the case solved, especially since her sister isn't the only victim."

"What do you mean?"

"Hally Leeds was found dead this morning. You know, she's the reporter who worked with Torrie at *Boca Style Magazine.*"

"Oh, my God. No, that can't be true." Leanne clapped a hand to her mouth.

"Maybe the killer thought Torrie had shared information with Hally. Why else would they both be murdered?"

Leanne's wide gaze looked like a deer in headlights. "It could be coincidence. I mean, they don't have any proof linking the two cases, do they?" Her hand trembled as she set her teacup and saucer down with a clatter.

"Probably it's too early to determine if there's a connection." Clasping her hands together, Marla leaned forward. "Who do you think would have a reason to want them both dead?"

"How would I know? I mean, I can understand Scott wanting to get back at Torrie, or even Hally wanting her post, but this?"

Marla jumped at the opening. "Tell me about Scott. Was he aware that his wife was planning to leave him for Griff Beasley?"

Leanne's jaw dropped. "Where did you hear that?"

"From a private source."

Leanne glanced over her shoulder, her expression guarded. "Griff worked with both women," she said in a lowered voice. "You might want to talk to him about it."

"That could be dangerous. Torrie knew something that he wanted kept underground, didn't she? Did she confide in you, Leanne?"

Her eyes bugged. "You're not implying that he—"

"I have no idea who killed them. That's for the police to determine. I'm just trying to get one step ahead so Jill can move on with her life."

"She and Torrie disagreed on many issues," Leanne stated. "Maybe Jill isn't as innocent as she claims. You might want to inquire into her past history before you jump to conclusions."

"Why, do you know something about her that I don't?"

"It's not for me to say." She glanced toward the entry.

"How about her Uncle Eddy? Did Torrie tell you about the property issue dividing the sisters? Their uncle is acting as attorney. I understand he was instrumental in your husband acquiring the land for Orchid Isle."

Leanne leapt up. "If you want to talk to Falcon, he should be downstairs at any moment."

"Do I hear my name mentioned?" The tall man sauntered into view, dressed in jeans and a sport shirt. His erect posture, confident air, and firm voice gave him an aura of power.

"Hello, Mr. Oakwood. It's nice to see you again." Standing, Marla stretched out her hand.

He gave her a lukewarm shake and a false smile. "Likewise. What brings you to our neck of the woods?"

"I have some sad news to impart. Hally Leeds is dead."

"Who?"

"She's a reporter for *Boca Style Magazine* and a colleague of Torrie Miller's."

"Oh, yeah, I remember. A redhead, right? She covered our grand opening." He regarded her from behind his spectacles.

"She and her photographer, Griff Beasley, were there," Marla reminded him.

"What terrible news. How did it happen?"

"I'm not sure exactly." Marla watched him carefully. She'd learned from Dalton not to reveal too much information. "Her body was found in the parking lot where she worked."

"So sad. I only met her that one time, but she did a nice piece on Orchid Isle." He shook his head, his expression revealing nothing. If that's how he reacted to emotional events, Marla pitied his wife.

"Torrie must have spoken about her colleague to you, Leanne."

Falcon shot a meaningful glance at Leanne, who stood primly by with her lips thinned. "My wife is still upset over Torrie's death. She has a delicate constitution. Like one of my orchids, heh heh."

Marla gestured at the moose head. "I gather you like to hunt game as well as rare flowers."

He stiffened. "It's a hobby. Now if you don't mind, Leanne should rest. Wouldn't want her lovely bloom to fade, you know."

Clear on her dismissal, Marla wished she could linger to question Falcon about his orchid collections. Not that she would know the difference between an ordinary orchid and a valuable specimen. She should learn more about them.

"That's a lovely flower arrangement," she commented on her way to the door. An accent table held a crystal vase with a fresh assortment of lilies and other exotics.

"Philip gets the credit," Leanne remarked in a quiet voice. "He's amazing. The man can get me anything I want."

Did Marla detect an innuendo in her tone? "He's very talented. I didn't realize he owns a nursery in Davie. He must have been a big help to you, Falcon, when you were drawing up the plans for Orchid Isle."

Falcon's eyes grew wary. "He made it happen. What Phil can't get from his suppliers, he grows himself. Stop by the park again, when you have time to take a guided walking tour."

"I realize the place hasn't been open long, but how is it doing? Are you getting a good crowd?"

Falcon squared his shoulders. "Yes, we are. Fortunately, the negative publicity over opening weekend didn't prove to be a deterrent. We've just opened up a new shop adjacent to one of the greenhouses where you can buy plants. Sales have been brisk."

"I'm glad to hear it." Marla shook their hands. "Thanks for seeing me, Leanne. I hope we'll run into each other again."

As she drove away, Marla considered Falcon's attitude. He didn't welcome her intrusion, nor was he forthcoming with information. She also got the impression he dominated his wife. She'd like to learn more about Orchid Isle's background and Eddy Rhodes's involvement in the land acquisition.

Checking in with Dalton, she asked about his investigation but received a curt reply. "Can't talk about it now. What have you found out?"

"I think there's some funny business going on between Falcon, Philip, and maybe Jill's Uncle Eddy," she concluded after describing her morning's excursions.

"You may be right." His deep voice poured over her like warm molasses. "Where are you heading now?"

She stopped at a traffic light on Route 1. A local commuter train zoomed by on the elevated rail to her left. Hot pink bougainvillea climbed a residential fence on her right.

"I need to stop by the bridal shop to pick up my dress. Then I have an appointment with the builder to show him where I want the hardware on our kitchen cabinets."

"Oh, yeah. Todd said the plumber is coming this week. Ask him if one of us has to be there."

"Okay." She hesitated. "If I have any free time, I'd like to learn more about orchids. I don't know enough about them to be able to distinguish between ordinary specimens and rarities."

"What for? I hope you're not planning on snooping into any greenhouses or nurseries."

"Who, me?" His words reminded her of Halley's office files and Griff's photos. She still had to find a way to get a sneak peek.

"Marla," he began.

She laughed. "Don't worry. I'll behave." *Yeah, right.*

"By the way, I returned that faucet we bought for the guest bathroom. I decided I liked the first one we looked at better. This is your last chance to change any of the plumbing fixtures."

"I'm okay with our selections so far. That's more your department."

"No, it isn't. You're the one who insisted on having a separate spritzer for the kitchen sink."

"That's because I'll be spending a lot of my time there."

"And you won't be using the bathroom?"

She gripped the wheel tighter. "It really doesn't matter to me. What time should I expect you for dinner?"

He cleared his throat. "I've got to work late tonight, so don't count on me. I'll call you later. Love you."

Marla clicked off her phone, eyes narrowed. First his obsession with home improvement stores, and now he was staying out late again. Last week she and Brie had eaten alone at least twice. True, Dalton could get crazy when he worked a case, but why did he have so many late nights now on top of everything else? Was he getting cold feet about their wedding?

Shrugging, she dismissed her concerns to plan the rest of her day. It was mere coincidence that at the bridal store, she overheard a woman talking about an orchid clinic being given that afternoon at a local park. And so she found herself, after stopping at her townhouse to drop off her wedding garments and to let Spooks out, at a classroom inside Secret Woods.

Marla hadn't been to the park hidden off old Route 84 in a while, but things remained the same from what she could tell. A few buildings in need of repairs housed a natural history display and park offices, plus the spare room for classes or social events. The faded boardwalk led toward a nature trail that branched in two directions.

She'd always favored the path on the left that wound along the mangrove wetlands to an overlook at the New River. She liked to look at the mansions with their private docks across the water and imagine what it would be like to live in a luxury home.

Too bad she couldn't take the time to relax, sit on a bench, and enjoy the view. Sniffing the earthy aroma of decaying leaves, she watched a raccoon survey her then scurry away into the woods. Not wishing to encounter any more wildlife, she entered the designated building and took a seat.

The room wasn't filled by any means. Two young women with notebooks, several retirees, a thin young man wearing glasses, and a jogger who'd come in for a rest occupied the other chairs.

A middle-aged woman strode in the door. She had graying temples on her jet black hair, a purposeful expression, and a pile of handouts, which she promptly distributed.

"Welcome to our Introduction to Orchids class," she said, facing the assemblage. "I'm your instructor, Diane Potts." She glanced at each one of them in turn. "How many of you are here because you'd like to learn more about orchids and how to take care of them?"

Everyone raised their hands.

"Good. Now how many of you've had experience cultivating your own blooms?"

The two young women plus one of the older couples responded.

"Very well. I'm going to give you an overview on what you'll need to know to get started. Usually, people gain an interest in orchid growing by going to an orchid show with a friend or by receiving a blooming plant as a gift and wondering how to take care of it. Then the bug bites, and you're hooked."

Not me, pal. Marla had received an orchid as a gift once and had killed it. Nothing green survived her black thumb. Dalton had better guard his tomato plants against her influence.

"Let's discuss the most common types of orchids people grow. You'll be most familiar with *Cattleyas,* the kind you see in corsages. *Phalaenopsis* are delicately pretty moth orchids. *Den-*

drobiums are long spikes of smaller flowers. *Vandas* are popular for their vibrant colors, and there are thousands more. It could take you years to study them. The orchid societies offer workshops, or you can attend various shows. There are lots of opportunities to create a new and absorbing hobby."

Marla raised her hand. "Isn't vanilla the only edible fruit of the orchid family?" She remembered her conversations on board the *Tropical Sun* with the French countess, a vanilla grower from Mexico.

"That's correct, although vanilla requires a tropical climate and the proper soil. It's a very valuable crop."

"What kind of cost investment will I have to make to begin an orchid collection?" the thin young man asked.

The instructor nodded her approval at his question. "To start, you'll need fertilizer to feed the plant. But then you may decide to buy another plant, or maybe a book to learn more. Soon you'll add some insecticide, fungicide, stakes and clips, potting material and pots. Often this hobby starts off slow and then expands along with your expense sheet."

"What kind of space would I need?" another woman said.

"You can start small, on a windowsill. With one or two plants, you'd use about a gallon of fertilizer a week. When you add more plants, you can expand outside or onto a patio. It's easy in South Florida. North of Orlando, people need greenhouses to keep orchids warm in the winter. Here we need shade houses to protect them from the sun."

"If I wanted to grow orchids as an investment, where would I get the stock?" Marla thought of Philip Canfield. Did he breed his own orchids or import them?

"You would buy seedlings from a wholesale grower and nurture the orchids from babies to blooming size. Keep in mind that plants in bloom are more expensive than out of bloom. Many growers live down in the Homestead area, and they often have retail outlets. Eventually, if you get proficient at it, you could do your own breeding."

"Do people buy and trade orchids as they do collectibles?" Marla persisted, after glancing through the handout and listening fifteen minutes more to a lecture on orchid varieties.

"I wouldn't say people trade them, but rare orchids can be as valuable as other collectibles. Most growers have Web sites and catalogs. Orchid shows are big business for them. They'll compete for awards, besides offering their plants for sale."

"What do you mean?" the young woman asked, busily scribbling notes.

"Different organizations give awards. For example, the American Orchid Society grants an Award of Merit, and the orchid would be tagged accordingly. This signifies to the buyer that this orchid merits special recognition. That doesn't make it rare, but definitely more valuable. It'll be more expensive to buy."

Marla raised her hand again. "How can I tell a rare orchid from a regular one?"

"Today, most orchids can be cloned, although this doesn't usually happen because then prices would fall. A few years ago in China, a new species was discovered. It was fabulously expensive and rare, but not for long. To me, a rare orchid signifies that it's in danger of being overcollected in the wild. There are laws regulating what people can take and from where. A well-known orchidist in Miami just got fined a hefty sum for illegally collecting specimens in the Philippines."

"Does this mean there's a black market for the more exotic blooms?" Marla folded her arms across her chest.

The instructor's eyes gleamed. "Sure, fanatics will pay anything. Call it *orchidelirium* if you will, but collecting orchids can become an addiction just as strong as alcohol or drugs."

"So how much money flows through this illicit trade?"

Pacing back and forth in front of the class, Diane snorted. "Trophy orchids, or rare varieties that cost thousands of dollars each, fuel a ten-billion-dollar orchid black market." She paused to survey them. "Look at the London pharmacist arrested for having six rare orchids in his luggage. He went to jail for orchid smuggling, and that's a minor case. Murder, greed, and betrayal are not uncommon among people passionate about their plants."

Chapter Twelve

"Orchid Isle sounds like a neat park." Brianna leaned against the kitchen counter in Dalton's house. "I'd like to go sometime. We could do lunch in Miami while we're there."

"Good idea." Marla stood at the sink, scraping their dinner dishes. They'd exchanged news while they ate, enjoying the private time together. Dalton hadn't gotten home yet, so she'd been discussing the case with Brie. Already the teen had a lurid fascination with detective work, probably because that often became their main topic of dinner conversation.

"I overheard two older women mentioning Orchid Isle in class." Marla stuck their plates in the dishwasher. "One of them said she'd spotted a rare orchid in the greenhouse. It had been written up in one of the journals. If true, it's illogical that Falcon would display the plant so blatantly. Someone might steal it."

"If he's an avid collector, he may want to show off his prize, like those moose heads in his living room." Brie's ponytail swung as she bent to pick up a crumb off the floor.

"I suppose. One of the women wondered aloud how the land deal had gone through when that property had been contaminated."

"Oh, yeah?" Brianna's gaze lit with curiosity.

"Your father checked the records as I asked and confirmed that Jill's cousin Kevin brokered the transaction. Eddy Rhodes was the attorney. They're mixed up in this somehow, along with Falcon Oakwood, but I haven't been able to get any more information on that strip of land."

"If Jill is going to them for advice on her property, you might warn her to be careful," the teen suggested, her eyes wiser than her fourteen years.

"Tell me about it."

After Brianna left to do homework in her room and no doubt talk on the phone with her friends, Marla let the dogs out and then glanced at the wall clock. It was eight already, and no word from Dalton. Her brow furrowed. What was he working on that could be keeping him this long? She hadn't heard of any difficult case in the news that might involve his unit.

She'd just sat at Dalton's desk to work on their seating charts for the wedding when her cell phone rang.

"Miss Shore? This is the alarm company. We have an alert at your salon."

"What?" She leapt to her feet.

"Could be a possible break-in, plus the smoke alarm went off. The fire department has been dispatched."

"I'll run right over there. Thanks for notifying me."

Clicking off her phone, she stuck it in her jeans pocket. She'd changed earlier into denims and a knit sweater. After explaining to Brianna where she was going and refusing the teen's offer of support, she charged out the front door.

Her heart raced. Maybe it was a false alarm, and she was panicking for nothing. But an inner voice hinted that the timing for this distraction wasn't any coincidence.

"Someone threw a Molotov cocktail in your front window," one of the cops said upon her arrival. "It started a fire, but that's been contained. You've got some water and smoke damage, and I'm afraid your reception desk will have to be replaced. But the guys got to it pretty quickly, so damage is minimal to the rest of the place."

"Thank God." Marla's stomach sank as she gingerly stepped

inside, careful not to crunch on any broken glass. More than her reception desk would need replacement. The entire waiting area was a soggy mess. Chairs, magazine tables, and display cases would all have to go. Not to mention the smell of smoke that lingered in the air, the water sloshing at her feet, and the grit that made her eyes sting. She blinked rapidly as moisture tipped her lashes. Who could have done this?

Her burdens suddenly felt insurmountable. She didn't need this trouble, not with everything else going on in her life. Is that why this had happened? Could it have been a purposeful act, rather than the random misbehavior of some young hooligans?

Gut instinct told her yes, she'd been targeted. But by whom? She'd rattled a few cages recently. Could it have been one of the people she'd visited in the past few days?

"I'm sorry, ma'am, but I'll need to ask you a few questions," the officer said in a kindly tone, pulling out a notebook.

"Of course, go ahead. I'd offer you a seat, but . . ." Her voice trailed off as she gestured helplessly at the ruined shop. *Lord save me, who am I going to get to clean up this mess before we open tomorrow? We'll have to cancel all our appointments. We could be closed for weeks.*

Dismay paralyzed her tongue and clouded her senses. The cop had to repeat his question before she heard him.

"Can you tell if anything valuable is missing?"

"What? Oh, Nicole would have emptied the cash register before she closed up on Saturday. Why, do you believe this was a robbery attempt? The guy had to know he would set off an alarm."

"Is there another reason why someone would want to destroy your place?" His pencil poised, he watched her intently.

Marla gave a wry chuckle. "Like, how many fingers do you have on your two hands, officer? I could give you more people than you can count who would be happy to see misfortune come my way, but many of them are in jail. *Or dead, but we won't talk about them.*

"Want to give me any names?"

She shifted feet. "Not at the moment."

"Does the parking lot have surveillance cameras?" He peered around. "Or the exterior of your building?"

"You'd have to contact our landlord." She gave him the information, then had an inspiring thought. "Maybe you can find witnesses who saw the car, if the fellow drove by and tossed the thing in my window." Shuddering, she considered what would have happened if customers had been seated inside.

"We'll ask around, but it's dark out. People's perception can alter. We'll check the asphalt for evidence, too, but these sort of malicious pranks often go unsolved. Usually it's teens out to prove themselves or have fun."

"I'll need the police report to file an insurance claim."

Oh, gosh, then she'd have to wait for the adjuster to come, and that could take days. Plus she'd have to get repair estimates from the contractors the insurance company recommended. She didn't have time, not when she had to accomplish so many last-minute wedding details, finish her packing before their closing date, and follow up on publicity for her spa debut.

"Are you all right, Miss?"

She glanced up, realizing she was shaking. "Did I tell you I'm engaged to Detective Vail on the Palm Haven police force? I should notify him."

"Okay. There isn't much more we can do here right now."

"Maybe it's related to one of his cases, you know, like a warning."

"Then he'd be the best person to call, Miss."

"I'll do that." If Dalton had been home for dinner, he would be with her now.

Too numb to take action, she answered a few more questions

from the officer, signed her statement, and stuffed the papers he gave her into her purse. After he walked away, she rubbed a hand over her face. What would she tell her clients? She'd have to notify her staff not to come in to work tomorrow and assign Luis to phone their customers from home. Lucky for them, he believed in backups. He should be able to access their client files from its online storage site.

Realizing their computer might need replacement, too, her knees buckled. She sagged against a wall.

In the parking lot, the firemen put away their equipment prior to departure. The smell of smoke stung her nostrils. Gathering her strength, she wandered outside. How much more could she handle? She'd need help boarding up the window until it could be replaced. Dalton would know who to hire.

When she called the station, however, the receptionist said he'd left more than an hour ago. Marla strode back to her car. Outside, street lights cast surreal shadows on the pavement. The air had grown chilly, making her realize she could have used a jacket. No matter. Soon she'd be safely back at their house.

Dialing Dalton's cell number, she figured he must have gone home. Brianna would have told him about the fire. So why hadn't he phoned her to find out what had happened? His house was only fifteen minutes from the police department.

"Hello?" he answered with a chuckle, as though she'd caught him midconversation.

Marla heard clattering noises and laughter in the background. Could he be watching television? Anger built inside her. Hadn't he cared enough to see if she was safe?

"Hi, it's me." She kept her voice even. "Where are you?"

"Uh, I'm still at work. I should be home by ten o'clock."

"What?" Sitting in her car with the engine idling, Marla gripped the receiver. "You're not in your office. I just called there and they said you'd left."

The background noise increased. Someone yelled, "Give me a corned beef on rye with a side of coleslaw."

"Say again, Marla," Dalton said, his voice muffled. "Better yet, I'll be home soon. I'll talk to you then." Before she could protest, he clicked off.

Where the hell are you?

Annoyed at his easy dismissal, she considered where he would go for a late-night snack that served corned beef on rye. TooJay's, maybe?

Switching the gear into drive, she burned rubber out of the parking lot and headed to the restaurant.

Pulling into the Fountains shopping plaza, she wound her way toward TooJay's and cruised past the vehicles parked nearby. Spotting a sedan that looked like his model, she pulled into an empty space a few cars down.

After she shut down the ignition, Marla took a couple of deep, trembling breaths. It wouldn't do to confront him with her nerves so shattered. She might lose control, and that wouldn't be a pretty scene. But she couldn't help wondering what he was doing having dinner out when he told her he'd be working late. This wasn't the first time he'd used that excuse, either. If she hadn't been so wrapped up in Jill's affairs, she might have remarked upon it sooner.

With a racing heart and icy fingers, she grasped her purse and emerged into the cool night air. He was probably just grabbing a bite to eat with a colleague. Cops got hungry, too, when they were concentrating on a case.

But she didn't like the looks of his companion when she finally spied them huddled at a booth inside the restaurant. Dalton was leaning across the table, patting the hand of an attractive blond woman with luminescent blue eyes.

"Well, fancy meeting you here." Marla sidled up to them.

Dalton jerked back, his face flushing. "Marla. I wasn't expecting you."

Obviously. "We need to talk. Now."

Dalton exchanged glances with the woman. "Uh, sure." He slid over to give her room to sit beside him. "Marla, this is Kathy Wilkinson. She's a PI from North Florida. Kathy, I'd like you to meet my fiancée."

Marla forced a smile to her face. "Nice to meet you. Am I interrupting a business discussion?" She glanced pointedly at their empty dishes. Apparently, they'd finished dinner and were lingering over coffee. The bill had already been placed on the table.

"We're discussing a case of mine that I feel is related to Dalton's," Kathy said in a smooth voice while giving Marla an appraising glance.

"Really? Which case is that?"

"You know I can't always talk about my work." Dalton's mouth compressed.

Oh? Since when?

"Don't let me stop you," she replied in a silken tone. "I could use a cup of coffee myself."

"Sorry, but I've got to go." Kathy opened her handbag, fished inside, and then tossed a twenty dollar bill on the table. "This should cover my portion. Dalton, let's resume this talk after you've checked the lab reports. I think you'll agree with me that we're looking for the same guy."

"Okay, I'll be in touch. Thanks for filling me in." Waving, he watched her depart before turning his attention to Marla. "Now what's going on? Why did you follow me here?"

"Can we leave? I don't really want to stay."

Signaling the waiter, he added his contribution to the bill and left a generous tip.

Marla pursed her lips, repressing her outburst until they stood by her car in the parking lot.

"You lied to me." Her heart thumped painfully fast as she faced him. He stood tall and brooding, his features sharply angular under the light cast by a street lamp. "How many nights have you been working late recently? Have you been to dinner with her each single time?"

"Marla, you're being ridiculous. We were discussing a case and got hungry, that's all."

"I saw you patting her hand as I approached. Are you as familiar with all your colleagues?"

He studied a lizard scampering into the grass. "We knew each other from before."

"Before when?"

He looked her squarely in the eye. "College. I didn't realize she'd moved to Florida."

"And she looked you up, did she? What exactly was your relationship in college?" Her voice rose. She couldn't help herself. A weight of self-doubt crushed her chest, making it difficult to breathe.

"We kinda, uh, hung out together."

"Oh, that's even better. An old girlfriend? And you didn't tell me?"

"We got together over a case, Marla. I didn't tell you about it because you've been busy meddling in Jill's life."

"Excuse me? Jill asked for my help."

His eyes narrowed. "She asked for your advice on her property issue. You've gone above and beyond, like you always do."

Marla's mouth gaped. "I thought you were encouraging me to find out things."

"Not to the exclusion of all else. You have a salon to run, a day spa to open, and a wedding to plan. You're running out of time."

"Aren't we losing focus here? This discussion isn't about me. I should have been informed about Kathy."

He put a hand on her shoulder. "I didn't mention it for this very reason. You're jealous."

She shook him off. "I am not. I'm pissed because you didn't tell me you were meeting an old flame from your past."

"That's irrelevant. I told you I was working late. It's the truth."

"I don't care. How can I trust you when you keep things from me?" Her lower lip trembled. Tears leaked into her eyes. Pressure built from within, torpedoing to the surface.

Dalton pulled her into his arms. "I'm sorry," he said into her hair. "I should have mentioned it. Okay?"

She sobbed against his shoulder, releasing her anxiety, her pent-up fears, her frustration.

"Me, too," she murmured through a series of sniffles. "I do trust you. I just don't want anything to come between us."

"Nothing ever will." He hugged her tight. "You're mine, for better or for worse."

"Gee, thanks," she said with a half-laugh, half-sob.

He held her at arm's length and regarded her seriously. "If I sound resentful that you're too focused on your friend, it's only because I want our wedding to be special. We still have so many details to finalize."

"I'd be all right if it wasn't for the break-in."

"Say again?" His grip strengthened.

She glanced away from his eyes, gleaming in the oblique rays from the streetlights. "Someone threw a Molotov cocktail into my salon window. Brie and I were just finishing dinner at home when I got a call from the alarm company."

"And you didn't notify me right away?"

"I tried, after I determined what happened. You were in there"—she pointed to the restaurant—"and couldn't hear me on the phone. I figured out where you were after I heard someone in the background holler for a corned beef on rye."

"Good detective skills, Sherlock."

She swiped at the wetness on her cheeks. "I know."

"How much damage was done?"

Reassurance flooded through her at his concerned expression. How could she have doubted him?

"The entire reception area is a mess. I don't know what to do first. I can't call the insurance people until the morning, and then they'll have to send someone out for a repair estimate. I'll need to call contractors and order new furniture and . . . you get the picture. Meanwhile, there's a gaping hole in the front of my shop and broken glass all over the floor."

"Let's go home and I'll make a few calls. We'll get someone to board it up."

Marla was more than willing to let him take charge. "What about my customers and staff? I think the salon stations are intact but the place smells from smoke, and I don't know how far the water damage extends. Some tiles might need to be replaced. We're going to have to close the shop until everything is fixed. I can't afford to lose so much business." *Not with all the upcoming bills to pay.*

"How about the day spa? Don't you have hair stations set up for overflow from your salon?"

"Well, yes, we have four of them, but—"

"You passed the inspections already, right? So why can't you open informally for now and send your customers over there?"

Thunderstruck, she gazed at him. "You're right. That may work. I'd have to call Luis so he can notify people."

"Good girl." He patted her arm. "Delegate as much as you can. Let's leave now, and we can make our calls from home. Brie must be worried about you."

After they arrived at Dalton's house, filled Brianna in, and made their initial phone calls, Marla and Dalton brought glasses of wine into the family room and settled onto the couch.

"Are you feeling better?" He tickled her thigh while the corner of his mouth turned up in a sexy smile.

She nodded. "I'm glad I don't have to face things alone anymore. I'm so lucky to have you." Leaning forward, she kissed him on his perfectly contoured lips.

He grabbed her head and deepened the kiss.

"I'd like to take that into the bedroom," he said after they separated, "but first, should I be worried that your place was targeted on purpose?"

"That thought had crossed my mind." She bowed her head. "I might have ruffled a few feathers recently."

"Why doesn't that surprise me?"

"You're right in that I have enough to do for the moment. I'm going to lie low. Jill has Arnie now. She has to learn to rely on him." *And not to keep secrets,* Marla added silently.

"I'm glad to hear you say that. Our family needs your undivided attention." Lifting her chin, he lowered his head and showed her what he meant.

Later, after their lovemaking, Marla vowed to concentrate on her own affairs and leave the investigation into Torrie's death to the police. Tonight's meltdown proved she'd been overtaxing herself, and she wouldn't accomplish anything if she lost her focus.

Her resolve lasted until the next day when Hally Leeds's assistant, Rachel, dropped by the day spa to share important news.

CHAPTER THIRTEEN

"Marla, there's someone here to see you," Jennifer called from up front.

"Sorry, will you excuse me a minute?" Marla said to her client.

Putting down her comb and shears, she wiped her hand on a towel before hastening to the front desk at her day spa. She'd assigned Luis to oversee repairs in the salon, and her youngest staff member was taking up the slack in the spa by manning the reception area. She dodged the painter carrying a bucket toward the massage rooms and a nail tech carting supplies from next door. New Age music played quietly in the background, while a citrus scent honeyed the air. She hoped the pleasant, relaxing ambiance would make people want to return.

As she came into view of the shop front, she stopped short. Fresh-faced with minimal makeup and her blond hair in a ponytail, Hally's young assistant looked like a recent high school grad.

"Rachel, what a nice surprise. How are you?"

Rachel glanced anxiously through the plate glass window toward the parking lot. "I'm fine, thanks. I need to talk to you."

Marla smiled encouragingly. "Do you mind if I finish a haircut first? Then I'll be free for a few minutes. Why don't you have a seat in our lounge?" she added, aware that Rachel might not want to be spotted by passersby.

She pointed to a room off to the side that held couches,

magazines, coffee, and Danish. She'd added a trickling water fountain to enhance the soothing surroundings. Feeling her neck muscles knot with tension, she yearned for a stress-reliever massage. When the rooms in the back were finished, she'd be one of their first customers.

Twenty minutes later, she filled herself a cup of coffee and sat opposite Rachel in the private lounge. No one else had come in, so they had the room to themselves. Marla glanced at her watch. She'd gotten a late start that morning, having had to move her roundabout and tools from the salon into the day spa, but then Grace Morgan had canceled her eleven o'clock appointment. She could always start her eleven-thirty a few minutes late. Hopefully, whatever Rachel had to say wouldn't take too long.

"So what can I do for you, honey?" Marla said softly.

The girl cast her eyes downward, wringing her hands. "Thanks for taking the time to see me. I thought you should know, since you're friends with Jill, and . . . and . . ."

"Yes?"

"Well, I found stuff around the office."

"What kind of stuff?" Putting her cup down on the coffee table, Marla leaned forward.

"After Hally's death, the police came and took her computer, looked through her trash, and examined her desk. But they forgot one place."

Marla's heart skipped a beat. "Where?"

"Hally must have used the copy machine last. She'd forgotten to take away the original inside. It was still in the machine when I went to use it. I dug a couple of crumpled papers from the trash can nearby, too. I just thought you'd like to know."

You said that already. Get on with it. "Can I refill your coffee?"

"No, thanks." Rachel shook her head, her eyes round. "I realize you're busy, and I don't want to bother you. The article in the copy machine must have been from our archives. It was dated years ago and tells about toxic waste on a piece of real estate. Real estate now occupied by Orchid Isle."

Marla straightened her spine. "No way." That confirmed what the woman in class had said. Had Falcon cleaned the site before he built his nature center? He'd have had to pass environmental inspections, unless Kevin and Eddy had played a role in skirting regulations. Would people come if they knew the park had been constructed on contaminated land?

Rachel opened her purse, then handed Marla a document. "Here's the original article. I made an extra copy for myself, just in case."

"Thanks." Marla rose and slipped the document inside a drawer for safe keeping. Returning to the couch, she sat and tilted her head. "You said there was also something important in the trash can?"

"That's right." Rachel retrieved a folded paper. "Sorry about the creases. I'm not really sure what this means, but I heard Torrie mention the guy's name before."

Taking the article, Marla scanned it. She didn't understand how a write-up on a polo club gala would be relevant, but—oh, wait. The accompanying photo had Grant Bosworth's byline.

She studied Rachel, who wouldn't quite meet her gaze. "This photographer works for a rival magazine. Do you have any idea why your colleagues might have been interested in him?"

Rachel shrugged, her brows furrowed. "Who knows? Maybe one of them wanted to make Griff jealous. They both liked him."

"Did you see Griff at the wedding?"

"He's so tall, it's hard to miss him." Her face paled as she realized what she'd said. "I mean, you could spot him anywhere in a crowd."

"Is there something you'd like to tell me, Rachel?"

Rachel's glance darted to the doorway as she squirmed in her seat. "I took a risk in coming here," she said, her voice trembling. "I should go now."

"Please don't be afraid. Let me help you. My boyfriend works for the police. Just tell me why—"

Rachel leapt up. "No, that's all I can say."

"Then I appreciate your bringing these to me." Marla stood, smoothing her skirt. "Can I share this information with Jill?"

The girl's eyes widened. "Of course. That's why I brought it to you."

"Why didn't you go see her yourself?"

"I-I'm not ready. Torrie knew that when she found me."

"And where was that?"

Rachel backed away. "It doesn't matter. Please don't tell anyone else I've talked to you."

"Where can I reach you if I have more questions?"

Full-blown panic entered the younger woman's eyes. "Don't try to contact me. It could be dangerous. Goodbye, Marla. Thanks for listening."

Rachel flew out the front door before Marla could stop her. Not having time to ponder the young woman's words, she proceeded to her next client. Greeting the middle-aged matron and mixing up a color solution took her mind off other matters. She even managed to avoid thinking about her conversation with Rachel during the subsequent cut and style, highlights, and blowout.

Finally able to steal a few minutes for lunch, Marla settled onto a stool in the storeroom, a turkey sandwich on a napkin in her lap and her cell phone in hand. Between bites, she called information and got the number for *Home & Style Magazine* in Palm Beach. She recalled that was the name of the journal that ran Grant Bosworth's byline.

"Hello," she said when someone answered, "I'd like to speak

to Grant Bosworth, please. He's a photographer on your staff."

The receptionist put her on hold. A minute later, another woman came on line.

"Hi, this is Angela Moran, senior editor. How may I help you?"

Marla swallowed. "My name is Marla Shore. I'm looking for Grant Bosworth in relation to a story he covered recently."

"I can take your name and number and pass it on to him."

"Thanks, but I'd really like to make an appointment to come and see him. Is he in the office today?"

The editor chuckled. "Are you kidding? Even I have never met the guy in person. We do all of our correspondence online or through the mail."

"Really?" She held the receiver closer to her ear. "You mean, you've never actually seen Grant Bosworth?"

"Between e-mail, fax machines, and video conference calls, personal contact isn't always necessary today. Bosworth does the work we assign him. We send checks to the address he specified. Both of us are happy."

"Could you give me his e-mail address then?"

"What did you say your interest was in Mr. Bosworth?"

"He knew a friend of mine. She's dead. I'd like to talk to him about her." Marla didn't know that Hally had ever met Grant in person, but the society reporter had definitely been interested in him for whatever reason.

"I'm sorry to hear that. As I said, I'll be happy to pass on your contact info to Grant and he can get in touch with you."

"Okay, thanks." Realizing she wouldn't get any farther along this route, she gave the requested information and hung up.

Her phone beeped. A text message had come in.

Mom called, Dalton wrote. *We got a couple more gifts. One of them was the crystal bowl you wanted.*

Oh, joy. More thank-you notes to write. Marla wouldn't send

them out until after the wedding. Meanwhile, she was trying to keep up with the flow so it wouldn't be so overwhelming later. Following the wedding was the day spa's official grand opening, then their move into the house, and no doubt something else would come along.

Rolling her shoulders to ease the tension, she hoped they'd have a chance to escape on a honeymoon somewhere along the way. She could sure use the break.

She tossed the remainder of her lunch into the trash and went next door to check on the progress of repairs with Luis.

Stepping past the open door, she regarded the floor warily. The broken glass had been swept away and the damaged furniture removed. A piece of plywood covered the front window space.

"Hey, Marla, how's it going?" Standing in the middle of the reception area, Luis regarded her with a broad grin.

She liked how nothing seemed to faze him. "The spa is working out just great. I am *so* happy we decided to put four hair stations in there. I'd never have thought we would be using them in this capacity. Did you get hold of the insurance agent?"

He nodded vigorously. "An adjuster has already been by, and I contacted a window person." He glanced at the boarded-up opening. "They'll take the measurements today, but it could be up to two weeks before the new one is ready."

"Will the insurance pay for hurricane-impact glass?"

"I'm waiting for an answer on that, but I told the window company to give us the pricing."

"Good man. I see you found someone to pick up the furniture."

"Yes. Your policy has full replacement value. I told the adjustor you'll want to order a new front desk, display cabinet, chairs, and a coffee table. Plus, we'll need a new computer." He made a sad face, obviously more concerned about his electronics than anything else. "I'm taking the hard drive to a guy I know. Maybe we can salvage the data."

"That would help. Did you tell the insurance man how we're losing business for each day the salon stays closed?" That was true, even if they'd moved their services to the spa. She'd had to rotate the hours of their staff members, since the new facility couldn't accommodate all the stylists.

"He said he'll look into compensation for lost wages."

"I suppose we could manage in here without the front area once the place is aired out." She wrinkled her nose at the lingering aroma of smoke. With the front and back doors both open, a breeze swept through. "What about the tile? Any damage from the water?"

"The cleaning crew took care of it pretty quickly, so that won't be a problem. Most of the stations are okay, since everyone packs away their tools before leaving. We'll keep the doors open while I'm here to give everything a good dry-out."

She gave him a hug. "Thanks, Luis. I don't know what I'd do without you. Have you had any trouble reaching our clients?"

"*Nada,* we're cool."

"Fantastic. Let me know if you need anything. I'm going to leave early today to take care of a few errands. You can reach me on my cell."

With the salon in his capable hands, she didn't have to worry. He'd make a good manager, she realized. She'd always considered Nicole her second-in-command, but Nicole had clients that demanded her attention. Should she ever decide to take an extended vacation, she'd feel confident assigning either one of them to take charge.

Her mood buoyed, she returned to the day spa just in time to greet the electrician who'd returned to install some dimmers she'd ordered.

After her last customer left at four o'clock, she called it a day.

It would be a rush to stop at the bank, the dry cleaner's, and the print shop before they closed, but she'd get it done.

Fortunately, Dalton was taking Brianna to dance class that evening, so she had some free time. Sitting in the car after her last errand, she dialed Griff Beasley's cell number.

"I was wondering if we could meet for a drink," she said after he'd answered and she identified herself. "I want to talk to you about something important that relates to Hally."

"Good God, I can't believe she's dead."

"Me, too. Have you heard anything about a memorial service yet?"

"No, that's up to her family. The cops have been all over the office since we got the news."

"I'm so sorry. It must have been quite a shock."

"You have no idea. Hally and I, well, we were close."

As close as you and Torrie? Marla wondered if the police had questioned him as a person of interest in the case.

"So are you up for a drink? I could be in Boca by six."

"Sure. Let's meet at the Ale House. You know the one on Glades Road?"

"Yes, I'll see you soon."

During the drive, Marla considered how to coax him to talk. She wanted to know why Torrie had taken an interest in a photographer from a rival magazine, and why she'd looked up an article on Orchid Isle's history.

At least, she assumed it had been Torrie. Rachel said she'd discovered those pieces in the copy machine and in the trash. Assuming Hally had found the articles among Torrie's files, did that mean someone at work had been keeping tabs on both women? Someone such as Griff Beasley? Was that why Rachel said it could be dangerous for Marla to contact her again?

Fingers of dread crept up her spine. Was she doing the right thing in meeting the photographer on her own? She'd just promised herself not to get any more involved in Jill's affairs, and here she was racing up the turnpike to Boca Raton.

Her fears quieted when she pulled into the parking lot of the Ale House. People milled about the front door and were coming and going from the busy parking lot. Even on a weekday, the place was hopping.

Spotting Griff inside on a bar stool, she slid onto the empty seat at his side. They shook hands, while a lady across the bar winked at him. It seemed he'd already attracted female attention with his dashing good looks. What single woman wouldn't be lured by his appeal?

She stiffened, imagining Dalton's reaction should he catch her there. Then again, hadn't she walked in on him dining at a restaurant with an old flame?

Pushing those thoughts aside, she gave Griff a brilliant smile. She might as well make the most of this opportunity.

She nodded at his glass, asked what brew he was drinking, and ordered the same, along with a refill for him. She'd invited Griff along, so she would settle the bill.

"What's up, Marla?" His laser eyes snagged hers. "You didn't ask me out for a drink just to socialize."

"As I mentioned," she said, adjusting her seat, "I have information on Hally. First of all, I suspect her death is related to Torrie's."

His gaze shifted to his glass. "They were both nosy. It goes along with their job. They must have both learned something that got them killed."

"Did either woman mention they were delving into the background on Orchid Isle?"

He shrugged. "Hally and I covered the grand opening together. Research is part of the game."

"How about the land deal that Falcon Oakwood made to acquire the territory?"

"What about it?"

"Could there have been anything underhanded going on?"

He squeezed his glass. "Look, if you know something, babe, spit it out."

"Torrie had copied an article, or maybe Hally copied an article that she found in Torrie's files, about toxic waste on the land. This was before Falcon acquired it."

"So?"

"So was any cleanup ever performed? What kind of toxic waste? Chemicals, fuel, biohazardous stuff? This may have been before environmental regulations got so much stricter."

His eyes narrowed. "Are you saying that Oakwood may have paid someone under the table to bury this subject?"

"It had crossed my mind. If not Falcon, then perhaps the real estate agent or lawyer involved. Namely, Jill's relatives."

"Ah, now I see why you're interested."

"I am assuming that neither reporter mentioned this matter to you?"

"Nope. How did you find out about this, by the way?"

"Never mind." She'd promised Rachel to keep silent about her source. "I don't see any other link between Torrie and Hally's murder. Do you?" She glanced at him pointedly.

"Hey, don't give me that look. I had nothing to do with it. I was just as shocked as everyone else."

"What do you know about Grant Bosworth?" Marla hoped to catch him with the rapid change of subject.

He jerked upright, nearly toppling his drink. "Who?"

"Grant Bosworth," she repeated. "He's a photographer for *Home & Style* in Palm Beach."

"How did you get his name?"

"Torrie was interested in him. She kept articles with his byline." At least, she assumed it was Torrie, and that Hally had found them later.

Griff swiveled away from her toward the bar. "Never heard of the guy."

"You must have met him in the photography circles. Probably you've covered the same stories for your respective publications?"

"Nope, never ran into the fellow. What does he have to do with anything?" Griff shot back.

"That's what I'd like to know. I phoned his office, and his editor said she'd never met the guy in person. He sends in his photos by e-mail."

"So? That's commonplace these days."

"I guess you're right." She tilted her head. "It still makes me wonder what Torrie found so interesting about his work. Hey, you don't suppose this Grant guy is the one who bopped you on the head at the Venetian Pool, do you? Maybe he hoped to get the scoop ahead of you."

Griff downed the rest of his brew, then gave her an oblique glance. "Hally probably got creamed because she snooped into Torrie's affairs. Torrie knew things about other people that they didn't like, and now you're butting your nose in the same dirt. If I were you, I'd watch my back, babe. Because if there is a killer out there, you could be next on his list."

Chapter Fourteen

Marla figured she wouldn't have a chance to follow up on any of her leads on Wednesday, but fate intervened. In the middle of the morning, an unexpected visitor strode through the front door.

"Jill, you're just the person I want to see." Marla put down the foils she'd been separating for her next client and hurried to greet her friend.

"I'm so sorry about your store." Jill gave her a hug. She'd twisted her blond hair into a chignon and looked comfortable in a sapphire sweater and black pants. The only betrayal to her state of mind were the dark circles under her eyes and her pallid complexion. "Did the cops catch the vandals?"

"No, but they're reviewing the surveillance videos from the parking lot." She held her tongue about the possible motive, positive she'd been targeted because of her inquiries.

"I hope your insurance covers the damage."

"It does. Let's go into the lounge where we can talk in private." After offering Jill some refreshments, Marla poured herself a cup of coffee and settled on the sofa. "Something has come to my attention that I'd like to share with you. Several things, actually."

Jill stiffened. "Is that woman's death related to my sister's? They worked together, you know."

"Yes, and I interviewed one of Hally's colleagues last night. You remember Griff Beasley, the magazine photographer? He accompanied Hally to your wedding, and they covered the grand opening of Orchid Isle."

"Right."

"He said Torrie knew things about people, and Hally may have recovered her files after she died. For example, the land on which Falcon Oakwood built Orchid Isle had once been a toxic waste site."

Jill's eyes rounded. "You're kidding."

"That's not all. It appears your uncle Eddy and cousin Kevin were involved in the transaction wherein Falcon acquired the land."

"Why am I not surprised?" Jill leaned forward. "That's the reason I'm here. I want you to come along when I talk to Uncle Eddy. Scott is giving me a hard time over our property issue, and I can't get any straight answers on what's happening with the oil people. I thought maybe you could help, since you've had experience with this sort of thing."

Marla resisted the urge to blurt a refusal. "Did Torrie ever mention someone named Grant Bosworth to you?"

Jill shook her head.

"How about Rachel, her assistant? Did you ever meet the girl?"

Jill's gaze flew to hers, then slid away. "I can't say that I have."

No? Then why did she send you a floral basket? "Were you aware that Hally had a thing for Griff but so did Torrie? And that Torrie planned to leave her husband?"

"What are you saying?" Jill's pitch rose.

"Both Hally and Scott had possible grudges against your sister."

"That's absurd. Hally is dead, and Scott wouldn't hurt his wife. I can't believe you suspect them." Jill twisted her hands. "Maybe I made a mistake asking you for help. I only wanted your advice on what I should do with my property. I didn't mean for you to go into sleuth mode, sugar."

Oh, so now I'm getting too deep into your affairs, am I? Friends can't maintain a relationship without trust.

"Marla, your eleven o'clock is here," Nicole shouted from the outer corridor.

Marla swallowed her coffee in a large gulp, tossed away the cup, and rose. "I'm not sure what you expect me to do, Jill."

"I'd hoped you would visit Uncle Eddy with me so I could be clear on the legalities of our lease. But I shouldn't impose when you have so much to do. Forgive me." Standing, Jill collected her purse.

Marla put a hand on her arm. "I'll go with you." Realizing Jill must be under tremendous strain, she cut her friend some slack. They could sort things out later. Marla couldn't resist it when someone needed her.

"Tomorrow is Thanksgiving," Jill murmured, her head down. "What are you guys doing?"

Marla's tone brightened. "We made a reservation for the buffet at Palm Haven Golf Club. Normally, I'd have it at my house, but I can't deal with the chaos this year, not with the wedding so close."

Kate and John were joining them, making seven people with Ma and Roger, plus she'd called Tally back and invited her and Ken.

It would be the only time they had to get together before the flurry of wedding activities began. Thank goodness Roger's son Barry was out of town. Her mother had tried to play matchmaker between them, but Marla had already made up her mind about Dalton. It would have been awkward to see the optometrist under the circumstances. When they met again, she'd be married.

"How about you?" she asked Jill.

"We're going to Arnie's parents." Jill gave a wan smile. "I don't feel like spending the holiday with my relatives."

Marla patted her arm. "That's understandable. When do you want to go see Eddy with me?"

"Can you get away on Friday morning? This is going to eat away at me until I get it resolved."

Marla compressed her lips. Her day off on Monday would have been better, but she could empathize with Jill's anxiety. "Let's go up front. I'll check my schedule."

She made a few calls and shuffled her clients around so that she had the morning free.

"I'll have to be back by one," she warned Jill.

"No problem. Let's meet at Arnie's deli at nine. I'll let Uncle Eddy know we're coming."

Time flew by the rest of the day. Marla finished her last client at six and then drove home to her townhouse, needing an evening to herself to relax and prepare for the family ordeal the next day. She'd barely flung her purse on the counter, scratched Spooks behind the ears, and refreshed herself in the bathroom, when the doorbell rang. Her stomach growled. She planned a quick frozen meal and then just wanted to crash.

She trudged through the foyer and peeked through the peephole. Her neighbor Kyle, a pet groomer nicknamed Goat because of his sparse beard and love for animals, greeted her with a silly grin. She flung the door open, noting his black poodle Rita straining on a leash.

"Hey, Marla. Wassup? Rita's been bugging me to play with Spooks but you guys haven't been around much lately."

"I know." Their doggy romance didn't have much of a chance, not when she'd be leaving permanently in a couple months. "Let me get him. We'll walk with you. He needs to go out anyway."

She retrieved her pet, locked the front door, then strode

beside Goat on the asphalt. The temperature was a pleasant seventy-four with a sweet scent in the air.

"So what's new with you?" She gave him an oblique glance. He wore a Cuban shirt over a pair of khakis. Scuffed sandals and a fur cap on his head completed his outfit.

"Ugamaka, ugamaka, chugga, chugga, ush." He danced a little jig while Rita ignored him and squatted on the grass. "The bells are ringing. My heart is singing. The lady and I are swinging."

Marla stood by while Spooks sniffed Rita's behind. "Stop that." She nudged Spooks away before turning to Goat. His riddles made convoluted sense to her now. "I gather Georgia is flying in as scheduled?" When Marla's former college roommate had visited her earlier that year, she and Goat had hit it off. Being on opposite coastlines didn't help their relationship, though.

Goat squared his shoulders. "Yep, and I can't wait." His expression sobered. "I've made a decision, Marla. I can run my mobile pet-grooming service anywhere." He swept an arm toward his van parked in the driveway. "You know how I've always wanted a bigger place on acres of land for all my animals?"

She nodded. He'd been yearning to move to the country.

"Georgia has a dream of opening her own salon. I'm going to propose to her that we get a place together."

Marla stared at him. "Why, Goat, that's wonderful. I hope it works out for you both."

"I need a favor. When she's here, call me by my real name, Kyle?"

"Sure, Goat. I mean, Kyle."

Taken aback by his news, she and Spooks had just picked up their pace when the door next to her townhouse opened. Her elderly neighbor, Moss, waved a paper in the air.

"Marla, come here. I've written a poem for your wedding."

She heaved a deep sigh. *An hour alone, that's all I want. I love these guys, but I desperately need some space.* Plastering a smile on her face, she took the paper from the man's extended hand. He tipped his customary naval cap at her with a grin.

"Thanks, Moss. Is it okay if I read it later? I need to get Spooks back inside. By the way, how's your wife doing?"

He stroked his white beard. "She has her good days and her bad days. We miss your company. It's going to be quiet without you around."

She chuckled. "Believe me, that's a good thing."

After Spooks did his business, Marla scurried inside. She'd see her neighbors at the wedding, but they wouldn't have these private moments anymore.

In the kitchen, she kicked off her shoes, released Spooks's leash, and gave him a treat. She listened to the news during dinner, wrote down a list of things to do tomorrow, then crawled into bed. Exhaustion took her into a world of troubling dreams.

She woke up the next morning eager to get a head start on her chores. As long as she had the principals from the wedding together later, she wanted to review the final details.

So it was that after they were seated in the country club restaurant, their plates laden with food, she broached the subject.

"We've turned our song list in to the DJ," she said to her family. "He'll coordinate with the violinist we hired for the ceremony."

"It would have been nicer if you'd gotten a live band." Kate took a sip of water. "I told you we'd pay for it."

"Thanks, Mom, but we wanted to keep things simple," Dalton replied between bites of grilled salmon. "This guy is very good. You'll like him."

"If you say so."

"Tell us about the rehearsal dinner," Marla said to her almost mother-in-law. She'd put Kate in charge so she wouldn't have any complaints.

"Yeah, what's the menu?" Roger bellowed. Shoveling a forkful of mashed potatoes into his mouth, he regarded the stiff couple across the table. John eyed him back, his disdainful gaze traveling over the older man's orange-colored sport coat.

Marla tuned them out, nudging Tally on her right. Dalton sat on her left, next to Brianna.

"What is it you wanted to tell me so urgently?" she said in an undertone. "I'm sorry we weren't able to get together separately, but things have been hectic."

Tally's clear blue eyes captured hers. "You've probably guessed it, but I'm pregnant."

Marla shrieked, throwing her arms around her friend. "Congratulations, I'm so happy for you."

Ken, her husband, grinned proudly. "I told her it would happen when we least expected it."

"No kidding. That's wonderful." Marla's spirits lifted.

Tally shared the news around the table, to a round of congratulatory remarks.

"You'll need to convert one of your rooms into a nursery." Dalton's eyes twinkled.

Ken stroked his jaw. "We've been thinking about getting a bigger place with the housing bargains out there."

"Kate and John have been looking for a condo. They can probably refer you to their real estate agent if you're serious." Dalton drank his coffee.

"That reminds me." Kate tapped Marla's arm. "I asked our Realtor about those guys in Miami like you wanted me to? She said Kevin Rhodes's name rang a bell. He'd been mentioned in one of those newspaper articles about mortgage fraud."

Marla and Dalton exchanged glances.

"Is that so?" Marla said. "Maybe I'll ask his uncle Eddy about that when Jill and I go to see him tomorrow."

Dalton gazed at her askance. "What?"

"Jill begged me to go with her." She could exaggerate a bit, right?

"Didn't you say you would step back from these extracurricular activities of yours?" His brows drew together like a line of storm clouds.

"Yes, but—"

"And don't we have a ton of things to do still?"

A wide smile cracked her face. "Indeed, we do, but I have it all under control." Rummaging in her purse, she withdrew a sheaf of papers. "Let's run down the list. First off, the flowers."

Reviewing the details took the heat off her and kept the peace through the rest of the meal. Dalton especially kept his mouth shut when she asked him about his case and his PI friend from up north.

"Did you tell the bus driver what time to pick up the guests at the hotel?" Marla asked her mother, concluding their discussion. Anita had taken charge of coordinating the out-of-towners and planning a postwedding brunch on Sunday.

Anita nodded, giving Kate a smirk. Marla hated how this seemed to be a competition between the two women but realized it was more of a big deal for them than for her and Dalton. They should've just gotten married in Vegas and been done with it. Or she should have hired a wedding planner and avoided this grief. Oh, well. This would be the last time she had to deal with her own nuptials.

Interviewing suspects took on a brighter prospect compared to family events. By the time Friday morning rolled around, she was actually looking forward to accompanying Jill to Miami.

"Hello, girls," Eddy greeted them at his corner suite in a high-rise building overlooking Biscayne Bay. Surrounded in his office by impressive legal tomes, he patted down his suit, tailored to fit his ample form.

"Thanks for seeing us. I know you have a busy schedule." Jill gave him a polite peck on the cheek.

In Marla's opinion, her friend looked worse than she had on Wednesday. Jill's hair was tossed about her head as though it hadn't seen a hair brush. She wore a smidgen of makeup that did little to hide her sallow complexion. Even her clothing, a pair of navy pants and a pale blue sweater, wasn't up to her usual style. This property issue must have been taking more of a toll on her than Marla realized, unless other factors were at play. Factors involving Rachel, perhaps? Marla sensed a connection between the two but couldn't fathom what it might be.

They seated themselves facing Eddy's wide mahogany desk. Marla's gaze roamed his framed photos, cherry wood pen case, silver desk clock, and other accouterments. She noted a bar in the back corner, too. Eddy's firm must do a bang-up job. He might be the lead attorney, but she saw other names listed on the door plaque. As their commercial real estate specialist, no doubt he landed some of their bigger clients.

"Scott says he can't afford to pay property taxes and liability insurance while we're waiting to get a tenant." Jill twisted her hands in her lap.

Eddy's chair creaked as he leaned back, folding his hands behind his head. "Nonsense. According to the early termination clause with the oil lube company, they owe you a year's worth of rental payments. That'll carry you through with the taxes until we get a new tenant. Did Kevin tell you we have a bank interested?"

"He said a lot of things, including the fees you're probably going to charge us for overseeing the termination clause, the environmental cleanup, and a new lease."

Eddy's double chin quivered as he smiled. "Of course, we'll give you a discount. And don't forget that any expenses you incur are tax deductible."

"Scott wants to sell the property."

"And what do you want, dear niece?"

"It's a tempting idea just to get rid of the aggravation, but even if we got a good market price, we could never invest the money to make the same income. Our corner location is ideal for traffic flow. I'd think a fast food place would do great there."

"Excuse me," Marla interrupted. "Wouldn't that require a drive-through? Does the zoning allow for it?"

Eddy shook his head. "Not presently. We'd pass that problem on to the new tenant, so it wouldn't trouble you," he told his niece. "Or you could exchange your property for another of equal value with the proper zoning variance."

"As in a land swap?" Jill flicked a spot of lint off her pants. "Kevin mentioned that idea to me. Torrie didn't approve."

"It's just another possibility, that's all." Eddy smoothed back some stray hairs on his receding forehead. "If you're looking for a buyer, Pete Schneider is interested. He'd give you a good price."

"He's the real estate agent who tipped us off that the property had been vacated," Jill reminded Marla.

"Right, and wasn't it Torrie who insisted on getting a new tenant rather than selling?" she replied, looking out for Jill's interests.

"Yes." Bending her head, Jill covered her face with her hands. "I don't know what to do. It's so confusing."

"Did you notify the tax office to send you the bills hereafter?" Marla said. "Have they been going to you or the tenant?"

"Who knows? Torrie took care of those details."

"Scott should have access to her records. Ask him." Marla leveled her glance at Eddy. "If you do find a new tenant, I'd think you could help with the clearances. After all, didn't you assist Falcon Oakwood get the proper approvals for his property?"

Eddy bristled. "That's different. This will require a traffic study. A new tenant has to hire an engineer and present his case to the city. He'll have to show that a drive-through would not obstruct traffic."

"That's not what I meant." Marla's mouth curved in a smile. "Jill's land must be contaminated from all that oil. You have ways of getting past environmental issues, yes? You did it for Orchid Isle."

Eddy's face reddened. "Where did you hear that?"

"I believe it was in Torrie's files. It's awfully coincidental that she died the same weekend as your attraction's grand opening. Imagine if the public found out what she knew?"

He stared at her hotly for a few moments of silence. "I've been around a long time. I know who to contact to get things done. That's why an eminent developer like Falcon Oakwood would come to me."

"If you say so." She maintained eye contact, challenging him to admit his dealings were legit.

Jill glanced at Marla. "I really should go see Kevin as long as we're in town. I'm more inclined to agree with Torrie now. I don't want to sell. Marla, would you mind if we stopped by his office? It won't take long."

Why not? I've already wasted half my day. "Sure, let's go." They were getting nowhere with this interview.

"Did you draw up my new POA?" Jill addressed Eddy, while tucking a strand of hair behind her ear.

"Yes, of course. You're in an awful rush."

"I've just gotten married. I need to add Arnie's name to everything. The power of attorney is the most important. I can change my other documents later."

Eddy called in two witnesses. Jill signed the form and took

the original for herself.

"I'll file a copy," Eddy told her. "Let me know when you're ready to amend your will."

Jill swung her purse strap over her shoulder. "Thanks, I appreciate it." She rose, and Marla followed suit while Eddy lumbered to his feet.

"Jill, a moment."

Allowing them a modicum of privacy, Marla left the room, leaving the door slightly ajar behind her.

"Did you tell your new husband yet?" Eddy said in a low voice, while Marla lingered in the hallway to eavesdrop.

"No, and don't you say a word to him. We're doing fine and, hopefully, things will continue that way for a while. Arnie doesn't need to know at this point. Let us get settled first."

"I beg to disagree. You realize Alexis and I have always been there for you, my dear, so heed our advice. What haunts you will come back to bite."

Chapter Fifteen

Marla, hovering in the hallway, hastened toward the reception area when she heard footsteps approach from the other side of the door. Jill bustled into view, her expression grim. She signaled for Marla to follow her outside.

They made desultory small talk on their way to Kevin's office, a modest building on North Kendall Drive.

As they pulled into the parking lot, she glanced at her watch. It would take forty-five minutes to drive back to Palm Haven, where her first client was scheduled for one o'clock. Forget lunch and her promise to stop off at her mother's place. Again, she had become so wrapped up in Jill's affairs that she'd neglected her own. She must learn how to say no.

Kevin greeted them with such an effusive show of welcome that Marla doubted he was overjoyed by their presence. After ushering them inside his comfortable office, he sat behind his desk and folded his hands.

"So what brings you ladies to our part of town?"

"I hear you've been soliciting a bank for our property." Jill smoothed her pants. "I'm thinking our site would be great for a fast food place."

Kevin's longish face turned shrewd. "We have a nibble from a bank. There are a couple of problems, though. I just talked to Scott about them."

Jill stiffened. "You called him, but you didn't notify me? What am I, chopped liver?"

Kevin's brow furrowed. "I meant to call you, but I remembered how insistent Torrie was on finding a new tenant. Since Scott will be in charge of her share, I thought I'd get his opinion first. I didn't want to come to you until I had something solid, with you being a newlywed and all."

"Hereafter, don't be afraid to consult me. I may be ignorant about commercial property matters, but I'm a quick learner." Jill lifted her nose. "Besides, I brought Marla along. She owns a duplex, so she understands this stuff."

Oh, joy. Put it on my shoulders.

"The bank people are worried about the environmental fallout. They're also not willing to give in on the vault removal."

"What does that mean?"

"It means you would be responsible for getting rid of the vault should they terminate the lease."

"Are you kidding?" Marla leaned forward. "Do you realize how heavy that thing must be? It could cost thousands."

"You're right." Kevin jabbed a finger in her direction. "Unfortunately, they're not willing to budge on the issue. They're also concerned it would take a while for you to get clearance from the environmental agency. According to your lease with the oil lube company, they're responsible for any remediation. The bank folks are skittish, though. I'd like to close the deal while we've still got them in our pocket."

"Is there anyone else interested in the property?" Jill asked.

"A guy who owns a Quik Mart in Perrine. I think we can do better with the bank, though."

"We've just been to see Jill's uncle Eddy," Marla inserted. "He said there could be a problem with the zoning in terms of a drive-through."

Kevin steepled his hands, regarding her from under a set of thick caterpillar brows. "We have two choices here. We could exchange the property for another of equal value with the proper variance. That's simplifying how it's done, but you get the idea. Or we could push for the tenant to assume responsibility for getting the zoning changed."

"I'm not giving up my piece of land." Jill folded her arms across her chest. "If the bank wants a drive-through, they'll have to get it approved."

"Okay, then what about the vault?"

"I'll have to accept their terms, I suppose. Marla, any suggestions?"

Kevin's arguments sounded logical to her. "Not really. I think you're making a good choice." She addressed Kevin. "Tell me, when Falcon Oakwood was looking for property on which to build his nature park, how did you come across that slab of land?"

Kevin's mouth tightened. "We're a commercial real estate firm. We know what's available."

"Wasn't there an environmental issue with his place, too? How did you resolve that one?"

"I have no idea what you mean."

Marla cocked her head. "I heard from a good source that his attraction was built on a toxic waste site."

Kevin's eyes narrowed. "If there had been any dumping going on, it would have been cleaned up. His land had a clean bill of health."

"I see. Maybe you could use the same leverage to clear Jill's land?" She held his gaze level with hers.

"Times have changed. Things are not so easy. Regulations have gotten a lot stricter."

Or maybe the people you bribed aren't around anymore. "It's interesting how you and Eddy were both involved in that transaction. I understand Torrie had been looking into it through the archives at her magazine."

Kevin bared his teeth. "Torrie had a bad habit of learning

people's secrets. Whatever she knew went with her to the grave. It's my guess that's why she died."

His words reverberated in Marla's ears all during the drive north. She attempted to draw Jill out, to get more answers, but her friend clammed up and kept silent. After thanking Marla for her company and promising to see her at the bachelorette party in two weeks, Jill dropped her off at work.

Annoyed that she'd wasted the morning and hadn't seemed to gain much in the way of information relevant to the case, Marla decided to focus on her own affairs from now on. Again.

Her one o'clock customer was already waiting when she walked into the day spa a few moments later. She'd checked in with Luis regarding the state of repairs, pleased to find he had everything in order. Their new furniture should arrive next week, and meanwhile, he'd diverted the work crew from her spa to finish the clean up in the salon.

Busy with her client, she barely heard the front door crack open later with a tinkle of chimes.

"Marla, come and see this," Jennifer, the young stylist, said from the reception area. "Someone sent you flowers."

At the next station, Nicole's eyebrows lifted. She paused, comb in hand, in the midst of doing a haircut. "How romantic! Dalton must know how frazzled you are with almost two weeks to go to the big event. He's so sweet."

It's more likely he's trying to make up for the other night when I caught him in the restaurant with another woman, Marla thought.

She glanced at the wall clock. It was only four o'clock. Two more hours to go before she could call it quits. At least Dalton had promised to take charge of dinner. She couldn't wait to tell him about her interviews with Eddy and Kevin.

As soon as she finished her blowout, she hastened to the front desk on which stood a glass vase with a spray of pink orchids and glossy greenery. A small card nestled on a stick.

For some reason, a shiver of apprehension scuttled up her spine. Dalton had never sent orchids before. Usually, he was a straightforward roses kind of guy.

Plucking the card from its perch, she schooled her face into a mask of pleasure while opening the envelope. Inside, bold printed letters met her stunned gaze.

STOP ASKING QUESTIONS OR THE NEXT FLOWERS WILL BE FOR YOUR FUNERAL.

Her smile withered and her blood ran cold. Realizing Jennifer was waiting for a flippant comment, she gave a strangled laugh.

"Aren't these delightful? I'll have to show the sender my special appreciation."

Jennifer chuckled. "You're so lucky, Marla. Dalton is a real gem. I envy you."

"Don't," she said in a harsher tone than intended. "I mean, flowers and chocolates and gifts don't count as much as actions. It pleases me more that he's making dinner tonight. Did you see who delivered these?"

The blonde's nose wrinkled while she thought hard. "Now that you mention it, I didn't see a logo on the van."

"What did the driver look like?"

"I dunno, he wore a cap and just sort of dumped these on the counter. Isn't there a company name on the card?"

"No, there isn't." Shoot, she should stick the card into a plastic bag so Dalton could check it for fingerprints.

"Leave these here for now. I'll take care of them later. Meanwhile, I'd better get back to work."

Gingerly stuffing the card back into the envelope, she held the latter by a corner and hustled to the storeroom where she scrounged for a sandwich baggie. After depositing the card inside, she stuck the sealed bag in her purse and proceeded to her next customer.

At fifteen minutes past seven, she finally pulled into the driveway at Dalton's house. She'd had a last-minute add-on and didn't finish until an hour past her expected time.

"We were just going to sit down to eat without you." Dalton turned toward her in the kitchen. He stood by the stove, wearing an apron and stirring something in a pot.

She sniffed garlic and tomato sauce. Standing on her toes, she gave him a quick kiss. "I'll be right back. I have to get something from the car." She dumped her purse on the counter then wheeled around.

A few minutes later, she plopped the vase near the sink. "These were delivered to me at the spa today. Everyone thought they were from you. I didn't tell them otherwise."

He turned down the burner. "I wouldn't send orchids."

"I know." She told him what the card said and watched his gaze darken. "It's in my purse in a plastic bag."

"Smart girl. So who do you think they're from?" He turned toward the hallway. "Brie, dinner is ready."

"Be right there," the teen yelled back.

Marla waited until they were seated and devouring their whole wheat spaghetti with Dalton's homemade sauce and turkey meatballs.

"Well," she said between bites after asking Brie how her day had gone, "Philip Canfield comes to mind immediately. He's a florist, after all. But that's too obvious."

"Falcon Oakwood?" Dalton sipped his glass of cabernet. "You said he was there when you visited his wife on Monday. Maybe he didn't like you snooping into his affairs."

"Yeah, but he doesn't seem the type who'd toss a bomb through my salon window. I have a hunch the orchid sender is the same person."

"Didn't you look into the property records, Dad?" Brianna cut in. "I thought you found out something about the land deal for Orchid Isle."

"Right." Dalton swallowed. "Oakwood got the island for a cheap price. I contacted the tax assessor's office in Miami and got more details."

"So we know the land had once been a toxic waste site, and that Falcon got it for a good price. Did you find out if it had ever been cleared by the environmental agency?"

Dalton shook his head. "Sorry, that information wasn't available."

"How convenient."

"So maybe Falcon sent you this bouquet as a warning to mind your own business," Brianna said. Her dark eyes filled with concern. "Marla, I don't want you getting hurt. Maybe you should back off and let the police handle things."

Marla glanced at Dalton, an ironic smile on her face. How many times had he told her the same thing?

"Don't forget, Jill's cousin Kevin and her uncle Eddy were involved in that transaction. Besides Falcon, they'd want to preserve their reputations, too." Marla told them about her trip to Miami. "I didn't mention what Kate had said about Kevin being mixed up in mortgage fraud."

"Good, because you've already stirred the hornet's nest," Dalton said morosely. "Two women are dead, and you're not going to be number three if I have anything to say about it."

She took a gulp of red wine, fortifying herself for what she had to say next.

"Uh, I didn't tell you about Griff." Both Dalton and Brianna shot her questioning glances. "You know, Griff Beasley, the photographer from Boca who worked with Torrie and Hally. Please don't get mad at me, but I met him for drinks the other day. I wanted to ask him about Grant Bosworth."

Before Dalton could admonish her, she rattled off what she knew about Rachel, the documents she'd received from the girl, and the connection between Griff and both victims.

"And you went to see him alone?" Dalton shouted, half rising from his chair. "Are you nuts?"

She held out a hand. "Relax. I didn't think he would do me any harm. Someone hit him on the head at the lagoon in Coral Gables, remember? Hmm, I seem to recall Alexis, Eddy's wife, telling us that's where they live."

"Oh, no," Dalton growled, his gaze boring into hers, "you are not going off by yourself again to interview Alexis."

"Why don't both of you come with me then? I want to revisit Orchid Isle and talk to the staff. We need more information on that waitress who disappeared. And actually, it was Alexis who told us that she'd seen Jill washing her hands in the bathroom. That meant Alexis had left the party for an interval also."

"I'd love to go to the park with you," Brianna chimed in. "Can we go on Saturday? And speaking of activities, Marla, isn't there something you want to ask Dad?" She blinked meaningfully.

"Oh. Yes." Marla beamed at Dalton. "Your daughter wants to take acting classes. I think it's a fun idea. She can learn all sorts of useful skills, including public speaking. Right, honey?"

"Sure, if you say so. My friend, Ashley, has signed up. The session starts in January at a studio in Davie."

A frown creased his brows. "Dare I ask how much it will cost? And then there's the matter of transportation."

Marla waved at him. "We'll work it out if you approve."

"Please, Dad. I thought I might join the drama club next year, but I don't have any experience. All my other friends have more activities than me."

"Let me think about it, okay?" He glanced at Marla. "In the meantime, let's go to Orchid Isle this weekend. I wouldn't mind scouting around while we're admiring the trees. But I'll draw the line at intruding on Eddy and Alexis at home."

"Good, that's settled then." Marla knew he'd come around. Scraping her chair back, she started collecting the dinner dishes.

"One more thing." Dalton fixed his gaze on her. She knew that look. It heralded unpleasant news. "While you've been running around town for your friend's benefit, I've discovered something you're not going to like."

Her heart sank. "What's that?"

"Jillian Barlow has a criminal record."

"What?"

"This goes back many years, but she'd been arrested on a kidnapping charge. She abducted some guy's daughter."

"I don't believe it." Her throat tightened. She knew Jill kept secrets but surely not something as bad as this.

"Apparently, the man dropped the case, although I don't know why. My guess is they recovered the girl, and she was okay. But it gives Jill a motive for killing her sister if she didn't want her new husband to learn about it."

"Then why murder Hally?"

"Because Hally found out what Torrie knew. It makes perfect sense. I hate to say this, but it's possible Jill could be the killer."

Chapter Sixteen

"I'm going to prove you wrong," Marla said to Dalton during the drive on Saturday morning. "Jill may have a shaded past, but she isn't a killer."

Marla still smarted from his accusation, especially because she had her own doubts. Finding evidence to the contrary would confirm her faith. She knew Arnie would do anything for her, and she'd been his friend way before Jill had come along. She owed it to him to learn the truth. Yes, Jill was hiding something, but it wasn't murder.

At least, she hoped not. Loyalty might be one of her virtues, but it could also be her blind spot. Well aware she could be wrong, she focused on the task ahead.

Peering out the windshield, she rolled her shoulders that bunched with tension. Dalton drove with a relaxed look on his face as though he hadn't a care in the world. She resented his attitude. Why should she worry about every little detail when he could be so blasé? But perhaps that's what had drawn her to him. He provided the calm eye in the midst of her hurricane-force life. She needed his steady rudder.

"What?" He caught her glance in his direction.

She smiled. "Nothing. It just feels good to be out with you and Brianna. Once we're past the wedding, maybe we can enjoy more days off together."

"Yeah, like that'll happen," Brianna piped up from the back seat. She'd been texting messages on her cell phone. "You guys must be the busiest parents I know."

"Would you rather I sit around the house, cook dinner, and clean all day?" Marla twisted her neck to regard the teen.

"Not really. You have a cool job. It makes you who you are."

"Exactly." She gave a nod of affirmation. She'd tried the housewife routine with Stan, and it hadn't worked for her. They had gotten their divorce less than a year later, for more reasons than one.

"Don't think I'm gonna want to go with you all the time," Brianna added. "I have friends. Once I get my driver's license, you won't be seeing much of me."

"God forbid." Dalton raised his eyes to heaven.

"It's not that far off." Marla poked him. "You'd better hire a driving teacher. I can't see you as her instructor."

"We'll cross that bridge when we come to it." He hunched forward, clearly uncomfortable talking about his daughter's future behind the wheel. "So besides taking a nice walk today, what are our objectives?"

"You're the detective," Marla replied, aware he'd blithely changed the subject. "You tell me."

"Brody has already questioned the staff, so we need to approach this from another angle. You're good with people. What do you suggest?"

"Why don't we say we were at Jill and Arnie's affair, and we're thinking of renting the hall for our own occasion? Or else we're gathering info for my hypothetical friend who's getting married. I used that excuse when I went to see Philip Canfield, the florist. He supplies flowers for Falcon's house as well as the gardens here."

"That guy gets around."

"Leanne thinks very highly of him." Hmm, he'd struck her as gay, but could she be wrong? Might Leanne's interest go deeper?

"So we're looking for details on Orchid Isle's history."

Marla's thoughts jolted back to the present. "Plus, we want to know about that waitress, if anyone's heard from her again. And if any of the staff noticed someone in the corridor between the kitchen and the ballroom right before Torrie died."

"Don't forget the napkin," Brianna cut in. "There weren't any prints on the knife handle. The guilty party had to ditch the item he used to clean it off."

"Did anyone take plastic gloves from the kitchen?" Marla sagged against her seat. "I imagine Brody has been asking the same questions."

Dalton gave her a playful punch on the arm. "You manage to get answers where detectives fail. We're counting on you to use your feminine wiles."

Her mouth lifted at the corners. "So be it. Wouldn't want to lose my reputation."

They'd chosen to come after lunch, because weddings and other events tended to happen later in the day. Marla approached the ticket lady at the reception desk after they parked and meandered through the front entrance. It was the perfect day for strolling outside: warm, sunny, with low humidity. The parking lot was already full, but she hadn't noted any vans emblazoned with logos for photographers, florists, or musicians.

"Is anyone available from the catering staff?" she asked the thin lady behind the desk, who wore a blue smock. "We need to talk to someone about holding an affair here."

The lady gave them a proud smile. "You're in luck. They're setting up for a benefit tonight. Ask to speak to Sandy. She's the sales director."

"Great, thanks."

After Dalton paid their fees, the lady handed them a park map. "Be sure to visit our new plant emporium. It's just beyond the greenhouse."

They passed the booth and halted in front of a gift shop. "I need to go to the restroom first. Wait here," Marla informed her companions.

On her way down the hall, she stopped abruptly. The bride's room was to her right. Had anyone thought to search in there after the murder occurred?

Hoping the door wouldn't be locked, she twisted the handle. No go. It was locked.

She took her time in the ladies' room, admiring the vase of flowers on the counter while she washed her hands. Orchids were among the blooms, making her wonder if Canfield supplied these as well. Why had Jill come into the restroom in the midst of her reception to scrub her hands? Had Alexis's observation even been valid? Or maybe Jill was afraid of germs. She must have shaken a lot of congratulatory hands that night.

Another thought struck, making Marla swallow convulsively. What if Alexis was behind the murders in an attempt to protect her husband? Perhaps she'd discovered Torrie had scandalous information on Falcon, and later that Hally knew about it? Had she done them both in? Remembering the woman's beefy arms, Marla figured she had the strength. Why hadn't she thought of this possibility before?

Rushing outside, she confided her notion to her soon-to-be spouse.

Dalton tilted his head, regarding her with a grin. "Good one, Marla. I hadn't thought of her as a suspect before. It's a stretch, though."

"Let's go find Sandy and see what she says."

They located her office off a small corridor that separated the kitchen from the ballroom. A bleached blonde, she glanced up at Marla's knock on the open door. Her face, overly made-up with crimson lipstick and copper eye shadow, reminded Marla of an aging movie star trying to hang onto her youth.

"Hi, may we have a few minutes of your time?" Marla stepped

inside without waiting for an invitation. "We're scouting locations for a friend who is getting married, and Orchid Isle looks like the perfect setting."

"Of course, please come in."

"I'll be in the gift shop, you guys." Brianna meandered off.

Dalton followed Marla inside, and they both took seats opposite the woman's desk.

"What's the date of your friend's wedding?" Sandy withdrew a blank form from a drawer. "I'll need to check the availability of our ballroom. I presume that's where she'd hold the reception?"

"It's the first Saturday in June. Her name is Nicole." Marla noted Dalton's twitch of the lips from the corner of her eye. "She wants the ceremony to start at six, cocktail hour from seven to eight, with a sit-down dinner for the reception."

"Okay. We have that date available, but she'll have to put down her deposit fairly quickly. June is a popular month for weddings. I'll give you a packet to bring to her."

"That would be great, thanks." Marla paused. "We're recommending this place because we were guests at Jill and Arnie Hartman's wedding. Your people did a wonderful job, up until that terrible tragedy. Such a shame their affair had to end that way."

Sandy's eyes filled with sadness. "I know, and it was our grand opening weekend, too. Not a very auspicious start, huh?"

"How did Falcon Oakwood take it? Isn't he the park's owner?"

"He may be the developer, but he's not responsible for the day-to-day running of the place. Mr. Oakwood has many other projects in the Tri-County area."

"It was very community-minded of him to turn this piece of land into such a beautiful attraction. What had been here before this?" Marla asked in a mildly curious tone.

Dalton sat twiddling his thumbs as though bored but she knew he'd kick in with the hard questions when ready. She got a swell of pleasure glancing at his broad-shouldered figure. Soon she could introduce him as her husband. A thrill rippled through her at the thought.

Sandy narrowed her eyes, regarding them both. "I think this place was barren before. There wasn't anything here."

Dalton hunched forward. "I heard talk it was a dumping ground," he said, his face impassive.

"If that's so, Mr. Falcon has done a marvelous job of reclaiming the land."

"How do you know it was cleaned up?" His jaw tightened. "People wouldn't be too happy to hear this was a toxic waste site. I mean, I don't know that Nicole would want to have her event here unless the site was proven safe."

Sandy bristled. "I'm sure the construction people would not have been allowed to break ground without having the proper permits. Now back to your friend's wedding—"

"Yes," Marla interrupted, "back to the wedding. Tell us about your catering staff. Wasn't there some waitress the police wanted to question from Jill's affair? How well do you vet the backgrounds of these people?"

"I'm not responsible for hiring. You'd have to speak to the catering manager." Sandy's mouth tightened.

"I see. Would we be able to take a look at the kitchen?" she asked sweetly. "With so many food-born illnesses going around these days, one can't be too careful."

Sandy flipped the folder closed on her desk and handed it to Marla. "Here's the information for your friend. If you were already here for an event, you're familiar with the ballroom and patio facilities. Let me see if Samuel is in the kitchen. He can help you with the rest of your questions."

Clearly eager to see them gone, she marched down the hall

with Marla and Dalton in her wake.

"Excuse me." Marla tapped her shoulder. "Isn't this the door into the ballroom?" She pointed to a closed door on her right. Examining the carpet underfoot, she noted a darker section that might have been a stain. Unfortunately, the wine carpet color hid many faults.

"Yes, and that's the kitchen entrance on the other side." Sandy poised to push open the double swinging doors.

"And that exit at the far end goes outside?"

"That's correct. I'll go see if Samuel is available. Please wait here." She left them alone.

Marla gave Dalton a meaningful glance. "Look, this door would have been directly behind the cake table. This has to be the spot where the murder took place. Or at least where Torrie was stabbed."

Brianna came sauntering into view. "Hey, why didn't you guys come and get me?"

"Sorry, we would have picked you up in a few minutes." Marla shifted her handbag. "We're waiting to talk to someone on the kitchen staff."

"Learn anything new?"

"Just that Sandy seems to worship Falcon Oakwood."

The woman with that name cracked open the door. "Come on, Samuel is here. He'll give you a few minutes."

"Thanks so much for your help, Sandy. I'll pass this information along to my friend. We have your card if she has any further questions."

Samuel, the executive chef, greeted them in his white uniform. He was a large African-American with a moustache and a sprinkling of gray hair on his head under a towering chef's hat. His wide smile put Marla at ease right away.

They asked a few innocuous questions, got a brief tour of the gleaming stainless steel kitchen, then veered the conversation toward their true purpose.

"We attended a wedding here a few weeks ago." Marla watched his expression. "I was wondering about a dark-haired waitress on staff at the time. I heard she disappeared afterward. Did she ever show up again?"

"You mean Susan." Samuel grimaced. "She was a temp hired to replace one of our girls who was sick." He stroked his jaw. "Seemed like a nice young woman, although a bit shy. Clumsy, too. You could tell she hadn't been at this job for long. Probably just wanted to earn extra money over the holidays."

"Did you hire her?"

"That would be Rhonda. Don't expect to find anything useful on her application. The cops already said the information given was false."

Dalton stepped forward. "Why do you think she ran off?"

The chef gave him a scrutinizing glance. "Who did you say you were?"

Dalton flashed his badge. The chef had no way of knowing this wasn't his jurisdiction.

"Who knows?" Samuel shrugged. "She witnessed the crime and got scared? She committed the act? You tell me. We haven't seen her again. She didn't even bother to collect her paycheck."

"Did you notice anything peculiar about her appearance?" Brianna chimed in, giving Marla a smug look. "Like, was she wearing a wig?"

Marla beamed at her in approval. The teen had a sharp mind.

Samuel scrunched his eyes. "Sorry, we didn't have much contact. My domain is the kitchen, not serving guests."

"Someone noticed her speaking to the bride's sister shortly before the, uh, body was found." Marla cleared her throat. "Was there any gossip in the kitchen about what they were saying?"

"None that I've heard. Anyway, my people don't talk about it. Bad karma, understand?"

"I don't suppose one of the guests came into the kitchen that day and swiped a pair of plastic gloves?"

"People come and go all evening at these events. It's impossible to track them all."

"Did anyone notice if the cake knife had been on the table with the cake before the reception began? It would have been decorated with ribbons and flowers." Or so Philip Canfield had implied. Another negative response. "How about the table linens? Did anything with red stains turn up? And I don't mean red wine."

Mute, Samuel shook his head.

"Where do the linens go to get cleaned?" Dalton inserted.

"A driver picks them up."

"Can you look up the company for us, please?"

Armed with the name and address of the place a few minutes later, they thanked Samuel for his cooperation and left.

"We weren't very subtle," Marla told Dalton as they headed outdoors. "He's going to report back to Sandy."

"So what? A murder was committed here. They have to expect questions."

"Then we should have identified ourselves right away rather than approaching her with a pretense."

"Who cares?" Brianna led the way on one of the walking trails. "Did you learn anything new?"

Birds twittered and branches rustled in a light breeze that caressed Marla's skin. She breathed in a deep breath of earth-scented air. Greenery flanked their path, palms and live oak trunks vying for space among the dense leafy undergrowth. Water trickled from a rocky stream as they crossed a planked footbridge. She remembered the fork ahead and led the way downhill toward the lakefront.

"We don't know anything more about the waitress except that no one has seen her since Jill's wedding." Marla ticked off the points on her fingers. "We have the address of the cleaners. And if anyone knows about Falcon's land deal, they're not talking. I still need to get a glimpse of the wedding photos. I can't shake the feeling that they're important."

"Which ones?" Strolling along beside her on the shady path, Dalton grasped her hand.

The warmth from his palm penetrated her skin. "I'd like to see the ones from the official photographer and the shots from Griff."

"You don't have time to track them down. May I remind you that we have only two weeks to go to our event?"

She squeezed his hand. "I know." Her stomach fluttered. It was easier dealing with someone else's affair.

After spending a couple of hours relaxing at the park, they drove to Coral Gables to check out the linen company. Located in the Hispanic district, the cleaners stayed open on Saturdays.

Brianna translated in halting Spanish. They concluded that the linens from Jill's reception had no unusual stains. No big surprise there. The killer had covered his tracks in a clever manner.

They decided to go for a meal at their favorite dim sum restaurant in Miami. Marla enjoyed the lively atmosphere and the tasty food. More importantly, she liked being with Brianna and Dalton. She hoped they'd have many more occasions when they could enjoy each other's company.

They were on the drive home when her cell phone rang.

"Marla, it's Arnie. Where are you? I have some bad news. Jill has been arrested for her sister's murder."

Chapter Seventeen

"Arnie, we're almost at the Palm Haven exit," Marla said into her cell phone. "What can we do to help?"

"I've got a lawyer for Jill," he said in a fatigued voice. "We're going to see if we can post bond."

"She didn't kill her sister. I know your wife hasn't been truthful, but I think it's because she doesn't want you to be hurt."

"We'll see." He didn't sound convinced.

"Do you want us to come over? This has to be hard on Josh and Lisa. We can babysit while you get things done."

"Thanks, but their nanny is managing. I appreciate the offer, though. You're a true friend."

"No problem. Will you do me a favor and call me when Jill gets out so I don't worry?"

"Sure, Marla. Take care." He clicked off.

"Arnie hung up," she told the others who were listening to their conversation. "He doesn't want our help and says he's hoping to get Jill out on bond. I wish he'd let me do something for him."

"It's not our business," Dalton reminded her in a soft tone.

"I know, but it hurts to be excluded. I could try to talk some sense into that woman."

"She has to confess to her husband before anyone else. Their marriage has to be based on honesty or it won't last."

"You're right." Marla stared at her hands folded in her lap. "I still feel bad for them." And angry at the real killer for bringing this upon them.

Marla wasn't one to sit idly by while her friends were in trouble. Nonetheless, she had too many details of her own to handle over the weekend to keep pestering Arnie for more news.

Happy to get a call from him on Sunday that Jill had been released from jail, she concentrated on her own affairs. She and Dalton had received a slew of gifts that had to be catalogued. They had an appointment with the clergymen who were to perform their interfaith marriage ceremony. Cousin Cynthia had phoned about their Uncle Moishe, who wanted to eat at a kosher restaurant while in town for the wedding. Then that afternoon, Marla's brother Michael and sister-in-law Charlene were coming down from Boca with their kids so Charlene could pick up her dress at the bridal shop. They'd all be meeting Anita and Roger for dinner. Meanwhile, Dalton's parents wanted their opinion on a new condo development on Nob Hill Road.

Monday arrived before Marla barely had a chance to blink. My God, were the next two weeks going to fly by this quickly? she wondered, after Dalton left for work and Brianna caught the school bus. She stood in his kitchen, wiping her hands on a towel after doing the breakfast dishes. Today she'd hoped to get things accomplished while she had time to herself, but Arnie's silence bothered her. She hadn't heard a word back from him since he'd told her Jill was coming home.

I am not nosing into their business, she told herself, picking up the phone later that morning. *I've had my salon partially destroyed, and a warning sent to me along with a vase of orchids. Two people have been murdered. Someone knows I'm getting close. And since Jill has confessed, Detective Brody might stop looking elsewhere for the guilty party. I'll only find peace when both murders are solved.*

Monday afternoon found her tooling down the turnpike

toward Coral Gables once again. Alexis was making good on her offer to show Marla her home, after Marla determined that Eddy had gone to the office for the day. She knew it was a risk going there on her own, but she felt if Alexis was going to talk, it would be woman-to-woman. Besides, she'd coaxed Alexis into issuing the invitation again after informing her of Jill's arrest.

Marla left a note for Dalton, informing him of her whereabouts just in case. He couldn't get mad at her if she said Alexis asked her to come by.

As her car wound through the streets of Coral Gables, she scanned the street signs painted on rocks by the ground, then turned right as directed through a neighborhood shaded by spreading oaks and graceful palms. She proceeded down the street, studying the mailbox numbers. Most homes in this community were two-story haciendas with lush lawns and tree-lined driveways.

Alexis greeted her under a portico with white columns. Her auburn hair hung in damp strands around her square-jawed face. Again, Marla was struck by her almost masculine features, the impression bolstered by her sculpted limbs and solid torso. She wore a towel wrapped around a swimsuit, and a pair of flip flops.

"Come in. You'll have to excuse me. I got a late start after you called this morning and just finished my swim."

Marla couldn't resist. "Would you like me to do your hair for you? I have tools in my car. Your ends look like they could use a trim. No charge, of course."

Alexis clapped her hands. "That would be amazing. Let me do a quick rinse off in the shower and get into some dry clothes. Meanwhile, I'll have Juanita prepare some tea and scones."

"Okay." Marla's fingers itched to hold a comb. "I'll get my kit." A few minutes later, she pushed inside through the open front door and hesitated in the foyer. Straight ahead was an expansive living room. High ceilings, polished wood floors, heavy Mediterranean furniture, and a magnificent view of the pool deck earned her attention.

She heard someone humming, presumably from the kitchen. A moment later a maid bustled inside, smiling at her. She was a short woman with dark, curly hair. "Missus say to go upstairs, *señorita.* She wait for you in bathroom."

"Okay, thanks." Hustling up the stairway, she admired the paintings mounted on the walls. Not that she knew much about art, but they appeared to be originals. These were certainly better than the dead animal heads she'd seen in Falcon's house.

After mistakenly peeking into several uninhabited bedrooms, she found the master suite. It took up one whole side of the house, a huge bedroom with a king-size bed, double walk-in closets, and a marble lined bathroom. This had both a generously sized stall shower and a deep tub with those side jets that squirted water at you.

With the air-conditioning temperature down low, the vents blasted away the steam rising from Alexis's quick shower. She'd dressed hastily in a simple shift, her hair knotted atop her head under the towel. Slipping her feet into a pair of sandals, she regarded Marla.

"Where do you want to work?"

"This is fine. You'll need a chair to sit on. Do you mind if the hair falls on the floor? We can sweep it up later."

Alexis seated herself facing away from the vanity. Studying the shape of her face and the texture of her hair, Marla decided on the type of cut. After fluffing the damp strands and towel drying them once more, she turned Alexis toward the mirror.

"So tell me what happened with Jill," Alexis began after Marla started snipping.

She'd hoped to hold this conversation later, when they

wouldn't be interrupted by the noise from the blow dryer, but Alexis had started the subject.

"Jill confessed to killing her sister."

Alexis's face tightened. "I don't know if I believe that or not."

"Didn't you tell me at one time that she'd had issues in her youth? What did you mean?"

"I don't suppose it would do any harm to tell you now, since you know so much already. But you have to promise not to say a word to Arnie until Jill tells him herself."

"Of course." Marla sectioned off another clump of hair with a large clip. Her fingers moved automatically, lifting one silky strand after another, cutting at an angle. Alexis should be pleased with the result. It would emphasize her eyes more and her thick neck less.

"Jill and Torrie were always competitive. Jill, five years younger, felt she never got the attention from their parents that Torrie did. Torrie could do no wrong in their eyes, while Jill often got blamed for things."

"It's sad when parents favor one sibling over another. I've seen it happen. People get lifelong hang-ups and often don't realize where they stem from."

"That's so true. A neighbor of mine is involved in a lawsuit because her wealthy mother left nothing to her and she'd been the one caring for her in the end. The old lady left everything to the brother who she thought needed the money."

"That will only drive her heirs farther apart. Was this unfairness why Jill felt estranged from her sister?"

Alexis gave a trilling laugh. "Oh, no. You see, just out of college, Jill married an older man who had a child. She couldn't have horrified her parents more."

Marla gasped, holding her scissors in the air. "Jill was married before? She led us all to believe Arnie was her first husband."

Alexis's gaze met hers in the mirror. "She was an actress, doll. Public relations may have been her specialty in college, but she caught the acting bug in junior high. Just look at how she changed her appearance. Her looks had been unremarkable in her teens, so it wasn't any surprise that she fell for the first man who paid attention to her. Whether she married him to spite her parents or because she craved affection, I can't guess."

"You don't think they loved each other?"

"Maybe she thought so at first. Jill didn't realize he had a temper or that he drank. All he wanted was a mother for his kid. She got disillusioned pretty fast."

Marla spritzed Alexis's hair with water again and took up her shears. "So what happened then?" she asked with a sense of dread. It couldn't be good, or Jill wouldn't have kept it a secret for long.

"This is what I heard, mind you. Eddy was the one who actually got involved."

"Go on." *Lift, snip, drop.* Marla applied her skill, shaping Alexis's hair into a more flattering style.

"The guy became physically abusive. By then, Jill had become fond of the little girl. She was afraid for her safety, so she took the child one night when he was stone drunk and ran away with her."

"That's why she was charged with kidnapping?" The pieces began to fall into place. Jill hadn't done a bad thing. She'd tried to save the man's daughter.

"When he woke up the next morning and they were gone, the husband filed charges against Jill. The cops found them. Jill got sent to jail and the kid went to a foster home. It was Torrie who posted bond. She and Scott offered a sum of money to the husband if he'd drop the charges and agree to a divorce."

"Torrie did that for Jill?" She wouldn't have expected such kindness, but perhaps Torrie's bitterness stemmed from Jill's ingratitude and not from any latent childhood rivalries.

"Yes, and she never let Jill forget it. Scott resented his wife's involvement, and that didn't help Torrie's relationship with Jill either."

Alexis examined herself in the mirror after Marla put her shears down. "That's really cute. My own stylist never suggested lifting the layers like this."

"She probably figured you were happy if you didn't say anything. If you want to change your style, it helps to say so. Hairdressers are not mind readers."

Alexis gave her braying laugh again, making Marla cringe inwardly. She picked up her blow dryer, plugging it into a wall outlet.

"So that's it? Jill married the wrong man, made a mistake in running off with the guy's daughter, and never did another bad deed?"

"As far as I know." Alexis shifted her position. "She should have told Arnie from the start."

"Absolutely. It isn't good to begin a marriage based on deceit."

She thought of her own past mistakes and how Dalton had been so understanding when he'd learned the truth. She'd been ashamed to tell him, having guarded her secrets for years, like Jill. It seemed only yesterday that little Tammy had drowned while under her care as a babysitter. If she could put that tragedy and her subsequent foibles behind her, so could Jill.

"Whatever happened to the little girl?" she asked Alexis. "She must have been traumatized by the situation."

Alexis shrugged her wide shoulders. "Who knows? Jill didn't need that kind of baggage. She was still very young. Thank heavens she's found a good man now, if she can hold onto him."

"Jill loves his children. Maybe she always regretted leaving her first husband's daughter behind."

"That was Torrie's condition. A clean break, or no money. Jill kept to the bargain."

Marla switched on the dryer, drowning out any further conversation until they were downstairs, seated in the living room where the maid had deposited a tray of refreshments.

"If you don't think Jill killed Torrie, who did?" Marla asked, after Alexis poured them both cups of brewed green tea.

"She confessed for a reason. You tell me."

Balancing her teacup in her lap, Marla bent her head. "Maybe she knows whodunit and wants to take the heat off them."

"Then it would have to be someone close to her. Who would she risk going to prison for? No one in our family, I assure you."

"Guess it's time I had a word with Jill myself."

Chewing on a scone, Marla redirected the conversation to idle chatter. She submitted to a tour of Eddy's wine cellar as promised then took her leave.

Armed with her new knowledge, she knocked on Arnie's front door at three o'clock.

A drapery at one of the front windows was pushed aside and let drop back into place. Moments later, Jill opened the door.

Her blond hair had been hastily twisted and clipped to her head, her makeup barely applied. Dark circles under her eyes and a pale complexion indicated a restless state of mind.

"Marla. How nice to see you," she said in a flat tone. "What brings you into the neighborhood?"

"Can I come in? I had a few minutes free and wanted to see how you're doing. And I didn't get to talk to Josh and Lisa last time I was here. Are they in school?" She held her breath, hoping she and Jill would be alone.

"Yes, their nanny should be in the carpool lane as we speak." Jill led her inside to the family room, where she plopped down on the sofa and slumped back on the cushions. Marla sat in an upholstered chair facing her.

"So tell me, Marla, why are you really here?"

"Why do you think? I'm worried about you. Tell me what brought you to the brink." She waved a hand as Jill's eyes widened. "Oh, I don't mean about killing your sister. Why did you confess when you're innocent?"

Jill hung her head. "What do you know? I might have had my reasons for wanting Torrie dead."

"Because she knew you'd married an older man and abducted his child when he threatened to harm you? All your relatives seem to know about it, so why didn't you tell Arnie? Did you believe he'd think less of you if he knew the truth?"

"I made a mistake, and I tried to put it behind me." Jill wrung her hands. "I should have told him I'd been divorced."

"But not about the kidnapping charge? Now I understand what Torrie meant when she said she hoped your vows meant more this time around, but it wasn't your fault that your first marriage failed. You did what you had to in order to protect that man's child."

"She was such a sweet girl, Marla." Jill's tone was so low that Marla had to lean forward to hear her. "I knew when I saw him smashing the chair in the dining room that we'd be next. I had a bag packed just in case. When he went into the kitchen to get another bottle, I grabbed Becky and ran."

"Becky?"

"Rebecca. That was his daughter's name." Her voice caught on a sob. "I missed her so when I had to give her up, but they wouldn't let me keep her. Torrie told me I had to let Becky go if I wanted her help. She regretted that decision to the end of her days."

I sat up straight. "What do you mean?"

Jill bent her head, stringy clumps of hair falling forward. "Torrie and Scott never had children, you know. They wanted to, but it didn't work out for them. She started volunteering in foster care, and when she saw what went on, she was sorry she had sent Becky away from someone who loved her."

"Didn't you resent her interference in your life?"

"How could I? If not for Torrie and Scott, I'd have been convicted of kidnapping a minor. They helped me get rid of that rotten egg of a husband. The price had been steep, but I'd been willing to pay it."

"So you're saying Torrie regretted that decision?"

"For a long time she held my actions against me. She had coughed up a lot of money on my behalf, and I'll admit I was less than grateful. We grew apart. Scott had never been fond of me, and any time we met, they never let me forget what I owed them."

Marla struggled to understand. "But when you both inherited that property, you and Torrie had to communicate with each other."

"Right. She saw how I'd changed and wanted to make amends, so she came up with the perfect idea for a wedding gift."

"Which was what?"

"Returning my stepdaughter to me."

Click. More pieces fell into place.

"Rachel," Marla murmured.

"Yes, Rachel is the name she uses now. Torrie told me how she'd found Becky through the foster care system and brought her to town as her intern. Becky hadn't wanted to see me, until Torrie explained that it was her fault we'd been separated and that I hadn't abandoned her."

"But she seemed loyal to Torrie when I met her at the magazine office."

"She came to realize Torrie only had my best interests at heart. She's at a similar age to me when it all happened, so it's easier for her to understand now."

"Were you aware Rachel, or Becky, disguised herself and got hired as a waitress at your wedding?"

Jill's eyes misted. "She wanted to get a glimpse of me without actually having to face me yet."

"I'm guessing Torrie found her out and yelled at her because someone heard them arguing." Her jaw dropped. "That's why you confessed? You think Rachel murdered your sister?"

"I know she did." Jill's lower lip wobbled. "We finally met each other in person. Oh, Marla, it was so good to see Becky again. Or rather, Rachel, since that's the name she prefers these days. Dear Lord, I couldn't believe how she'd grown. But then she told me how Torrie screamed at her at the wedding and said she should never have come, that it would ruin things between us. Rachel got angry and blamed Torrie for everything that had happened. Somehow she got hold of the knife Torrie was carrying."

"Wait a minute. What knife?"

Jill's face scrunched. "Our wedding cake knife. Don't ask me how Torrie got it. Anyway, they struggled, and the knife ended up in my sister's chest. Rachel told me how she panicked, afraid she'd killed Torrie. She ran away to get help but decided it would look too incriminating. So she kept going."

"Oh. My. God."

"You see why I had to turn myself in? If Detective Brody learned our story, he'd figure Rachel took the job as Torrie's intern to exact revenge on her. And when Hally learned her true identity, Rachel killed her, too."

"She sent you flowers after Torrie's funeral."

"Rachel wanted me to know she was out there."

"This is important information, Jill. You should tell the detective these things and let him uncover the truth. Maybe Torrie wasn't dead when Rachel left her."

"I can't take that chance. I'm just now discovering my stepdaughter again. I don't want her taken from me."

"She's not the only suspect. Other people have motives." Marla's mind raced. Rachel had means, motive, and opportunity, making for a strong case against her. "Did you hear anything about the medical examiner's report?" Jill shook her head. "Then you don't know what really killed your sister."

"Who else do you suspect?" Jill's eyes filled with hope.

"Aside from your uncle and cousin who are trying to convince you to sell your property? Torrie wasn't happy with Scott's business decisions and hinted at leaving him. She was having an affair with another man. Jealousy could be Scott's motive. Or greed, since he's inherited Torrie's share of your land." Except he didn't leave the ballroom in the midst of festivities. Jill did, as had Alexis. But Jill would have had blood on her gown if she'd stabbed Torrie.

"Scott is too meek." Jill's lips compressed. "That man wouldn't hurt a fly."

"Sometimes people can appear calm and hide a volcano inside. Think of all those workplace shootings."

"If Torrie was seeing another man, Scott wouldn't do anything about it. He's not the type. Who was it, do you know?"

"Griff Beasley, the photographer from *Boca Style Magazine*. Thing is, Hally considered him her territory." As quickly as possible, Marla ran down her list of suspects. "So you see, Rachel isn't the only person with a motive for murder."

"No, but she was there at the right time holding the weapon." Jill squeezed her eyes shut. "Please, Marla, prove she isn't guilty. I'll be forever grateful."

I'm trying to prove you're *not guilty,* Marla thought.

"One item I meant to look into was the seating charts. Do you still have them? I'd like to see whose table was next to the one with the cake."

"Sure." Jill rose and scurried from the room. She returned a few minutes later carrying a folder. "Here, take it, but I'd like them back later for my records."

"Thanks, this will help." Leveraging to her feet, she accepted the packet.

"So what now?" Jill tucked a loose strand of hair behind an ear.

"Now I track down the cake knife. Philip Canfield implied he put it on the table, but then how would Torrie have gotten it? The wedding photos are the key. Either I have to get a look at your proofs, or I have to get into the office at *Boca Style Magazine*. They may still have Griff's digital photos on file. Besides, Griff is hiding something. He worked with both Torrie and Hally, and now they're dead. Rachel works in the same office. We don't want her to be the next victim."

Chapter Eighteen

Marla stopped by the wedding photographer's place first, hoping for a glimpse of Jill's proofs. Luck followed her into a private alcove with a computer where the receptionist brought up the digital files.

"Here's what we have so far, but the polished proofs won't be ready for another couple of weeks at least," the woman said in a friendly tone. She wore a smart belted black dress with a V neckline and chunky jewelry. "When did you say your date was?"

"In June." The lie rolled off Marla's tongue.

"We have various packages available. Stop by the front desk before you go and I'll give you the information. Were you interested in video as well?"

"Oh, yes."

"Our guys do a great job. I don't have the one available from the Hartman affair, but we have other sample videos to watch if you're interested."

Marla gestured. "Not right now, thanks. These are fine."

She turned to the monitor after the lady strode away and flicked through dozens of pictures. After fifteen minutes or so, she finally spotted the wedding cake. It was a beautiful three-tiered confection with buttercream icing, decorated with candied violets and Philip Canfield's orchids. Unfortunately, she couldn't find a single shot of the entire table. Either they were close-ups of the cake itself or views of Jill and Arnie at the head table cutting the cake together and feeding each other.

Gritting her teeth in frustration, she collected her purse, breezed through the lobby, where she collected the promised information, then left.

Sweat beaded her brow outside, where the temperature had risen into the low eighties. She wasn't perspiring from the heat, though. It was the lack of evidence exonerating Jill and Rachel that gnawed at her. She must be missing something important. And what of Detective Brody? Did he suspect Jill hadn't been telling the truth? The news reports all said an arrest had been made, but the police were still following leads in the case. That must mean he wasn't convinced by her story.

Marla shoved aside her theories for now. She and Dalton had a social event to attend that evening. Meanwhile, some repairs in her salon needed supervision and so did a supply delivery at her day spa. Neither were open to the public today, but work crews were there waiting for her approvals. Heaving a heavy sigh as she slipped into her Camry, she wished there weren't so many burdens on her shoulders.

Dalton helped relieve the pressure later, when they were both dressing for the dinner party benefiting the Child Drowning Prevention Coalition, Marla's pet charity.

Smelling like soap and his favorite spice aftershave, he kneaded her tight muscles and trailed his fingers down her bare arms. Privacy enclosed them in his bedroom, while Brianna did her homework in another part of the house. Marla stood in her underwear, her hair damp from the shower. She murmured with pleasure as he attacked the knots in her neck.

"Mmm, that feels so good."

"So do you." He turned her around and kissed her. "Do we have time?"

"Not now. I've got to do my hair. Sorry." With genuine regret, she withdrew from his embrace and padded into the bathroom. She looked forward to this annual event and the fashion show that accompanied it. It helped them raise thousands of dollars to put into educating the public about child drowning prevention measures.

Several hours later, she put down her dinner fork and signaled to Dalton. "Look, do you see who's taking photos? It's Griff Beasley!"

Dalton's head whipped around. "So it is. You can't miss his tall figure."

Marla got up to greet him. "Hi Griff." She tapped the blond man on the shoulder. "It's nice to see you again."

His cobalt eyes widened, then narrowed in displeasure. "Marla. What a surprise."

"Likewise. I'm glad to see you're covering this event. We could use the publicity. By the way, when is the article coming out on Orchid Isle?"

"Our magazine is bimonthly. Look for it in the bookstore." He grabbed a passing couple, the woman wearing a billowy taffeta creation. "Excuse me, can I get your photo, please?" He snapped a few shots then copied down their names.

"It must be difficult for you, working without Hally or Torrie's input. Who's covering the write-up tonight?"

He jabbed his thumb toward a statuesque brunette. "Jessica has been assigned the fashion beat. Why don't you ask her about the show?"

"No, thanks. I feel like you and I still need to talk." She stared him down.

A flush darkened his face. "Look, babe, whatever you think this is all about, it isn't."

He strode off. Marla thought about following him to ask further questions but a woman she knew accosted her.

"Marla," exclaimed the fashion boutique owner. It was Yolanda's line of clothing that was being shown tonight. "I should have brought in your people to do the models' hair. Those stylists backstage are too slow." Black hair in a tight bun, she pressed her wide red lips together.

"We'd be honored to be included next time."

"Have you met my husband?" She pointed to a man who swaggered over, his Asian features cold as iced plum wine. After introducing them, Yolanda inclined her head. "We're opening two new franchises," she stated proudly. "I must get you involved in my shows, yes?"

Marla lifted her chin. "That would be great. I've been wanting to do more photography work, too, so please keep me in mind for any photo shoots at your stores."

"Speaking of photographers, I saw you talking to that Beasley fellow. He's a sly one, although he has a sharp eye with the camera."

Marla's heart skipped a beat. "What do you mean?"

Yolanda chuckled, a sound deep from her throat, while her husband gave a grunt and wandered off. Taciturn guy. With his stocky build, he reminded her of a thug in a James Bond film.

"Beasley knows how to butter his bread. A man like him can always find use for his skills."

Marla hadn't a clue how to decipher the woman's words, but Dalton came to sweep her away to the dance floor and she had to drop the matter. It wasn't until she was on her computer the next morning, checking e-mail and browsing the Web before heading into work, when she got an inkling of what Yolanda had meant.

She'd put Grant Bosworth's name in her search engine, and it popped up with a series of photos. The pictures accompanied an article on *Home & Style Magazine*'s Web site. Marla scrolled down, noting Yolanda and her husband's proud grins in one of the digital shots.

A shock of recognition jolted her.

No way.

That was Griff's secret? That he and Grant Bosworth were one and the same? Now Yolanda's words made sense, and so did the reason why he'd want his colleagues to keep quiet. But had he murdered them? It didn't seem a strong enough motive, but there was only one way to find out.

She needed to revisit *Boca Style Magazine,* see if she could talk to either Rachel or Griff, and get a look at his photos from Jill's wedding.

Neither one would answer if she called them, but they might respond to Jill.

"Why is it so important?" Jill asked when she reached her friend at home. "You have enough to do with your own wedding in a week or so."

"Yeah, but you won't be there if they cart you off to jail again. We have to solve this now."

"And you think Griff Beasley has the answers?"

"Some of them. Don't you want to know what was going on between him and your sister?"

"I suppose."

"And wouldn't you like to give Rachel a defense against a murder charge if she's ever arrested for Torrie's death?" *Once you admit to Detective Brody that you were lying.*

"Sure, but—"

"Then call Griff, tell him you know what his deal is and that you'll expose him unless he meets us."

"Is that safe?"

"Make it a public place. And tell him you want a copy of his digital photos from the wedding. You're aware the magazine owns the rights, but you only want them for your private use."

"Will he buy it?"

"There's only one way to find out."

She didn't have to offer any excuses to Dalton, who was working late on his case, and Brianna, who had dance class that evening. Marla drove the teen to the studio a bit early, then hightailed it to the Seagrape Café at Sawgrass, where Griff had agreed to meet her and Jill. They got a table at the outdoor patio overlooking the lake. After ordering drinks and appetizers, they stared at each other in pregnant silence.

"Well?" Griff slumped in his seat, his hand cradling a beer.

Jill cleared her throat. She looked pale but attractive in a wrap dress and heeled sandals. Her wedding ring glinted in the light from flaming torches. The moon had risen, casting a golden glow over the water. A light breeze stirred the current, bringing a faint floral scent their way. It blew away the stench of cigarette smoke coming from another patron.

"I'd like to know what your relationship was with my sister." Jill drummed her fingers on the table.

Griff shifted uncomfortably. "We worked together."

"Come on, Griff, we know it was more than that." Marla's lips compressed. She wouldn't let him dodge the darts this time. "Torrie knew you were taking photos as Grant Bosworth, didn't she? Is that why you played up to her, so she'd keep quiet?"

Griff's expression changed into a sneer. "Good work, babe. You should get a job as a journalist."

"I saw your photos online from the party last night. Does your editor at *Boca Style Magazine* know you're moonlighting for a rival publication?"

"Nuh uh, and you're not gonna tell her."

"Why shouldn't I? Two reporters are dead who worked with you. Did you kill them so they wouldn't wreck your cozy arrangement?"

He gazed at her in genuine surprise. "Are you nuts? I wouldn't murder anybody over an assignment. The worst that can happen is that I lose my job, but so what? I'm good at what I do. Someone else would hire me."

"Then how about this." Marla hunched forward after the waitress delivered their drinks. Jill seemed content to let her do the talking. "You and Torrie were having an affair. Maybe you truly cared about her, or maybe you just cared about preserving your job. What promises did you make? Did you say you'd marry her if she left her husband, and then you went back on your word?"

He shot her a sheepish glance. "Torrie shouldn't have taken me so seriously. We had a good thing going the way it was."

Schmuck, Marla thought. *You probably said that to get her into bed.*

"Did she threaten to expose your little secret? And Hally, what about her? She liked you, too, and got jealous. Then she discovered what Torrie knew and became a threat as well."

"I'd signed an exclusivity clause," Griff said with a snarl. "If one of those snoops ratted on me, I'd get fired. Still, I didn't kill anybody."

"Did you bring the photos?" Marla snapped.

He handed over a disk. "Keep this between us, okay? The magazine owns the rights."

"Jill, is it all right if I look at these first?"

"Of course." Jill focused her determined gaze on Griff. "Did you know I'd been arrested on the charge of murdering my sister? If there's anything in these photos that will help my defense, I intend to use it."

He gave a curt nod, a clump of hair falling across his forehead and giving him a rakish look. "You should check out that girl who worked for Torrie. Something strange going on there."

Jill's eyes iced. "You keep away from her. Give us a better reason why we shouldn't believe you're the murderer."

"Did you ever think maybe it was something Torrie and/or Hally were investigating?"

Marla's lips parted. "A fashion reporter and a society

columnist don't do investigative journalism. You're just trying to throw us off your trail."

"Oh? Well, check this out, babe."

Reaching into his pocket, he drew out a folded paper and tossed it to her. Although it was rumpled, she could see that it was a copy of an article from the *Miami Herald.*

"I don't get it." Her brow furrowed as she scanned the print. "Carl Woods Homes is being sued in a class-action lawsuit by homeowners for using defective building materials? What does that have to do with anything?"

"Keep reading. Look whose name is mentioned."

Her eyes scrolled down the page. "Holy highlights, Falcon Oakwood owns the company."

Jill, leaning over her shoulder, pointed further down the page. "Isn't that the name of your housing development?"

Marla felt the color drain from her face. "Oh, no. Does this mean Carl Woods is the umbrella company for our builder? I have to tell Dalton. There's no way I'm moving into a house constructed with Chinese drywall." Her heart sank at the implications.

Jill put a calming hand over hers. "Maybe it doesn't apply to your place. So, Griff, you're saying Torrie had been aware of Falcon's dirty dealings? She may have told Leanne."

"Leanne said something about being free of his mother's influence. I wonder what she meant," Marla mused.

Griff reached for a coconut shrimp when the waitress delivered the platter. "Just remember, ladies, you didn't hear any of this from me."

Always looking out for your own skin, aren't you?

Marla glared at him, unable to think of any other questions to ask while he ate. After finishing his beer, he burped and lumbered to his feet.

"See ya around," he said before striding away.

"I hope your house isn't affected, Marla." Jill leaned back in her seat with a weary sigh. She'd already emptied her glass of chardonnay.

"I'll let Dalton deal with it. I have too much to do." Her head spun with confusion and dismay.

"Assuming I'm not back in the clinker, I'll see you next week at your bachelorette party." Jill gave her a broad smile.

"Right." Her stomach churned at the reminder. "Twelve days to go to the Big Day."

One week. That was all she'd give herself to find the killer and absolve Jill from guilt.

Maybe Griff's photos would shed some light on the case.

She gathered her purse, threw enough bills on the table to cover the tab, and gave Jill a farewell embrace.

Chapter Nineteen

Marla squinted at the computer screen in her townhouse home office. She didn't see any evidence of a cake knife on the decorated table. Philip Canfield hadn't actually come out and said he'd put it there, but he had let her assume as much. How, then, had it ended up in Torrie's hand?

Could he have been mistaken? Had Jill entrusted it to her sister to bring to the wedding?

She viewed the photos again, looking for clues, noting who was present in the vicinity of the cake table. Shaking her head, she was ready to give up when she remembered the seating charts. They'd gotten lost in the pile of papers on her desk.

Shuffling through the lot, she found the folder Jill had given her. Ah, there was the diagram. Now, who was seated at which table? There were essentially two rows, tables next to the stage and then a second tier behind them. According to the charts, Jill and Arnie's relatives held the prime spots, followed by their close friends. Marla and Dalton's table was toward the rear, the second from the end to the right facing the stage. The first ones in either row would be closest to the cake table.

She didn't recognize any guests from the back row, but the table closest to the stage was where Leanne and Falcon Oakwood sat. Their names jumped out at her.

Of course. If Falcon had for some reason accosted Torrie in the hallway, then shoved her body under the table, he could have just sauntered to his seat afterward with none the wiser.

Marla still wasn't sure what he might have done with the cloth that he must have used to clean his hands. She'd have to ask Leanne if there had been any unusual stains on his tuxedo. Maybe this is what Leanne had meant when she said she'd soon be free of his mother's influence. Did she intend to turn in her husband, seek a divorce?

The phone rang, jarring Marla's senses.

"Marla? It's Leanne Oakwood."

"Omigosh, I was just thinking about you. We need to talk."

"Right." The woman's voice sounded strained. "I heard what happened to Jill, the poor thing. I have some information that might be useful in her defense."

Marla's breath hitched. "Sure, Leanne, go ahead. I'm listening."

Leanne cleared her throat. "It involves Orchid Isle. I found some documents in my husband's files that are relevant. You'll know what to do with them. Do you have some free time this week for us to meet so I can hand them over? I know you're busy with your wedding and all, but it's important."

"What did you learn, Leanne?"

"I can't take time to explain. Falcon might walk in at any moment." Leanne lowered her voice to a hushed tone.

"Is it about the toxic waste? I know he acquired the land for Orchid Isle when it was contaminated. Did he skirt regulations? Did Torrie find out?"

"No, this involves something else. The proof is at Orchid Isle, along with these files. Let's meet there, and I'll show you everything."

"Proof about what?" Marla persisted, unwilling to make the trip without further information.

"Oh, God, I hear footsteps. He's coming this way! Please, Marla, it's not only for Jill's sake. This will help me, too."

Marla swallowed a sigh as she reviewed her mental schedule.

"I'm free on Thursday morning. I don't go into work until one o'clock that day."

"The park opens at ten. Come at nine, and I'll arrange for you to be let in. We'll meet inside the greenhouse. And Marla, please don't tell anyone. Word gets around, and I don't want Falcon to get wind of what I know."

"All right. See you then." Marla hung up, a grim smile on her face. What else could this be about besides her husband's dirty land schemes?

Increasingly nervous as the week progressed and her wedding date approached, she managed to juggle family demands, drop off the place cards and table favors at the country club, and confirm the music selections with the DJ. Luis told her the salon could reopen on Tuesday, relieving her of that problem. Meanwhile, the day spa's grand opening loomed closer and so did the holidays, making her regretful that she'd planned so much at the same time.

Finally, on Wednesday when she had a free moment, she picked up the phone to call Tally. Maybe her best friend would take a ride to Orchid Isle with her in the morning. Marla didn't think it wise to go alone. But when she remembered Tally's pregnant state, she put the receiver down. It wasn't a good idea to involve her in case the encounter with Leanne turned ugly. The thought crossed her mind that Falcon's wife could be the guilty party.

Marla finally confided her plan to Dalton that evening.

"Are you crazy?" He faced her in his kitchen, spatula in hand. "I'll go with you. You should have told me sooner."

"Sorry, I just became involved in so many other things that it slipped my mind until now."

"What are these files she discovered? And what's the proof at Orchid Isle?"

Marla shrugged. "Leanne wouldn't say on the phone. I'm

thinking it's a ploy to be free of her husband." She described her findings to date.

"You mean, Leanne wants a divorce and needs some leverage, so she snooped in her husband's office to get evidence against him?"

"Could be. We'll see what she has to offer."

Thursday morning, Marla pulled her car into the empty parking lot at Orchid Isle, claimed a space, and turned off the ignition. After pocketing her wallet and cell phone, she stuck her purse under the seat.

"Shouldn't you wait here?" she asked Dalton. "Leanne thinks I'm coming alone."

"It's a ways to the greenhouse. I'll accompany you there and then wait outside. She won't see me." His firm tone told her arguing would be futile.

They advanced toward the front doors past a cluster of blue plumbago and white pentas. The lights were off inside the two-story white building, but when Marla twisted the doorknob, it opened. She eased inside, calling out a greeting. No one answered. Leanne must be waiting for her at the designated location.

It had been smart to wear a sweater over her knit top and jeans. The sweet-scented air felt cool against her skin as they proceeded out a side door onto the winding path. Birds twittered in the trees and leaves rustled overhead. They crossed a small arched bridge as water gurgled and danced on the rocks below.

A few more paces ahead, they came to a fork in the path and halted.

"Do you remember which way to go?" She peered in one direction then the other.

Dalton's brow furrowed. "It's not toward the lake, so let's go the other way."

She stepped past a red-tipped Chinese fringe plant. An airplane droned in the sky, the only sign of civilization. Its sound tapered off with the vapor trail, leaving them alone with lizards and other jungle creatures. "It's so quiet here."

"Too quiet. I don't like it." Dalton's shoulders hunched as they followed the trail. "Maybe I should call Brody."

"Why? I'm meeting a friend in the park and we're exchanging information. What would you tell the detective?"

"Good point."

A squirrel darted by in the undergrowth. Branches provided a canopy overhead that filtered the morning light. Cascades of moss trailed from the tree limbs like old men's beards. Cobwebs glistened between broad-leafed plants and prickly tree trunks.

A yellow and black butterfly soared in front of her. Banana plants grew alongside gingers, ferns, liriope, and palms. They passed through a cycad collection and entered a grove of bamboos that creaked like an unearthly chorus. If this had been a toxic waste site, Falcon had done a stupendous job in recovering the land. She could believe it had taken years to get to this level of growth. Maybe she'd been maligning his character wrongly. Maybe he had gotten the proper clearances.

Or not. Why else would Leanne be meeting her? She knew her husband was guilty. Torrie, and later Hally, must have discovered his schemes, and that's why he killed them.

"There's a sign." Dalton pointed beyond a tall laurel fig tree.

The sign was nearly obliterated by a hanging vine, but she determined the greenhouse was in the same vicinity as a cemetery. A cemetery? Who could be buried there? She pursed her lips as she trudged on.

Dead pine needles crunched underfoot as they headed over a less-traveled path. An evergreen stand brought a fresh pine scent to her nose. It mingled with a wet earthy aroma and chased away the stench of something rotting in the shrubbery.

A cracking noise overhead made her leap aside just as a large branch fell to the ground in a gust of wind. The breeze picked up, ruffling her hair. She hastened along, aware of clouds accumulating in the wakening sky. Dalton remained silent, his gaze wary as they covered ground.

Straight ahead was the greenhouse, the cemetery off to their left. Marla paused to peer at a memorial plaque in front of the grassy area.

"Dear Lord, it's a pet cemetery, of sorts. Eww." Dead animals found on the grounds were buried here in accordance with state regulations. A gruesome tribute, to be sure, but one that respected their natural habitat. With a grimace of distaste, she turned away.

The greenhouse appeared to be a series of connected domed structures with walls of white opaque glass stretching from floor to ceiling.

"I'll wait out here," Dalton said. "If you're not back within fifteen minutes, I'm coming inside. Holler if you need me." He leaned against a solid oak trunk and folded his arms across his chest.

"Right. Let's hope I can make this quick."

She pushed through the main entrance and paused inside as steamy humidity hit her in the face. The moisture was so thick, you could almost cut it with a knife. Her lungs breathed it in, along with a heavy floral scent.

A rocky waterfall gushed across an expanse on her right, and on her left stretched a tropical jungle-like growth of plants alongside and in between two concrete aisles. Underfoot, winding rivulets wet her running shoes. Visibility was practically nil from one end of the greenhouse to the other, where it opened into the next big space. Leafy banana plants, spindly palms, hanging vines, and dangling blossoms obstructed the path in what she could only describe as ordered chaos. She paused to admire a variety of vividly colored orchids.

"Leanne, I'm here," she called. "Where are you?"

A rustling noise off to the left startled her. Brushing aside branches, she plunged in that direction. She ducked through an open door into the next hothouse, dodged hanging plants from above, and stepped over a hose coiled on the ground.

She stumbled to a halt when Philip Canfield slithered into view like a garden snake. His dark hair in his usual ponytail, he grinned at the sight of her. Black seemed to be his favorite color, as his outfit matched his hair.

"Marla, my dear, what a pleasure." The way his eyes gleamed said otherwise.

"What are you doing here? Where's Leanne?"

"I'm afraid she couldn't make it, but she was most obliging in summoning you." He held one hand behind his back as he sauntered closer.

"What do you mean?"

"I needed to tie up a loose end. You did come alone, didn't you?"

"Sure," Marla lied. Her eyes narrowed. "Wait a minute. You're not her ticket to freedom, are you?" She had thought Leanne meant to expose her husband's wrongdoings to get him off her back, but maybe she'd been planning to leave him all along. Leave him for Philip Canfield.

"Leanne is very special to me. She's a good girl who will do anything I require, unfortunately for you. She didn't ask me why I wanted you to come here."

"And why is that?" Marla's heart thumped wildly. This was a trick? Leanne hadn't intended to meet her at all? Her gaze darted toward the exit, but Canfield blocked that route. She could only go deeper, trapping herself further.

Her trembling fingers clasped the cell phone in her pocket. If she could speed dial Dalton, he'd overhear their conversation. Whatever Canfield had to say, she wanted to listen first before Dalton burst upon the scene. He would intervene if she was in danger.

Canfield sneered. "You know too much. Such a shame. Torrie had a lot going for her, too, although not everyone would agree. Like her, you've become a thorn in my side."

"Many people disliked Torrie. What did you have against her?"

The florist's eyes turned glacial. "Torrie threatened to expose me unless I set her up in her own apartment. She couldn't wait to dump her husband. She'd counted on Griff's support, but she should have known he's just a player."

Expose what about him? Marla didn't want to ask, afraid she'd provoke the guy. She didn't know what he held behind his back but hoped it wasn't a gun.

"I suspected Griff." Marla backed away, her gaze level. "Torrie knew he'd been violating his noncompetition agreement with their magazine. Then I wondered if maybe Hally had done it out of jealousy, because she wanted Griff for herself."

"You're totally wrong. It was me all along. I couldn't let Torrie put a stop to my lucrative side trade." He sneered. "She just got in the way."

Marla's lips parted as understanding dawned. "You supply collectors like Falcon with their orchids, obtaining specimens and smuggling them into the country." In a way, Leanne had been truthful. The evidence *was* here, among the flowers.

Canfield pounded his chest. "Orchid enthusiasts will do anything, pay anything, to get what they want. Falcon is a fanatic. He's my best customer. And Leanne is too stupid to realize what's going on beneath her nose."

I wouldn't be so sure. She knows more than she lets on.

"Do you really love Leanne, or are you pretending to care for her in order to stay close to her husband?"

"She has her uses, although I'll admit she's pretty damned good in bed."

Bastard! Marla gained another few inches away from him. Plants stood in pots all around her. Those would make a good weapon if she could get her hands on one. Where was Dalton? She didn't want to cry out and alert Canfield. Dalton should know by now something was wrong.

"Did Leanne tell you about the affair between Griff and Torrie?"

Canfield nodded. "That's right. I couldn't be sure what Torrie had told him, so I tried to get rid of the photographer during an event he was covering at the Venetian Pool. Someone came along, and I wasn't able to finish the job. I hoped I'd scared him enough to keep quiet if he knew anything."

"You disguised your voice and called him on the phone to find out where he'd be that day." She resisted the urge to wipe her sweaty palms on her pants. "I thought you might have been after his camera," she continued, her voice raspy. "Weren't you afraid someone would notice the cake knife missing from the table at Jill's reception, after you'd said you put it there?"

"I'd forgotten to lay it on the table, so I gave it to Torrie, who was going that way. She said she'd deliver it."

"Then what happened? I don't understand."

"It doesn't matter, Marla. Your time has come." He brought his arm around. His hand gripped a mean-looking knife. "Are you aware I enjoy fishing?" he asked in an idle tone, while she stared at the sunlight glinting off the steel. "I can describe how we gut our catch, if you're interested."

She swallowed. "No, thanks. But tell me this: you'd left the cake knife in the van, went outside to retrieve it, and . . . ?"

"And you're dead, Marla. That's enough questions."

He lunged, the blade slashing through the air. Ducking

sideways, she elbowed his arm out of the way. Then she charged up the aisle in the opposite direction to the main entrance. If she could reach the bend ahead, she'd come down the row on the other side.

Grunting, he darted after her. She kicked a planter into the path, tripping him. She gained a few feet before he caught up, hooking her by the wrist. Struggling to free herself, she bit back a sob when he brought the knife within range of her abdomen. Would he stab her there, or slice between her ribs? The blade looked to be several inches long, with a serrated edge. Her breath came in short, panting gasps as she sought to remember her self-defense lessons.

"Torrie snagged me at the wedding." He grasped her tightly, pulling back his lips in a feral grin and looking nothing like the fop he pretended to be. "She said that unless I shared some of my profits with her, she'd alert the customs people to my shipments. She'd have made a hell of an investigative journalist. Too bad she was stuck doing a fashion column."

He appeared willing to talk, so Marla pressed her advantage. "So you told her no, and she got angry?"

"I lied and said sure, I made enough so that I could give her a cut. Then I asked her to take the cake knife I'd forgotten and put it on the table inside. I'd figure out a way to deal with her later."

"So what happened? Did Rachel catch you talking together?"

"Who?"

"Rachel, a waitress at the affair. She worked as an intern at Torrie's office and had disguised herself as a temp hire."

"I don't know who you're talking about. All I know is that Torrie grabbed the cake knife and walked away. I followed her to make sure she didn't mess up my decorations."

"And then you found her in the hallway, didn't you? With the knife in her chest. Was she still alive?"

His face contorted at the memory. "She tried to speak to me as I bent over her. But this was an opportunity I couldn't resist. Someone else would get the blame, so I twisted the knife until her last breath left her lips."

"Wasn't she bleeding? Didn't you get blood on your clothes?"

"Only on my shirt. I buttoned my jacket until I could get back to the van to change. I always show up in work clothes and change into my formal outfit before guests arrive."

"Why didn't you leave her in the corridor? You took a risk shoving her under the cake table. Someone in the ballroom might have seen you."

"I heard footsteps and panicked. I needed to get rid of the body before her blood stained the carpet. The door was right in front of me. I opened it and no one was around. All it took was a few seconds."

"How did you wipe the knife handle clean? There weren't any prints."

His glance dropped to his hand holding the dagger. "The seats at the table closest to the door were empty. Guests must have been out on the dance floor. I took a water glass and rinsed my hands, holding them over the centerpiece. Then I wet a napkin, crouched down, and wiped off the knife handle that was still lodged in Torrie's chest. I made sure to wipe off the door handle on both sides, too. Anyone looking my way would have thought I was just fussing with the decorations."

"Where did you put the soiled napkin?"

He gave a proud grin. "Inside the flower arrangement on Leanne's table, after wrapping it inside another clean cloth. I told her to take the centerpiece home. I'd accidentally spilled some red wine inside and the alcohol would kill the flowers. She should discard the entire vase. The little lamb was happy to comply."

"And then where did you go?" Marla asked, aware he liked to

brag about his accomplishments. "Into the banquet hall, or through the side door into the park?"

Canfield waved the knife. "I was afraid someone would see me in the corridor so I slipped into the crowd in the ballroom until I could go outside to change." He hesitated, confusion clouding his expression. "What I don't understand is why Jill confessed. Tell me how much she knows, and I'll make your death quick."

Marla slipped a hand behind her and grasped a heavy pot holding some kind of spiny cactus. "I told you about Rachel, the waitress, who was really an intern in Torrie's office. She was Jill's estranged stepdaughter. Torrie meant to bring them together as a wedding gift to her sister. But Rachel jumped the gun to get a glimpse of Jill beforehand."

"What's your point?" His face twisted with impatience.

"Torrie was furious when she spotted the girl at the wedding. They argued in the hallway. Somehow the cake knife became embedded in Torrie's chest. Rachel ran away, afraid she'd killed her mentor. I gather this is where you came along."

Were those sirens she heard in the distance? Dalton must have summoned backup, but why hadn't he come to her aid? Had something happened to him?

She talked faster, hoping to keep Canfield distracted. "In case you're not familiar with Jill's history, her marriage to Arnie was the second time around for her. She didn't want him to know and with good reason. She'd been married very young to an older man with a daughter."

"This girl Rachel?"

She noted the calculating gleam in his eye, as though he were assessing this new threat. Rachel would know she had left Torrie alive and that she hadn't been the one to push her under the table.

"Jill grew very fond of the girl but less so of her husband, who turned out to be a drunken abuser. She was afraid he'd harm the child, so Jill ran off with her."

"Plucky thing, eh?"

"Her husband didn't think so." Marla's palms grew slippery with sweat. "He accused her of kidnapping his daughter. Jill got caught, arrested, and the girl was placed in foster care. That's the last they saw of each other until Torrie came into the picture."

Canfield raised his eyebrows. "How so?"

"Torrie and Scott were the ones who bailed Jill out of trouble, but only on the condition that Jill divorce the man and leave the child behind."

"So Jill was indebted to her sister."

"Who never let her forget it. Jill feared Torrie would say something to Arnie about her past mistakes, but she didn't realize Torrie really wanted to make amends."

"You're kidding, right? Torrie liked to cause friction between people, not dissolve it."

"This was different. Torrie always wanted to have children but wasn't able to conceive. The property issue was bringing her closer to her sister for the first time in years, and she wanted to give Jill a wedding gift that would break the ice between them for good."

"Get to the point. How much does Jill know?" His hand tightened on his weapon, while his hard gaze dropped to her midsection.

"Wait, you'll understand in a minute. Jill had always longed after the stepdaughter she'd abandoned. Meanwhile, Torrie began volunteering for the foster care program, making inquiries as to the girl's whereabouts."

"So Torrie found Rachel?"

Marla nodded. "Torrie contacted Rachel and told her how much Jill missed her and that it was her fault they'd been separated. She offered Rachel a job at the magazine as her intern while Rachel got up the nerve to meet Jill again. It would have to be after the wedding. Jill still hadn't told Arnie about her first marriage."

"So what happened to make Jill confess? She met the kid, who told her what happened with Torrie?"

"Right. Jill figured Rachel had killed Torrie, who must have bled to death after Rachel fled the scene. At least it would look that way to the police. She didn't want to lose the daughter she'd just rediscovered."

"So Jill didn't even think about someone else coming along, finishing what Rachel had started, and hiding the body?"

"We were looking for that napkin, because we figured the killer wiped his prints clean. Even if it wasn't Rachel who made the killing blow, she'd be questioned by the cops. Jill wanted to spare her that trauma."

A relieved grunt escaped his lips. "Good, so they don't know anything about me, right?"

The sirens had stopped. Marla glanced toward the exit, praying help was on its way and worried about Dalton's silence. She only needed to divert Canfield a few more minutes. "I'm not aware of how much the cops suspect. How about Hally? Why did her life have to end?"

"She shared an office with Torrie and got wise to my import business. Damn nosy females. Just like you." His muscles tensing, he raised the knife.

Sensing the thrust that was about to come, Marla jammed the ceramic pot into his solar plexus. With a howl of rage, he bent over, his grip on her wrist loosening.

She twisted herself free, turned, and ran. Branches and vines stung her face as she charged blindly forward. She'd made it into the greenhouse nearest the exit when a large force collided with her from behind.

Crying out, she toppled to the ground, almost smacking her chin on the coiled green hose. Canfield leapt on her, his knee pressing into her spine. Screaming, Marla bucked, trying to throw him off. He grabbed her hair, yanking her head back with one hand while his other hand gripped the knife.

Good Lord, he's going to slit my throat.

Heavy footsteps sounded outside then crashed into the greenhouse. "Philip, stop!" yelled Falcon Oakwood, waving a gun. "You don't want to do that."

The florist hesitated, while Marla prayed silently. Cold steel pricked her skin, sending shivers through her body.

"Come on, Phil, we can talk about this. I don't need any more bad publicity for my park."

Canfield cursed aloud. "You have just as much to hide as I do. She knows everything."

"I don't care. When Leanne told me what you'd had her do, I figured it out. I'm losing my wife, Phil, and I've realized she matters to me more than anything. You're not going to take her from me."

"Oh, yeah? And what will Mummy say when her precious son goes to jail for building this place on contaminated land?"

"Let me handle things my way. Get off her." Falcon aimed his weapon. "Her boyfriend is outside. I tranked him but he'd already called the cops. They'll be here any minute."

Falcon had tranquilized Dalton like one of the animals he hunted? Rage surged through her.

"Come one step closer, and I'll kill her." Canfield's arm tensed.

"No, you won't, or you'll deal with me next."

"You're making a mistake. You should want this." Canfield's hand inched away while he talked.

Marla took advantage, twisted her head, and chomped her teeth into his flesh until she tasted blood.

"You bitch!"

He sprang back, giving her the chance she needed. She scrambled to her feet and fled in Falcon's direction, blocking his aim at her assailant. She bumped his arm as she brushed past, making the gun drop from his fingers.

With a growl, Canfield launched himself at the park's owner. Ceramic pots crashed to the floor as they fought.

Outside in the bright sunlight, Marla raced toward Dalton's still form on the ground. She sank to her knees, feeling for his pulse. Her heart soared when she detected a steady beat. Thank goodness, he'd be okay. And so would she. People sprinted toward them from a distance.

"Over here," she yelled.

Something warm trickled down her neck. Her fingers, touching it, came away stained with crimson.

"Are you all right, Miss?" the first officer on the scene asked, while other men in uniforms rushed inside the greenhouse.

"I'll be okay. This is my fiancé. He's been drugged. Please take care of him."

Her head swam dizzily, and then the lights went out.

Chapter Twenty

"So tell us what happened after the cops arrived," Tally said at the Friday evening rehearsal dinner.

Brushing a strand of hair behind her ear, Marla regarded her best friend. She blinked wearily. Last night her bridesmaids, with the exception of Brianna, had taken her to a lounge on South Beach with some exotic male dancers. Blood rushed to her face at the memory.

"I passed out. Later, I learned that in their struggle, Falcon accidentally stabbed Philip Canfield with his own knife. It was a fatal wound." Marla didn't say aloud that she felt it a fitting end for the florist. His demise reflected Torrie's tragic death.

"How did Falcon know you'd be there?" Kate asked from across the table.

Marla felt a swell of warmth toward her. She'd done a bang-up job in arranging this dinner party.

"Leanne told him. At the last minute, she had misgivings and confessed to her husband that she and Philip were lovers. Her plan was to leave Falcon, move in with the florist, and go back to school. She'd trusted Canfield, and as a result she believed he murdered two women, and I might be next."

"Canfield did all this to protect his orchid-smuggling business?" Brianna chimed in.

"That's right. Leanne had been so starved for affection from her husband who doted on his mother and his plants that she'd fallen for Philip's advances. Out of spite, she told Torrie what she knew about Falcon's dealings. She wasn't as naïve as he assumed. Leanne gathered information so she'd have leverage for a divorce."

"So Leanne told Philip Canfield that she'd confided in Torrie?" Tally regarded her with rounded eyes. "Didn't she suspect him when Torrie was killed?"

"She thought her husband might be guilty. But when she considered why Canfield wanted to meet me at Orchid Isle, she put two and two together and told Falcon. For his part, Falcon realized he'd better take action or his marriage would fall apart. He really does love Leanne."

"That man should go to jail." A muscle twitched in Dalton's jaw. "We're lucky his company didn't use Chinese drywall for our development, but other homeowner associations have filed suit against him. Not to mention building his park on a former toxic waste site."

Marla gave him a wan smile. "He's promised to take any necessary remedial actions. He really wants to win Leanne back. He's told his mother she has to move and will even take down those animal heads around the house to please his wife."

"Sounds like he's ready to change," Anita intoned. At her side, Roger nodded, his mouth too full for him to speak. He'd emptied the bread basket before anyone else had a second chance.

"He's not the only one." Marla took a sip of water. "Griff decided to go freelance. He quit his job at the magazines. This way, he won't have to worry about any noncompetition clauses."

"How's Jill handling all this?" Tally's blond hair fell across her face like a curtain.

"Jill had a long talk with Kevin and Scott. It seems Eddy was the one who negotiated the land deals with Falcon and Philip Canfield. Kevin found the properties and Eddy did the rest. Eddy was also the one pushing for Jill and Torrie to sell their property. He had Pete Schneider lined up as a buyer. Both of them would profit from the sale.

"Kevin agreed it would be in Jill and Scott's best interest to retain a different attorney. He truly does want to help them secure a new tenant. Now that they've cleared the air, hopefully the commercial property issue can be resolved. And Kevin never was involved in mortgage fraud. That news article Kate mentioned had a quote from him on the subject, that's all. So he's clean."

"What of the child?" Brianna asked in a small voice.

"You mean Rachel? Jill finally confessed everything to Arnie and introduced him to her former stepdaughter. Rachel is going home and agreed to keep in touch. She's relieved that Canfield was ultimately to blame for Torrie's death."

"And Hally's," Dalton reminded them.

"I fear my loose lips were responsible for sinking that ship." Marla hung her head. "I'd mentioned somewhere along the way that Hally may have discovered Torrie's files on people."

Dalton patted her arm. "You didn't know about Canfield. It's not your fault."

"You're right." She'd blamed herself for enough things in the past. Now it was time to embrace the future.

She smiled at Dalton, her heart swelling with love and affection. Tomorrow was the big day, one that would alter their lives forever. Like Falcon, she was ready for a change. The next phase of her life was about to begin.

"Jill was cleared of all charges by the police," Marla concluded. "She and Arnie are looking forward to their honeymoon. So all's well that ends well."

The next evening, Marla swallowed nervously and prayed that things would go well. She stood outside the room set up for the ceremony at the country club, clutching a traditional nosegay bouquet of roses and stephanotis in peach and white. Her ivory gown flowed to her ankles with a sweep train. With its ruched bodice and jeweled halter neckline, the slim chiffon dress had cost more than some fancier gowns with billowing skirts and beading. Her choice suited a second marriage, being simple yet elegant. Better still, she had the bust line to pull it off.

She'd borrowed her mother's cultured pearl necklace and had worn pearl and diamond earrings to match.

Her heart thumped rapidly as she waited for the catering director to signal her to proceed. Strains of violin music reached her ears from inside, where chairs were set up facing a gazebo. Decorated with white tulle and tiny lights, it would serve as the chuppah, the canopy under which a Jewish couple were wed to symbolize their new home. Although they'd mixed their religious traditions for the ceremony, this was one she'd kept. She and Dalton had also each signed the *ketubah* brought by the rabbi to their respective dressing rooms.

Waiting by the double doors, she gulped, hoping she was doing the right thing and that this marriage would be her last. Her mother and Dalton's parents had already walked down the aisle, followed by the bridesmaids and her matron of honor. Her turn came next.

Peering through a short gauzy veil, she strained to listen to the violinist for her cue. Her knees wobbled under the dress. This might be her second time, but she felt like a total novice. Maybe it always felt like this to be a bride.

She wanted more than anything to be a good wife and mother and had promised herself to focus on family hereafter. No more running around town chasing after suspects. That was Dalton's job. She had a new one now, taking care of him and Brianna.

Her thoughts evaporated when she heard the beginning of the wedding march.

"Here you go." The director, a highlighted blonde, nudged

her. She'd helped things run smoothly so far, and Marla cast her a quick grin that probably came out more like a grimace.

Freezing a smile on her face, she stepped forward onto the white carpet strewn with rose petals. At the far end, Dalton stood proudly watching her, dashingly handsome in a tuxedo. Their attendants flanked him, facing the congregants.

Marla's pulse thrummed in beat to the music. She walked slowly, letting her train trail behind, careful to step across any folds in the fabric underfoot. Nodding here and there to people she recognized, she glided as if in a dream past white columns lining the aisles. They were topped with floral bouquets and had tulle with tiny lights strung between them.

The rabbi and reverend waited under the chuppah. Marla focused on Dalton's craggy face, which split into a happy grin as she approached. As rehearsed, she paused before joining him while her mother rose from her seat in front.

"I love you, *bubula,*" Ma whispered in her ear as she folded back Marla's veil.

Anita kissed her, then took Dalton's hand and put it into hers. Anita resumed her seat while Marla and Dalton faced the clergymen together. Marla held onto him tightly, her hand trembling. He gave her a gentle squeeze and a reassuring glance. Tally came forward and took her bouquet. Marla spotted Brianna and gave the teen a wink, glad she'd consented to stand here with her. They'd come a long way together and both had benefited from their relationship.

She tried to concentrate while the rabbi greeted the guests then read some psalms and traditional blessings. The reverend led them in the Lord's Prayer and the lighting of the unity candle. Most of the prayers flew past her ears. She quaked in her ivory shoes, holding onto Dalton like a lifeline.

Before she knew it, the words "I do" came from her lips. Dalton, facing her, repeated them when it was his turn.

His eyes glowed warmly while he recited the passage he'd personally written for the ring ceremony. She thought she'd burst with joy when he slid the gold ring on her finger.

Her voice shaking, she said the words she'd memorized and slipped the ring on his sturdy finger.

With proud smiles, the rabbi and the reverend pronounced them man and wife.

Following Jewish tradition, Dalton stomped on the cloth-covered glass at his foot.

Shouts of "Mazel tov!" and "Congratulations!" rang forth. They turned in unison to face the congregation. The violinist struck up a tune and they marched down the aisle to a round of applause.

"I love you," Marla told Dalton as soon as they passed beyond the doors.

"I love you, too." He gave her a long lingering kiss and then they were swamped by guests.

The cocktail hour flew past while the bridal party posed for photographs and then mingled.

"Wait out here," the hostess ordered before ushering everyone else into the ballroom.

Marla had gotten a glimpse inside. Tulle draped from the ceiling. Tiny lights shone from potted plants and the sheer fabric overhead. Crystal gleamed on tables decorated with white cloths, tall floral centerpieces, and candlelight. Ribbons circled each of the draped chairs, matching her peach and cream color scheme. Music played from the DJ set up on stage in front of a wooden dance floor.

A moment later, she and Dalton paraded into the ballroom, where floor to ceiling windows looked out on a view of the lake and golf course and stars twinkled in the night sky.

Everyone stood and clapped their hands. She beamed with joy, especially seeing everyone she loved in one place:

Her new family: Brianna and Kate and John, plus Dalton's relatives that she'd only just met.

Anita and Roger, both of them wearing broad smiles. Marla no longer begrudged her mother a beau. Maybe their nuptials would be next.

Her brother Michael, and sister-in-law, Charlene, who looked stylish in her persimmon bridesmaid dress.

Her local cousins, Cynthia and Bruce, and her out-of-town relatives.

Her friends Tally and Ken and Jill and Arnie.

Nicole, Jennifer, Luis, and the rest of their salon staff.

And not to forget her neighbors: Moss and Emma had made it, the elderly couple expectantly waiting for Marla to read aloud the poem Moss had written for the occasion. Even Goat looked spiffy in a suit. Beside him stood Marla's friend Georgia from California, who'd flown in for the occasion.

She'd take time to speak to each one of them in turn, but first she and Dalton had to begin the dancing. She swept into his arms, looking into his eyes, feeling so much in love that the rest of the world dissolved.

Held in his embrace, she was barely aware their feet were moving, barely aware of the voices around them, of dishes clattering, of music thumping from the speaker system. All she saw were Dalton's smoky gray eyes regarding her in a manner that took her breath away and filled her with rapture.

"You're mine," he said, his voice husky. "My wife."

"Yes, I am. Now and forever, my husband."

Her eyes filled with tears of happiness as he lowered his head and kissed her.

They twirled around the dance floor, completing a circle.

A circle symbolizing their love, their union, and their new family.

ABOUT THE AUTHOR

Nancy J. Cohen is a multi-published author who began her career writing futuristic romances. Her first title, *Circle of Light,* won the HOLT Medallion Award. After four books in this genre, she switched to writing mysteries. Her popular Bad Hair Day series features hairdresser Marla Shore, who solves crimes with wit and style under the sultry Florida sun. Several of these titles made the IMBA best-seller list. *Shear Murder* is her latest release. Active in the writing community and a featured speaker at libraries and conferences, Nancy is listed in *Contemporary Authors, Poets & Writers,* and *Who's Who in U.S. Writers, Editors & Poets.* When she's not busy writing, Nancy enjoys reading, fine dining, cruising, and outlet shopping. She likes hearing from readers. Please contact her at nancy@nancyjcohen.com or visit her Web site at http://nancyjcohen.com.